FACELESS

A TROPICAL AUTHORS NOVEL

AJ STEWART CHRIS NILES NICHOLAS HARVEY

NICK SULLIVAN

Copyright © 2023 by Down Island Publishing, LLC

All rights reserved.

No part of this book may be reproduced in any form or by any electronic or mechanical means, including information storage and retrieval systems, without written permission from the author, except for the use of brief quotations in a book review.

Printed in the United States of America

First Printing, 2023

ISBN-13: 978-1-956026-57-3

Cover design: Harvey Books, LLC

Editor: Gretchen Tannert Douglas

This is a work of fiction. Names, characters, businesses, places, events and incidents are either the products of the author's imagination or used in a fictitious manner unless noted otherwise. Any resemblance to actual persons, living or dead, or actual events is purely coincidental.

1

He watched the people moving in and out of the ballroom with the dispassion of a rancher at a cattle sale. The meeting and greeting, the fake smiles and handshakes offered in hopes of doing business rather than making any kind of meaningful connection. The logos on their polo shirts were the only way to tell one group from the next. Boxes of pamphlets and corporate swag—pens with floats, ball caps, and T-shirts—were lugged into the large room that was transforming into a trade show of everything nautical.

As he moved easily through the construction of corporate booths and product demo stations, he reflected on the irony of his own name. His call sign was Angler, and in a business where not having a fixed identity was a competitive advantage—if not a lifesaving necessity—it had become who he was to the point where even he sometimes struggled to recall the name on his birth certificate.

But despite his call sign, he wasn't in the market for a new boat or a bimini canopy or a fish finder. He didn't spend his spare time on a Jet Ski or pontoon boat. For a moment he wondered what that might be like, to actually hang a pole off a deck and sip on a cool drink while not caring whether he caught anything. Perhaps one day. Perhaps after this job. This last job. He felt his teeth grind involuntarily at the thought. One last job. The mercenary's lament.

Angler wandered out through the exhibit space into the broad South Florida sunlight and flicked his sunglasses down. The small marina at the resort at Tarpon Point was being transformed inside and out. Older private craft were being shuttled out to moorings and docks further up the Caloosahatchee River and replaced by gleaming new demonstration models of speedboats and bass boats and Jet Skis. A shining silver pontoon boat with a deep bass sound system eased into a slot beside Angler as he ambled out toward the water.

The docks reached out like fingers into Glover Bight, a small natural harbor near the mouth to the river that split Fort Myers from Cape Coral. The end of each dock formed a T, allowing larger vessels to moor in the shallow waters without having to access a slip. Angler stood on the T at the end of the longest dock and looked back at the resort. A team of men with a hydraulic lift were erecting a banner that read *The Great American Boat Show*. To Angler it meant nothing more than a crowd and all the advantages and disadvantages that entailed. And it meant one more thing: that this was where the job would take place.

He watched for a while to understand the traffic patterns of the people moving in and out of the buildings, and scoped out a couple of paths around the complex that were lightly used. They might be dead ends or clear exit paths. He would walk them to confirm. After a few minutes he turned back to the water. There was one way in and one way out of the bight, at least to the untrained eye. From his position he could see out toward the southern reaches of Pine Island and the eastern end of Sanibel. Boats coming in and out stuck to the marked channels that directed vessels around the many shallows and sandbanks. More opportunities and threats in Angler's eyes. He knew beyond the barrier islands were the open waters of the Gulf of Mexico, and to the south, beyond Naples and Marco Island, the wild coastline of Ten Thousand Islands. Then onto the Keys and the Caribbean.

He saw many ways in and many ways out. A few ways to get the job done successfully and a longer list of how it could go wrong. Especially now the method had been changed and become more complicated. He had been given direction on the how and when of the operation, but he would make up his own mind. Too many times Angler had relied on the intel of others only to realize the gaps in the information too late.

Not this time.

He captured the surroundings in his memory and then turned back toward the hotel complex. He wanted to know every way in and every way out, by land and sea and any other means, and the lanyard around his neck and the polo shirt on his back would provide him with the unfettered access he needed.

Deek Morrison watched the man on the dock from the shadows of the rear entrance to the hotel. The guy looked the part—trade show lanyard, corporate polo and chinos, clean-cut hair and well-tended goatee, both with a touch of salt and pepper. Deek wasn't any kind of military guy, but he lived and worked in the Washington, DC bubble, so he saw plenty of uniforms, and this guy walked like he had once worn one.

He might have looked the part, but there was something off about him, something that set Deek's imagination running. The resort was a hive of activity, setting up for the coming boat show. Everyone had somewhere to be or someone to meet or something to do.

Except this guy.

He was watching the work happen but not doing any of it. He didn't stop at any particular corporate booth to check on preparations and he hadn't shaken a hand or handed out a single card. Instead, he was looking around like a home buyer at an open house, walking the grounds and checking out the rooms.

Deek wasn't worried about setting up his booth. He had come

early on a hunch—no, it was more than a hunch. It was a solid working theory, even if his boss couldn't see it. Didn't *want* to see it. Deek knew what he knew. And this guy might be the guy. There would be time to do the less important stuff. The stuff that had gotten him to Florida in the first place.

He watched the man turn from the dock. Deek glanced down at his trusty Omega Seamaster Professional watch as the guy strode by, then he followed him back inside.

Boring, boring, boring.

It was the only way to describe the fire department lieutenant's briefing. Sam Waters looked around the room at the assembled first responders. Who would have thought that being a firefighter could be so dull? She had figured it was all dashing into burning buildings and saving kittens from trees. But this was not that. This was traffic patterns and flow rates, marshaling and exit strategies for large crowds, hallway widths and logjam points. The lieutenant walked them around the hotel describing how they should be prepared for anything that could induce panic, not just fire. Sam wondered if that included trying to get away from the lieutenant's monotonous deadpan delivery.

Sam shot Dusty an eye roll and got a shake of the head in return. He could be such a killjoy. He was the reason she was at the walk-through. Part of the reason, anyway. The blame part. When he had suggested she take on the role of citizen deputy with the Lee County Sheriff, he had sold it as a chance to spend her days out on the water. For the most part that had turned out to be true. She cruised around in a sheriff's launch checking fishing permits and safety violations on the waters around Cape Coral-Fort Myers and the barrier islands just offshore. It was largely sunshine and the rush of sea spray through her hair. But if the tradeoff was doing these event gigs and listening to the most boring man in the world, she might have to reconsider.

The lieutenant was pointing out each and every exit from the exhibition hall when Sam's attention wavered and landed on the blond guy. He stood in the corner of the room trying to look like he was working a phone, but was really watching someone else that Sam couldn't see. He didn't look like anyone else in the room despite trying to do so. For a start he wore a button-up shirt instead of a corporate polo—the only other button-up shirt in the room belonged to the fire lieutenant—and over the shirt he wore a blue sports jacket that was a thirty-four long when the guy really needed a thirty-two regular.

Sam watched him until the lieutenant led the group away to the restaurant across the marina. She pushed him from her mind. All these guys probably did a circuit of trade shows and knew each other, so he was no doubt looking at his business archnemesis or some woman—or hell, some guy—who had spurned his advances at a past conference drinks session.

They walked across the concourse and around the marina to the restaurant. The fireman droned on and Sam looked out at the glistening water. It called to her, and she wondered why she was landlubbing with Dusty.

"Blimey, this is dull," she whispered in her English accent, as the lieutenant went on about the nature of kitchen fires. "Why am I here?"

"The show has to pay for law enforcement presence, and you are part of that presence."

"But I'll be on the water, won't I?"

"They might put you on parking lot patrol."

"I resign."

"Or there might be a fire that you need to attend."

"I already know how to extinguish a marine fire. Kitchens are well outside my domain, mate."

"I know."

"Do you?"

"I've seen where you live, remember?"

Sam shrugged. "What are you doing here, anyway? You're a

detective. Aren't you supposed to arrive after the crime has been committed?"

"Captain Cross asked me to attend."

"So you're smooching your boss's—"

"I am representing the department. So are you."

Sam said nothing more. There was no point. She tried to focus on the ins and outs of grease fires but found her attention wavering. Even through the tinted windows in the restaurant the water sparkled. She wondered if the windows had been polarized. The color of the water really popped, and—

There was that guy again. Standing by the entrance to the main building, his hand shading his eyes as he looked out onto the marina. Sam tracked his focus and found another guy standing at the end of the dock. This guy looked the part. The polo and the chinos. He was standing at the end of the dock looking out onto the water, which was a perfectly reasonable thing to do, for a guy working at a boat show.

The guy in the polo turned from the dock and strode back toward the building. Sam noted that he didn't walk so much as march, his posture high, his shoulders back. He walked like Dusty, as if spinal alignment were mission critical. As the guy reached the resort entrance, Sam looked for the blond man. There he was, fussing with his watch, until the second guy passed by, when blondie turned and followed him inside.

"Any questions?" asked the lieutenant.

There was shuffling of feet but no one spoke. Dusty made to raise his hand but Sam grabbed his wrist before the damage was done.

"In that case, thank you all for your diligence. Your departments will forward assignments for the event by day's end." The lieutenant nodded to suggest this was the end, and they were dismissed.

Sam smiled at Dusty. "What are you doing now?"

"Back to the office. You?"

"Same." Sam's smile widened. His commute entailed a good

forty-five minutes in Cape Coral traffic. Hers was a cruise in her launch back up the sound to the sheriff's Gulf District office on Pine Island.

"Jerry's later?" he asked.

"I'll save you a seat."

Angler did his walk-throughs and then headed back to his rental jon boat. It was clear from the moment his aircraft came in for landing at Southwest Florida International Airport that a boat was the smart way to get around. The cities on either side of the river were a tangle of streets packed with slow moving vehicles. Everything about this job said water was the fast way around, so he had found a low-key marina to hire a boat, and the place had provided even more.

Angler stepped down into the aluminum jon boat and pulled on the cord to fire up the tiny eight-horsepower outboard. He eased the tiller around and cruised slowly away from the dock and into the channel. The boat was small enough to get across the shallows and he could even drag it across sandbars if he had to. The only downside was the speed. Right now it didn't matter, but later it would. An old, dented jon boat would not do.

He motored out past the Sanibel Causeway and St. James City at the southern end of Pine Island. He cut north between the islands and into Pine Island Sound. It was a wider expanse here, room for bigger craft to maneuver, but far from deep. He passed the populated islands of Sanibel and Captiva before easing off the throttle as he reached Baskin Island.

His intel had suggested this island as a suitable base from which to launch the operation, but Angler would make his own call on that. The place had its merits: it was only sparsely populated and even then, mostly at the north end. There was no bridge across from Pine Island or the mainland, so emergency response was limited. The subdivision at the north end was actually a fly-in fly-out community with a small grass landing strip. Angler would confirm the suitability of all that. For now he floated in the sound, his focus on the south end of the island, where his intel said he should be.

Deek handed over his credit card and threw up a prayer. He was confident there was enough credit on it for now, but it was dependent on how big a hold the hotel had placed. Deek was aware of the irony of someone with his qualifications struggling to manage a credit card, but living in DC wasn't anyone's idea of cheap, and the federal government didn't exactly pay like Morgan Stanley.

The woman at the boat rental stand offered him a smile as the charges were approved, and Deek let out a sigh that he hoped she couldn't hear.

"Now, the rental will need to be back by dark, otherwise you will have to return it to the dock on Pine Island. Because of the boat show, see."

"Got it," said Deek, handing over the pages of waivers. He felt like he had taken responsibility for the national debt.

"Are you familiar with outboard dinghies?" she asked, as she slowly looked over the paperwork.

Deek repeatedly checked his watch, but the woman failed to get the hint. "Sure am. I'm on the water all the time," he lied.

"Awesome. Well, Jonathon can run you through it if you want."

"I think I'm good," he said, tapping his foot.

"All right, then. It's that one there, skiff number six."

"Perfect, thank you." Deek rushed out toward the little boat and could feel his stomach turning a touch already. He tried to tell himself it was because he had lost sight of his quarry. The guy he was following had his own boat already so he had just taken off. Deek had to hire one and that took longer than the rental car line at BWI. Now he faced the real test.

Deek didn't do boats. He didn't really do water. He had grown up in a small town where the biggest patch of water was a swimming hole in the nearby river, and Deek had not been part of the crowd that hung out down there. Living in DC meant he knew people who spent their leisure time on the Chesapeake Bay, but Deek wasn't part of that crowd, either.

He climbed down from the dock into the small fiberglass boat and settled himself on the bench seat. The boat rocked from side to side as Deek turned to the outboard motor. He knew plenty about how boats worked—more than most people. He just didn't have a lot of practical experience. He was more a theoretical guy. But his theories were being ignored by people who could do something about them, so Deek pulled on the cord and started the little five-horsepower motor. It spluttered to life and he let out another sigh.

Deek turned the throttle and the little boat eased out into the bight, then he checked his phone and made his heading for the causeway. There was no telling where the other guy had gone but chances were it wasn't out into the Gulf. His boat wasn't that much bigger than Deek's and he had no fishing gear.

Deek followed the path of least resistance around the bottom of Pine Island and up between it and Captiva. There were a good number of boats cruising the sound but few of them were dinghies. Most seemed to be center consoles with bimini tops, so Deek took out his field glasses to scope the water for a smaller vessel. He was at the north end of Captiva when he saw something familiar.

An aluminum jon boat sat on the Pine Island side of the channel. Through his binocs Deek could see that the boat wasn't moving, but no fishing rods hung out over the water. The man in the boat had no field glasses of his own but he was definitely focused on the island on the Gulf side of the sound.

Deek checked his phone. Baskin Island. Not much to it. Shaped a bit like a seahorse. A small community, a little marina, a long beach on the Gulf side. The man was looking at the south end of the island but to Deek's eye there wasn't anything of note there. He looked again through his field glasses. Now he could see it. Some houses. The scale was difficult to discern but the homes were clearly large, each with a dock. Only one home had a boat. It carried the shape and white hull of a luxury motor yacht. Deek moved his view along the row of homes, noting four of them. They looked the same, as if they had been built as one development. He saw no people. Not around the houses, not on the docks, not on the boat. He wondered what the guy in the jon boat was looking at.

Deek cast his glasses back across toward the other boat but with the limited field of vision he couldn't pinpoint it. He dropped the glasses and looked across the water.

The other boat was gone.

Deek scanned the water again, and then a third time. The jon boat was nowhere. He twisted the throttle and headed toward where the other boat had been but didn't get there fast. When he reached the point across from the south end of Baskin Island, Deek cut the motor and scanned the area but saw no sign of the other boat.

He wondered if the other guy had gone over to the homes he had been looking at. Deek snatched up his field glasses and scanned the island. The bulk of the shoreline was mangrove and scrub. The homes at the south end were the only visible buildings. Three empty docks led to three lifeless homes. He focused on the boat behind the second home from the south. The sleek lines and wide entertaining decks were familiar to Deek. He knew the model and he knew the manufacturer. He moved his view to the transom of the vessel. He read the name.

Aeolus.

Deek knew the very boat. And suddenly all the theoretical strands came together. He was right. He had been all along. This thing was really happening.

Sam eased her patrol launch out of the resort marina and headed for the sound. Traffic was heavy on the river but craft moved slowly, the channels having been disturbed and the sandbars moved around during Hurricane Ian. The charts were not completely accurate anymore, and the dredging of the channels only half finished, so she headed for the channel that led to the deeper water around Pine Island. She took a deep breath of briny air and banked around St. James City and headed north. The boat was a rigid inflatable center console, one of the smaller vessels in the marine unit, but it suited Sam just fine. The twin outboards could open up and get her where she needed to be plenty fast if she wanted, but mostly she took it easy and tried not to harsh anyone's mellow by creating too big a wake.

There were a few recreational boats out and she considered checking them for safety gear, but Sergeant Mulligan had asked her to be prompt in returning from the briefing—overtime was not in the unit's budget. Sam would have done this part of the job for free, but now she was officially on the payroll—albeit the lowest of the low in the ranks—the sergeant had ruled out unpaid overtime, at least as long as she was in an LCSO vessel.

She ran up the west side of Pine Island toward Pineland, but just as soon as she opened up the throttle she eased off it again. Ahead she saw a small fiberglass skiff, the kind of thing they rented by the day out of Tarpon Bay resort. There was only one occupant and no fishing gear. That in itself was not so suspicious—lots of tourists hired the little putt-putts to spend a few hours on the water, taking in the sanctuary around Pine Island. But this guy had binoculars out, and they were pointed directly at the houses at the end of Baskin. Houses that belonged to her friend, Enoch Brookes.

As she got closer she recognized the blond hair of the guy from the resort. This guy seemed to enjoy watching other people, which was fine sitting at a café in Paris but started to edge into creepy when he was scoping out a house through binoculars. She slowed and eased the patrol boat between Baskin and the guy with the binoculars, and he didn't look up until her hull blocked his view.

The guy squinted into the sun and up close she noticed the man's blond hair crept over the tops of his ears, and his nose looked like he had a deviated septum. Sam pushed her throttle into neutral and tossed a mooring line around a cleat on the smaller boat's bow.

"Afternoon," she said.

"Hello," said the guy. "Is there a problem?"

"Lee County Sheriff. This your boat?"

"No, it's a rental."

"Right. Did you do a safety briefing?"

"They gave me a form to sign."

"I'm sure they did. I just need to check you have all the right safety equipment. Do you have your rental agreement?"

The man pulled a sheet of paper from inside his jacket pocket. The sports coat had felt like overkill at the resort but really didn't suit the skiff. He handed the agreement over and Sam gave it a cursory read.

"What's your name, sir?" she asked.

"Are you English?" he replied.

"I am. And your name is?"

"Deek Morrison. What's an Englishwoman doing in a police boat in Florida?"

"Keeping you safe. And I'm with the sheriff's office."

"You said."

"So what are you doing out here, Mr. Morrison."

"Just boating."

"Just boating? Not fishing?"

"No. Just looking around."

"Sure. You got a PFD in there, Mr. Morrison?"

He looked under the seat and caused the boat the rock, then produced an orange life jacket.

"What's your interest with the houses over there?" Sam asked.

"What houses?"

"The ones you were looking at through your little binoculars there."

"I was just looking at birds."

"Birds? What kind of birds?"

"Egrets?"

He didn't sound too sure.

"Egrets," said Sam. "And what were you looking at back at the Tarpon Bay resort?"

"Where?"

"I saw you at the resort earlier. You were watching someone."

"Was I?"

"Yes, you were. And I have to tell you, Mr. Morrison, you were acting a little suspiciously."

"I don't know what you mean."

"Fair enough. How about I just tow you into the sheriff's office and we talk to my sergeant."

"No, you don't need to do that."

"All evidence to the contrary."

"Okay, look, can you keep a secret?"

Sam raised an eyebrow.

"I'm a federal agent," he said.

"A federal agent?"

"That's right."

"Do you have some ID to that effect?"

Morrison leaned to the side and reached into his trouser pocket. Sam remembered that Dusty had said to be careful when people reached into pockets—they might produce guns. Sam had never carried a gun. Not as a police diver in Britain and not here. As a civilian deputy she wasn't authorized to carry and had yet to feel the need.

Morrison took out a card and handed it to her. It read *Deek Morrison, Maritime Administration, Department of Transportation.* There was an official seal on the card and everything. Sam figured she could have knocked one up on a computer in about five minutes.

"You got anything with a photo?"

"No. I didn't bring my actual ID. I'm technically not on the clock."

"But you are technically following people and looking at private homes through binoculars."

"Yes, I was doing that. But listen, there's a reason."

"I'd love to hear it."

"I am a federal agent. I'm trailing someone I believe to be about to undertake a terrorist attack on American soil."

"Mr. Morrison, are you armed?"

"It's Deek, and no ma'am, I'm not carrying."

"You're a federal agent tracking a terrorist and you're not carrying a weapon? I thought all federal agents were armed."

"I'm not that kind of agent."

"Well, I don't know what that means, Deek, but I think you should come and talk to my sergeant. If there's a terror attack about to happen, he needs to know."

"He won't believe me."

"Why?"

"Because they never do."

2

Sam checked the bow line of the little skiff and helped Deek across into her patrol boat. She was tempted to leave him in his own boat but she didn't want him trying to motor away. She needed to figure out what she was dealing with before she got back to the sergeant with either a warning about a possible attack or, more likely, to handover another Florida crazy.

Sam eased the throttle forward until the towline was taut but kept it slow so she could hear what the "federal agent" had to say.

"So why do you think there's going to be a terrorist attack?"

"You wouldn't believe me if I told you." He had his eyes on Baskin Island as they motored past.

"Yeah, you said that. You were watching that guy. You're still looking for him. Who is he?"

"I don't know. Not exactly."

"So how do you know he's a terrorist?"

"The evidence."

"Let me guess, you can't share."

Deek turned and looked at Sam. He was a little green around the gills but that might have been the water reflecting off his pale skin.

"What do you know about Azerbaijan?" he asked.

"Azerbaijan? The country?"

"Yes."

"Not much. Eastern Europe, former Soviet territory, I think. On the Caspian Sea, isn't it?"

"You know more than most."

"Don't they have oil?"

"They do. And natural gas. That's what drives their economy."

"So?"

"So do you know much about Armenia?"

"This is going to go faster if you quit the Trivial Pursuit bit and just tell me what you think is going on."

"Okay. Armenia is the next-door neighbor to Azerbaijan. Landlocked between it and Turkey. The Azeri and the Armenians have a long history of acrimony. Even today there is contested territory between them. They're pretty much constantly in conflict."

"You mean war?"

"They try not to call it that. But the Azeri have to get their oil and gas out to Europe, and they have done that for a long time using pipelines via Russia. That relationship is proving problematic these days. There's another pipeline—an EU sanctioned one—that runs through Georgia and around to Turkey, then on to Europe. There have been a number of 'accidents' on that pipeline—sabotage might be another word, so the Azeri are looking at backup plans."

"Through Armenia?"

"Exactly."

"But they're at war."

"In conflict, yes. It's a problem. But I've uncovered information that a meeting has been arranged between the ambassadors to the United States of both countries to attempt to broker a peace, or at least an economic detente. I believe that meeting is due to take place later this week at this boat show you're having."

"International peace talks at a boat show? I can see why you're having trouble selling this to your people."

"The boat show is a cover. The whole thing is being brokered by the industrialist Harold Hildebrand."

"Who?"

"He's one of the fifty richest men in the world. A billionaire twenty times over."

"I don't read *The Economist* as much as I used to."

"You read *The Economist*?"

"No, agent. It was a joke."

"Oh. I see."

"So you think someone's going to disturb these peace talks?"

"I do."

"Who? The Azerbaijanis or Armenians?"

"People from Azerbaijan are called Azeri, but no, not one of the sides. A third party."

"The Georgians with the pipeline? No, the Russians. If you tell me it's the Russians I'll be sad."

"Are you Russian?"

"No, but it would be horribly cliché."

"Well it's not the Russians."

"Who then?" Sam turned the wheel toward Pineland and headed into a small marina with an expansive boat shed.

"Where are we going?" asked Deek.

"I told you, to see the sergeant."

"No offense, but this looks like a backwater."

"None taken. It is. That's why we like it. But this is where the local office is."

As Sam eased in against the dock with a practiced hand, Deek pulled his feet up onto the seat and tucked his chin into his knees. She cut the motor and tied off and then turned to him.

"You okay?"

"He's not going to believe me," said Deek.

"You could work on your story, I gotta admit."

"They don't want to see it. Not my boss, not your boss."

"Listen, I'm going to let him know we're back, and you can work on your sales pitch. Just a tip—get to the point." Sam climbed up onto the dock and walked along past the boatshed. The doors were closed up for the day. Sam took a look back at her patrol boat before she turned the corner to the office. The agent was still semi-fetal in the boat.

Sam reached the glass door that read *Lee County Sheriff's Office Gulf District* and pulled at the handle. It didn't budge. She tried again with the same result. She cupped her hand and peered inside. It was dark, as if everyone had quit for the day. The office wasn't a twenty-four-hour operation but it wasn't that late. As she stepped back she saw a note taped on the inside of the glass. It told whoever cared that the duty officer was on the water and left the non-emergency number to call for assistance.

Sam didn't call for assistance. She strode back around to the boat where Deek still sat. He had put his feet down but his face was etched in uncertainty.

"Strikeout," she said. "The sarge is on the water."

"So what do we do?"

"I got someone else. Someone better. But first, you gotta explain this stuff to me."

"Explain what?"

"The why, the who, the how?"

"I have no idea how. But the why? It's all oil and gas. See, Harold Hildebrand owns oil and gas operations all over the world. But he's smart. Do you know the California Gold Rush, the forty-niners?"

"I've heard of it."

"From 1848 to 1855. Lots of fortunes were made. But not by the gold diggers."

"By whom?"

"The merchants. You don't make money digging for gold, you make money selling the shovels and buckets and denim jeans. And Harold Hildebrand knows his history. Sure, he's right into the oil and gas business, but he also owns businesses that make the specialized drilling equipment, and build and manage pipelines, and he builds the ships that transport the stuff all over the planet."

"So?"

"So he has businesses everywhere, but not so much in Europe, especially Eastern Europe, where most of the EU's energy comes from. It's dominated by Eurasian businesses, not surprisingly. And Hildebrand wants his piece."

"You remember the bit I said about getting to the point?"

"There's a breadcrumb trail that suggests that Hildebrand is hosting the peace talks on his new super yacht that will have its maiden voyage at the boat show."

"Still don't see any terrorism."

"It's all a lie."

"What is?"

"Hildebrand's goal to get into the European supply pipelines, setting up the peace talks."

"Hang on. You've come up with a theory about peace talks that no one in your agency buys and then you say the theory is bunk? Are you dizzy, 'cause you're walking around circles, mate."

"No, the peace talks are real. It's Hildebrand's motive that I'm saying is a lie. I think he's setting up the talks in order to sabotage them and drive the two parties further apart, not closer together."

"The point, fella. Why?"

"Because he controls the transportation of liquified natural gas. You'd call it LNG."

"I'm not sure I would, but so what?"

"When the Georgia pipeline was attacked and Russian supplies were limited, the EU had to find alternatives. One of those was US LNG. Hildebrand owns the rights to some of the fields and pretty much all the specialized vessels to ship it over to Europe. He made a bundle from it. But then the pipeline was repaired and the EU looked at other options because piped natural gas is much cheaper than shipped LNG. Hildebrand's business should have taken a hit when things went back to normal."

"And they didn't?"

"The share prices on a couple of his businesses did, but then he did something counterintuitive. He started building more LNG transport ships. Demand for US LNG was going down but he was acting like it was going up."

"Like he knew something?"

"Right. And I think he knew about the Azeri-Armenian pipeline talks. I think he's organizing the peace talks so he can disrupt them and drive Europe toward more dependence on US gas."

"That's a stretch."

"That's what my boss said. But the Azeri ambassador has a vacation home in Miami, and he grew up in Baku, on the Caspian Sea. He's a keen sailor, both in South Florida and on Chesapeake Bay. And the Armenian ambassador grew up in a resort village on Lake Sevan. I don't have any intel on whether he sails here, but it's not a stretch for two guys who love boats to meet up under the cover of a boat show."

Sam frowned. There were more loose ends in the story than a Scottish tapestry, but there was just enough to make her wonder. If she did nothing and something happened, then what?

"Okay, follow me. There's someone who needs to hear all this."

Sam led Deek to her personal boat—a Frankenstein's monster of a vessel, cobbled together from used parts that didn't really belong with each other. She carefully opened the throttle and puttered across the sound and over to Baskin Island. Deek focused on the inlet at the north end, where the small marina and most of the houses were. Sam moved her eyes between the agent and the mangroves that enveloped the east side of the island. When she saw the tiny cut of beach in the middle of the island she changed heading.

"Where are we going?" asked Deek.

"Home, first."

"There's nothing there."

"I know." Sam smiled. The mangroves acted like sentries either side of a small beach which Sam coasted in toward. A weather-beaten stilt house sat to one side, otherwise the place felt like the end of the earth.

Sam coasted into the beach and tilted the outboard as Deek jumped onto the sand.

"What is this place?"

"Home," said Sam, jumping from the boat, and dropping an anchor into the sand. She didn't stop, instead leading Deek into the foliage. In a couple of minutes they came upon an old shack that looked in worse shape than the stilt house.

"Is this where you live?" Deek asked, running his hand along the rough top of an old wooden picnic table.

"No, this is Herm's place. Come on."

Sam led Deek on through the bushes and broke out onto a long wide stretch of white beach. Deek stopped when his feet hit the soft sand and looked both ways. There were no buildings or people to be seen.

"Wow," he whispered.

"Yeah," said Sam, marching on down the beach. They headed south toward the point where the island thinned out like the tail of a seahorse. At the far end of the beach several pilings stuck out of the water as if there had once been a dock of some kind, but whatever had been there was long gone.

Except for a pontoon boat. It was grimy and the canvas top was bleached to a color that was as much blue as pink. The vessel had twin pontoons as its hull, on top of which was a flat deck surrounded by railings. On one railing someone had attached a sign painted in a 1930s Hollywood marquee script. It read: *Jerry's*.

"Who's Jerry?"

"You don't want to go down that rabbit hole," said Sam. "Just stick to your knitting."

Sam stepped onto a gangway that led up from the beach to the boat. There were people on board, and they each had a drink in their hand as if a party cruise was about to get underway.

"Hey, Shaq," said Sam to a guy behind a makeshift bar. He was blending something with ice, and as Deek got onboard Shaq poured two tall glasses of yellow liquid which he garnished with a piece of pineapple.

"Pineapple margaritas," he said with a beaming smile.

"Lovely," she replied after a sip. "Shaq, this is Deek."

"Hey, Deek. Margarita?"

"Um, sure?"

"This one's yours."

Sam led Deek onto the boat where four people had been chatting. Now they all stopped and stared as if it was a western saloon.

"What are you all gawking at?" she asked.

A man with a long gray ponytail and an acoustic guitar across his lap smiled. He was north of sixty but the smile still made Sam catch her breath every time. "Who's your friend?" he asked.

"Jo Jo, his name is Deek, and you can all wipe the silly expressions off your faces. It's not what you think."

"It never is, darlin'."

Deek peered at the older man. "Do I know you?"

He smiled again. "Were you there that night I woke up lying in the gutter on the Sunset Strip with Jon Bon Jovi?"

"Ah, no."

The man shrugged.

"Deek, Jo Jo Tanner. He was a rock star, a *long* time ago."

Sam shook her head and sat on a side bench seat and gestured for Deek to join her. He sat down between Sam and a dark-haired guy in a polo shirt.

"Deek, this is Detective Dusty Rodriguez. Tell him your story."

"He's not going to believe me."

"Deek, no one is ever going to believe you if you start every story with that. Just tell it, will you?"

Deek took a sip of his drink and turned to the detective who watched him with a frown. He told Dusty what he had told Sam, about the oil and gas and the tankers and Harold Hildebrand. He explained the links with the ambassadors, and the anticipated maiden voyage of a new super yacht where the meeting would take place.

Dusty listened without interruption, then when Deek was done he spoke.

"And you're a federal agent?"

"Kind of."

"Being an agent is not really a *kind of* thing."

"I work for the federal government."

"You got ID, a card, something?"

Deek pulled out his wallet and handed Dusty a business card.

"Maritime Administration."

"That's right."

"Okay. Let me make a couple calls." Dusty stood and walked down onto the beach and headed away.

"Where's he going?" asked Deek.

"Reception's not much cop here," said Sam. "Sometimes you get lucky on the other side."

"Listen, I can't hang around. I'm supposed to return my boat rental before dark."

"Right." Sam leaned across to a woman on the other side of the boat. "Hey, Chris."

"Hey, Sam. How was the briefing today?"

"Boring as hell. Listen, Deek here rented a boat from Tarpon Bay, but he's not going to get it back tonight."

"No problems. They've already moved a few of their other boats to our marina, so I'll just give Tania a call later and let her know I've got it."

"Great. It's tied up at Pineland right now but I can bring it down in the morning."

"Sure."

"You full up?"

"Pretty much. They're moving everyone out so they can bring in all the trade show boats. Seems like a big deal. You know we had a break in?"

"No. Did you call it in?"

"No point. I told Dusty. Someone cut their way into the caged space out the back where we keep the scuba gear."

"Anything missing?"

"Looks like an old tank, mask, some fins. Honestly, if someone's that desperate to dive around here, I would have lent it to them for free."

"That kit's not exactly new."

Chris shrugged.

"Nothing else? No cash or anything from the store?"

"The back door wasn't touched."

"Weird."

"Florida."

Sam nodded, then she turned to the sound of Dusty walking back up the gangplank.

"An agent? Really?" He frowned at Deek.

"I'm a federal employee."

"You're an economist. A paper pusher."

"Yes."

"You're an economist?" spat Sam.

"Yes, but that doesn't make me wrong. In fact, it's why I'm right."

"You got thirty seconds before I boot you from this boat and you can swim home, mate."

"Okay, I'm an analyst for the Maritime Administration. I track ship building around the world as an economic indicator, and for potential national security implications."

"You follow who builds boats?"

"And their movements around the globe. Ships change hands more often than you'd think."

"So you're a boat spotter?" said Sam.

"I wouldn't put it that way." He sucked on his drink. "So what if I am?"

"Well, I grew up on the Isle of Wight, and half the people I knew were boat spotters. And they didn't miss much."

Deek paused. "So you believe me?"

"How do you know about the oil and gas pipelines?" asked Dusty.

"I didn't, at first. I noticed Hildebrand building his new gas tankers first. It raised the question, why. So I did some digging."

"How about this super yacht?" asked Sam.

"I was already watching that. It's technically not my job, it's not merchant marine, but I track super yachts for fun."

"For fun?" said Dusty.

"Yes. I tracked it being built in Italy. It's a special design, low draft to travel easily across the Bahamas bank. I knew it belonged to Hildebrand."

"But how did you put these ambassadors on board?"

"I can't, not a hundred percent. But I have a friend at the State Department. We were at Georgetown together. He connected those dots for me."

"Does he believe your story?" asked Sam.

"He wants to be head of his department someday, so he's keeping his head down."

"Smart," said Dusty. "You don't want that?"

"I don't want someone blowing up a super yacht with people on board."

Dusty took a deep breath. "I don't know, pal. I don't see any connection to this Hildebrand guy. This super yacht isn't even here."

"It will be. It's arriving during the show. And Hildebrand already has a boat here."

"How do you know that?" asked Sam.

Deek pulled out his phone. "See this? It's a boat tracking app. I built it."

"You *are* a boat spotter. What's it do?"

"Anyone who likes to track boats can enter the details—registration, names, dates, routes, that sort of thing."

"Any boat?"

"Any boat. Some people follow interesting aircraft too. Most of us only track bigger boats—the super yachts, shipping, cruise ships. But many people log pleasure cruisers and sailboats, basically anything that moves across the ocean. The commercial vessels have transponders much like aircraft, so there's other software that can track them in real time, but we like to log things we see for ourselves."

"So what's this got to do with Hildebrand?" asked Dusty.

"I logged a motor yacht—sixty-footer—that came up as owned by him."

"Where?"

"At a dock right over there." Deek point across the island toward the sound. "There are four houses at the end. It was at one of them. It's called the *Aeolus*."

"Enoch's houses," said Sam. "I saw it, too. And you're sure it's Hildebrand's?"

"Yep. But I'm sure the detective can look up the Coast Guard records."

"I can and I will," said Dusty. "Did you know anything about someone staying at Enoch's place?"

"No," said Sam. "But I can call his office tomorrow and find out."

"Yeah, do that."

"So you believe me?" asked Deek.

Dusty shrugged. "I'm having a hard time seeing a billionaire blowing up his own yacht, especially if he's going to be on it."

"He's the money, not the one doing the job."

"So who's doing the job?"

Deek shifted in his seat. "This is where it gets hard to believe."

"This is where?"

"You ever heard of Şeytan Taciri?" Deek asked, pronouncing it Shay-tahn Tah-jeer-ee, doing his best not to mangle the Azerbaijani.

"No. Who is he?"

"He's a shadow. Part myth, part legend. Thought to be behind everything from corporate espionage to acts of terrorism. He's believed to come out of Eastern Europe. Maybe Romania, maybe Bulgaria. Some say he's a mercenary for hire, others believe he's the mastermind. He's been credited by European authorities with political assassinations and corporate boardroom takeovers. The word is that he was behind the Georgia pipeline sabotage."

"Hold on a tick," Sam said. "Şeytan? Satan? Is that really his name?"

"Well, I doubt it's on his birth certificate. In Azerbaijani, it means 'devil,' and Taciri means 'merchant.' I've always assumed it was a nickname he got from his enemies, given his reputation."

"Who has a file on him?" asked Dusty. "Interpol?"

"Almost certainly. Most European security agencies will. FBI and DHS as well, I'm guessing. But from what I hear, they'll all be pretty thin. No one even knows what this guy looks like."

"You know someone at Interpol?" asked Sam.

"No," said Dusty. "Why would I know someone at Interpol?"

"You said it."

"I'm asking. I'm sure someone in my office has a contact, or maybe the local Feds. But I still don't see the Hildebrand connection."

"Hildebrand doesn't want the Armenia-Azerbaijan pipeline to become real," said Deek. "If Şeytan was behind the Georgia pipeline sabotage, then maybe he doesn't either."

"It's thin," said Dusty. "How do you know about this Şeytan character? You're not in law enforcement."

"I told you, I have a friend at State."

"Another economist?"

"Yes, as it happens. But he says the story of Şeytan Taciri is the kind of thing that gets whispered about in the corridors of power. He operates in high places."

"And boat shows, apparently."

Sam shook her head. "So you're chasing a guy who isn't here and is being assisted by a ghost."

"I said you wouldn't believe me. What are you going to do?"

"I'm going to verify whether what you're saying is the rambling of an unhinged nobody," said Dusty. "And if it is, I'm going to call your boss and make you somebody else's problem."

Angler cruised along Pine Island Sound in the gathering darkness in a long coat despite the mild weather. As he followed the channel markers up the Caloosahatchee River he glanced at the Tarpon Bay resort but motored past. He puttered up toward Redfish Cove, keeping to port and heading up into the manmade canals that cut through the Cape Coral shoreline like veins. Warm light glowed from the canal-front homes, except the one where Angler stopped. He cut the motor and coasted into the dock behind the house he had selected. No lights penetrated the house's storm shutters that told Angler on his earlier pass that no one was home.

He quickly tied up, stepped up onto the dock, and moved out into the dark backyard. He jogged across to the next house. It wasn't dark. The ambient glow of a television shone through the sliding doors. Angler paused for a moment to ensure no one was standing in the backyard enjoying an illicit cigarette. With the coast clear, he tiptoed down the dock to where another small boat was tied up.

The second vessel was similar to his rental jon boat except the hull was fiberglass. It was well used and smelled of fish. Not a tender used to reach a bigger, nicer vessel. This was an old man's fishing boat. It probably never ventured further than the wide river mouth. Angler figured in an accident it would be cheaper to replace than to cover any insurance deductible.

Angler untied the boat and pushed away from the dock. He floated for a moment, back past his own boat, then he used the old rope that had replaced the pull cord to start the ancient outboard.

He moved slowly across the water, out of the canals and back into Redfish Cove. The water here smelled different than out around the barrier islands. Less briny, more vegetal. He saw the small public beach to port and followed its lines a couple hundred feet offshore, toward the six-hundred-foot-long fishing pier at the end. Taking a long fake beard from his coat, he stuck it to his face, covering up his own goatee, then he pulled a beanie down over his hair. He felt like a member of ZZ Top. The disguise wasn't going to fool anyone up close, but he wasn't planning on stopping for chitchat—and he knew from experience that any clever law enforcement officer who heard about a long beard was going to assume the changed look from that was a clean shave, not his salt-and-pepper goatee.

Angler eased in toward the end of the beach. The fishing pier was T-shaped, and he could see people standing under the lights at the top of the T, some with fishing lines and others watching the city lights twinkle across the water.

Cutting the motor, he let the old boat drift toward the pier, reaching it about halfway along its length. His approach would not have gone unnoticed, but he could use that to his advantage. He hit the timer on his watch and got to work.

He moved fast now, tying the vessel to a piling and then pulling the line from the old fuel tank and letting the excess spill out into the well the tank sat in. Then he took a doctored flare with a fuse that made it look like Wile E. Coyote TNT and wedged it into place. Angler lit the fuse then grabbed hold of the pier's balustrade and hoisted himself up.

Angler glanced both ways to see if his climb had been noticed but saw no one paying him any attention, so he flicked his coat collar up like it was freezing out, and he shuffled toward the shore like a man thirty years his elder. He passed a couple walking arm in arm out toward the end of the pier, and he fought the compulsion to run, keeping his eyes down and his movements slow.

There was a restaurant to his right, chatter and laughter and glasses tinkling. He went the other way, off the dock and into the darkness between the pier and the parking lot. There were no people here, so he ripped off his beard and shoved it into a trash can. He stopped underneath a palm tree up from the beach, took off his coat and beanie and dropped them at his feet, then leaned against the tree to wait.

He had timed it for three minutes but these things were never that precise. As it was, his timer was on 2:39 when the fuse hit the flare and a bright spark burst from the waterline, then with two percussive thumps—first the fuel in the well followed by the tank itself—the old boat exploded.

Angler hit his timer again as all the people at the end of the pier turned to the explosion. For a moment no one moved. Angler recognized the deer in the headlights posture, but soon people were reaching for cell phones and moving off the dock and away from the fire that engulfed the small boat.

The roads to the pier were a tangle of surface streets and canals, making fast access complex. It was a similar situation at the resort, which was the reason why Angler stood in the darkness under a palm tree watching the first responders arrive in a small fire department rescue vehicle.

A couple fire fighters strode toward the pier carrying fire extinguishers and one other ran away across the parking lot. As the first men reached the flaming boat, a fire engine screamed into the lot, sirens blaring.

The fire was out within a minute of the first arrivals, but the emergency vehicles continued to come. First a police unit and then a fire department marine unit—a Boston Whaler that Angler knew was kept at the yacht club marina just across the parking lot. Angler watched all the emergency personnel appear, then mill around, then start asking people around the dock what they saw.

The fire engine departed, and the Boston Whaler towed the smoldering boat around to the marina behind the restaurant. Before anyone got any ideas about checking for watchers in the shadows, Angler picked up his coat and beanie to dispose of on the walk back to the closed-up house where his jon boat waited for him.

3

Deek used the sad little soap to wash in the dribble that passed for a shower in his motel room. It was a mom-and-pop-type operation, that kind of place that looked like a Motel 6 but didn't quite meet their quality standards. The bedspread had cigarette burns and the carpet held dark stains that made Deek think of serial killers.

He used a towel with the absorbency and weight of tissue paper to dry himself, then he pulled on some pants and sat on the bed and listened to the police scanner. A half-eaten sub sat beside the television, which showed a hundred channels of static.

The department budget extended to better hotels than this but he wanted to keep costs to a minimum in case he needed to fudge his expenses later. He had never chased down a terrorist plot before and he wasn't sure what it might entail, but he knew as an economist that an empty bank account limited the options.

Deek was toweling his hair and wondering whether Sam and Dusty were going to help or send him packing back to DC, when he heard something on the scanner. The usual chatter was replaced by an emergency call to a fire on the water.

Deek focused on the call by staring at the scanner as if it had a screen. An explosion at a fishing pier. Something about it set Deek's imagination running. He needed to see this for himself. But he couldn't.

His rental car was at the resort where the boat show was to be held. He had hired a boat that was now tied up at the marina on Pine Island. Dusty had brought him back over to Pine Island after the party broke up at the strange pontoon boat that never moved, and then the detective had given Deek a ride back to his motel.

Deek checked the map on his phone. The pier with the explosion was several miles away and was going to require a taxi ride, and although he could expense the ride when he got back to DC, Deek wasn't sure how much more his credit could take. The app said not much, but he hoped there was some kind of wiggle room in those numbers.

He listened to the chatter on the scanner as he hung his towel and put on a shirt, then he sat back on the bed. It took him a few minutes to realize that he was tapping his foot like he was in an electric chair. He had to know. Explosions didn't happen on the water for no reason. Was it a test run for the terrorists?

Deek grabbed his wallet and was calling a taxi as he stepped out the door. Twenty-five minutes later he arrived at the marina. It looked like the fun was over. There were no lights, no sirens, no tactical teams in body armor. He walked over to a guy in shorts and a tank top who was watching a cop talking to a woman at the entrance to a long pier.

"What happened?" asked Deek.

"Some dude's boat blew up." The guy sniffed. "I left my damn rod on the pier. Cop won't let us back on until he's spoken to everyone. What's there to say?"

"Anyone hurt?"

The guy shrugged. "Didn't see them taking a body away, so…"

When the cop finished talking with the woman, the guy in the tank top approached him and Deek followed.

"Can I get my fishing rod now?"

The cop looked down the pier and then back. "Go on. But come straight back. Fishing's done for tonight."

The guy took off and the cop looked at Deek. "You see anything?" he asked.

"No, I just got here. I'm Morrison, Maritime Administration." He tried to make it sound like he was FBI or something, but he wasn't sure he nailed it.

"Maritime Administration? Never heard of it."

"Accidents on the water are something we track. What happened here?"

"A leaky fuel line on an old boat. It blew up."

"Casualties?"

"Nope."

"Who owns the boat?"

"Dunno. It's an old fiberglass thing, no registration decal, so no telling. I'm gonna wait here a while to see if the guy turns up, otherwise I guess he'll come looking for us when he finds his boat gone."

"What guy?"

"Whoever owns it."

"You get any kind of description?"

"Old guy, with a beard. Maybe. Nobody actually saw him get out of the boat, and I don't know how an old guy gets up onto this pier from a boat anyway. But that's what the witnesses saw. An old guy walking off the pier shortly before the explosion. Crazy old loon probably didn't maintain his tank. Was probably lucky he didn't get blown up too."

Deek thanked him and walked away. He'd wasted good money on a cab ride for nothing, and he couldn't blow any more on another taxi. He would have to walk back to the motel. Or was his car closer?

Suddenly Deek felt the world spinning. Maybe he was chasing shadows like his boss said. Maybe he was seeing things that just weren't there. He was risking his career—whatever that meant—on a flight of fancy. He felt the compulsion to throw up, so he ran toward a garbage can. For some reason that felt better than vomiting on the ground. He gripped the can and convulsed as he dry wretched. The taste of an hours old meatball sub burned his throat but nothing else came up.

He couldn't even vomit right.

Deek wiped his face as he looked down into the dark trash can. He saw something furry and recoiled when he thought it might be a raccoon. After he had pulled his heart from his throat, he looked back into the can. It wasn't a raccoon. He reached in and pulled out something dark and soft. It was like hair, but not real hair. He turned it around and straightened it out.

It was a long fake beard. The kind of thing a person might wear for Halloween if they were dressing up as a lumberjack. Only it wasn't Halloween, not even close. Then he recalled what the cop had said. An old guy with a beard. Only now the beard was in Deek's hand.

Deek strode away. He had something, he knew it. He wasn't sure what, and he wasn't sure how he would sell the idea of a fake beard meaning anything, but his gut was telling him it was something. He had to tell Sam. He had to tell Dusty.

He had to get back to his room. He checked his phone and found that his car was about the same distance away in the other direction. A two-hour walk around the maze of canals. But at least then he'd have his wheels.

As he walked, he processed what he knew and what he thought he knew and his confidence ebbed and flowed like a vicious tide. By the time he was halfway there he knew only two things for sure: he was going to devour what was left of a crusty old submarine sandwich and he was going to sleep like the dead.

A few hours later, the morning spread bright and warm across the second-floor balcony of the safehouse, where Angler sat drinking coffee. His first safehouse had been arranged for him, and it was still available should he need it, but Angler preferred staying under everyone's radar.

The house sat on stilts with a golf cart parked underneath, in a small subdivision of houses at the north end of the Baskin Island. He had tied up his rental boat at an empty pier on the back bay of the island and walked to the house along quiet, sandy tracks. The house was vacant—such was the benefit of home rental websites with calendars—so it was just a matter of walking the area until he found the place that matched the online photos.

The balcony was separated from the homes around it by a thick canopy of shade trees and cocoplum hedges. From his vantage point he overlooked a grass airstrip that cut roughly east-west through the trees like a scar. His attention was drawn to the sound of an engine starting up with too much choke, a spluttering that firmed into the solid throbbing of a small aircraft.

A couple minutes later a four-seater Cessna rolled out from beside another house and motored to the end of the runway. It sat for a moment—Angler assumed the pilot was doing his final checks. Although there was no tower, the pilot was probably getting clearance from the local commercial airport in Fort Myers.

Then the engine roared and the aircraft bounced along the strip and took off well before it got anywhere near the end. Angler watched it bank away to the north, then looked back to the airfield, where a man walked a French bulldog onto the strip and away toward the east of the island.

Angler sipped his coffee and thanked the homeowner for leaving the house well stocked. Plans were forming in his head. Ways in and ways out. Staging points and entry points. Threats from security and law enforcement. There were only a few more boxes to check, and Angler planned to check those after he had a second cup of caffeine.

Sam took her boat over to Pineland. Hers was a part-time role with the sheriff's office, so she had no rostered shift, but she towed Deek's rental skiff back to Chris's marina on her own time. She took a quick look at the scuba storage where someone had broken in and found Chris had repaired the cage with baling wire. Then she sipped a hot tea and used her cell phone to call Enoch's office while she had reception.

Enoch Brookes was a wealthy investor who split his time between the hubbub of New York City and the quiet anonymity of Baskin Island. He had been friends with Sam's uncle, Herm, for decades. Together Herm and Brookes had scuppered attempts by developers to overturn the nature conservancy on Baskin Island. To that end, Brookes had purchased the four homes that had been built at the south side of the island to prevent developers buying their way in. Brookes stayed in the southernmost house when he was on the island, and the others remained vacant, though maintained.

"Brookes Capital," said the woman who answered the phone.

"Margaret, this is Sam Waters. I'm a friend of Enoch's from Baskin Island."

"Yes, Sam, of course. How are things in Florida?"

"Monotonously sunny."

"Careful what you wish for, the other option might be a hurricane."

"Oh, I don't wish for anything else. But I wondered if Enoch was available?"

"I'm afraid not. Can I help?"

"Maybe. Does Enoch ever rent out his house on Baskin?"

"His private home? Never."

"What about, how do I put this, his spare houses?"

"On Baskin? No, not as a rule."

"It's just that there seems to be someone docked at one of the homes, and I wanted to check before I barged in on someone to whom he gave permission."

"Let me check with him. He's in Asia right now so it might be a few hours."

"No problem, thanks, Margaret."

"Thank you, Sam. Enoch appreciates you all keeping your eye on things."

"No problem. Bye."

Sam ended the call as she saw Dusty motor over from the island into the commercial dock where he left his police-issue SUV overnight. She wandered over.

"I called Enoch," said Sam. "He's in Asia but his secretary said she'd get back to me."

"I think Margaret's a personal assistant, but okay."

"What's the difference?"

"Perception, I guess. I thought you'd be all over that."

"If it's the same job I don't see how playing semantics helps."

"If you say so, Sam." Dusty tied up his skiff and walked toward his car. "I looked up the boat this morning. It's registered to a holding company that is owned by Harold Hildebrand, so I guess the economist's intel is good. On that at least."

"What do you make of the rest of it?"

"It's thin bordering on crazy. I put in a call to the FBI field office just to cover my bases."

"Your bases? More like your ar—"

A horn blared from a small car tearing into the gravel lot. It skidded to a stop near Dusty and Sam, and Deek Morrison practically fell out of it.

"You're both here. Cool. Did you hear about the explosion?"

Dusty and Sam traded a look. "Explosion?" they said in unison.

"Yeah, last night. You didn't hear about it?"

"No," said Sam. "Where?"

"The fishing pier up at the Cape Coral Yacht Club."

"I know it. The pier blew up?"

"No. A boat did."

"Someone blew up a boat?" asked Dusty. "How do you know this?"

"I was listening to the police scanner."

"Really? You don't have a TV?"

"I do, but it doesn't work. But that's not the point. I'm telling you there was an explosion."

"Give me a minute," said Dusty, walking away with his phone to his ear. For a moment Deek and Sam watched him having a conversation.

"This might not be related," said Sam.

"It is. Listen, I went to—"

"What do you think this was?" asked Dusty, returning to them. "An old boat with a faulty tank blew up. Nothing suspicious."

"Oh, it's plenty suspicious," said Deek. "If a boat blew up, where's the owner?"

"Might have been stolen."

"Then it's suspicious."

"But not terrorism."

"I'm telling you, I went to the scene. The officer there told me witnesses reported an old, bearded man walking away from the boat shortly before the explosion."

"So?"

"So, I found this." Deek stepped back to his car and returned with a plastic freezer bag holding what looked like a dead squirrel.

"What is that?" asked Sam.

"A fake beard. I found it in a trash can near the dock."

"You took evidence from a scene?" said Dusty.

"No. That's my point, there was no scene. No one else was looking for anything. I found it and now I'm turning over to the police." He handed it to Dusty.

"What do you want me to do with it? The chain of custody is a disaster. It could be yours."

"It might not be evidence, but it might tell you something about the guy who was wearing it."

Dusty glared at Sam as if it were her fault for bringing this lunatic into his life. "It was a decrepit, old boat, Deek. Not a super yacht."

"Maybe it was a practice run."

"Terrorists do their practice runs in Afghanistan or North Africa, not a couple miles from the target."

"Unless they have a reason to practice nearby."

Dusty shook his head. "All right, I'll have it tested. But when it gives up nothing, I need you to crawl back into your cave and leave me to do real detective work."

"Whatever," said Deek. "I'm telling you, it fits."

"You're making the evidence fit the hypothesis. It's a rookie mistake. Now, I've got to get to work."

Dusty took the bag and drove away, leaving Sam and Deek looking at each other with nothing to say.

"What now?" asked Deek.

"I've got things to do." Sam turned toward the dock. "Oh, and Deek. Don't go doing anything stupid."

"Did you check the boat?" He nudged his head toward Baskin Island.

"We did. It's Hildebrand's."

"See?"

"He might have a legit reason to be there. Just let us check it out, Deek."

She walked toward her boat and Deek kicked the gravel. Then he got back into his car and headed for the only place he could think to be.

4

Sam motored back over to Baskin and tossed the anchor on the beach beside her stilt house. She walked through the trees to Herm's camp and found him cleaning a gas generator.

"Morning, pet," he said through his thick beard. He had so much hair on his face and head he wasn't much more than a pair of eyes. "Cuppa?"

"Yeah, I'll do it." Sam filled the kettle from a water canister, put it on the camp stove and lit the flame. "Uncle Herm, have you heard anything about Enoch renting out one of his houses?"

"Here? No."

"There's a boat docked down there."

"His place?"

"No, the second one along."

"He's had people stay before but he always tells me."

"That's what I figured. I'll wander down and take a look."

"You want me to come?" he asked, hunched over the generator and looking like a bear mauling a salmon. If Harold Hildebrand was a rich guy, it was possible he and Enoch moved in the same circles, and she didn't want to cause unnecessary alarm. "No, I got it."

They drank their builders' tea and nibbled on some digestives that Sam's mum had mailed over from the UK, even though they could get English biscuits in the Publix in Cape Coral.

Sam cleaned up and then walked along the beach to the south end of the island, where it was only a rise of grassed dunes that separated the houses on the sound side from the beach on the Gulf.

She walked down the far side of the southernmost house—the one that Enoch Brookes used as his Baskin home. At the rear Sam could see across the backyards and docks of all four homes. There were now two boats at the second dock: Hildebrand's motor yacht and a twenty-foot center console fishing boat.

Sam retraced her steps and made for the second house. She figured she didn't have to go in as a county deputy of sorts, all official. There was another option.

As she reached the space between the two houses, Sam noticed a woman walking toward her along the line where the dunes met the lawns in front of the houses. There was no sidewalk or road. The sand just bled into the grass and was kept from taking over by regular visits from the gardeners.

Sam stopped outside the second house and watched the woman approach. She was taller than Sam's five-three, and her light cotton blouse and linen trousers gave her a stylish look. She saw Sam waiting and offered a smile as she approached.

"Good morning," she said as she reached the house.

"Morning," said Sam.

"Nice day for a walk," said the woman, brushing a fallen black hair from her face despite her modern bob cut, and offering her hand. "I'm Laura Smythe."

"Sam. Waters." Sam shook Laura's hand. She had pianist's fingers, slender and oddly strong.

"You're English," said Sam.

"Sort of. I grew up in Germany, actually. But my father was English."

"Your accent's BBC World Service."

"I went to secondary in London. My dad wanted me to speak with a proper English accent."

Sam had never heard such a perfect English accent, except maybe on the news or during the Queen's Christmas message. This woman could have been aristocracy. With her tanned face, large eyes and sharp nose she might have been from Munich or Manchester, Stockholm or Stevenage, Bratislava or Basingstoke. Sam suddenly felt self-conscious of her unkempt hair and Isle of Wight caulkhead accent.

"Are you staying on the island?" asked Laura.

"No, I live here, actually."

"How marvelous. It's paradise."

"That it is. And what about you?"

"I obviously don't live here. I'm setting up the house for my boss to come and stay."

"Here? I know the owner. He doesn't usually rent it out."

"No, I expect not. I don't think my boss is even paying for it. More like a favor, I suppose, from Mr. Brookes."

"You know Enoch?"

"Not personally. But my boss does."

"Harold Hildebrand?"

Laura nodded. "You know quite a lot, Sam."

"I'm the observant type. I noticed the boat."

"Ah, right. Well, would you like to come inside?"

"Sure, why not."

Laura led Sam inside the house. She had been inside Enoch's house only once, but the layout was the same. It was fully furnished with stuff Sam had seen in fancy catalogs. Laura didn't offer Sam a seat in one of the plush sofas. Instead they took stools at the marble kitchen counter.

"I'd offer you tea but Mr. Hildebrand doesn't drink it. Would you like some water?"

"No, I'm good, thanks." Sam noticed some boxes with wires hanging from them at the end of the counter.

"Security cameras," said Laura. "Mr. Hildebrand is quite particular about security, so when I come ahead of him I have them installed if they are not already in place. The technician is working on them now."

Sam glanced around but saw no cameras. Clearly rich people liked having security but didn't like the feeling of being watched.

"Is that the other boat out there?" asked Sam.

"You are observant."

"Occupational hazard."

"What is it you do?"

"I'm with the sheriff's department, part-time. I kind of look after things on Baskin. It's not always easy to get law enforcement out here."

"I see. Well you're right, that's the technician's boat. And it's also not easy getting tradesmen out here."

"Tell me about it. So what is it you do for Mr. Hildebrand?"

"I'm one of his personal assistants."

Personal assistant. She wouldn't mention that to Dusty. She'd never hear the end of it.

"One of?"

"Yes, he's a very important man, so he has a team. Part of my job is to arrive early to anywhere that he plans to go so we can ensure all his needs are met."

"Like the Secret Service do for the President?"

"Something like that, but it's just me."

"Can I ask when he's coming?"

"I can't say exactly, you understand, but he will be here for the end of the boat show."

"I heard something about a super yacht?"

"Yes. *La Fiamma Azzurra*, the blue flame. She will undertake her maiden voyage as the highlight of the end of the show."

"She's coming from Italy?"

"That's right."

"Wouldn't that have been her maiden voyage?"

"I'm not much of a boat person, but I believe the maiden voyage refers to a vessel's first trip in its intended duty. So technically the trip from Italy was a positioning voyage."

"Ah, got it. So if Mr. Hildebrand is staying here and has his super yacht over at Cape Coral, why is his other boat docked outside?"

"Oh, Mr. Hildebrand won't be staying here. He prefers to sleep on the *Aeolus*. But he needed somewhere to dock it, and he will use the house for entertaining."

"Wow. It's a real glimpse of how the other half live."

"I can assure you, Sam, it's all that and more. My dad was an English teacher, so it's quite something to me, too. But despite it all, I have to tell you, Mr. Hildebrand is actually a pretty normal man. He enjoys a barbecue and watching American football and spending time with his family, just like anyone."

"I bet his TV is pretty impressive."

"In New York, it's a twenty-seat media room with theater seating," she said, raising her eyebrows. "Anyway, Sam, I must get about my work. Thank you for dropping by."

"No, thank you, Laura." Sam slipped off her stool and walked to the door. "Let me give you my number in case you need anything."

"That's very kind."

As Sam recited her number, Laura punched it into her phone.

"I hope you enjoy your stay," Sam said.

"It's work, but it's not exactly digging in a mine."

Sam waved and walked back across the dunes. As she reached the peak the wind blew in the right direction and her phone got some reception and it bleeped that she had a voicemail.

"Hello, Samantha, it's Margaret. Just to let you know, I heard from Enoch and yes, he did offer one of the four houses to a business associate, a Mr. Hildebrand. Apparently the house is being prepared by an assistant. Her name is Laura. He apologized for not letting Herm know. If you have any problems, call me any time."

Sam ended the voicemail and walked back down onto the beach

and watched her bars drop to zero. So it was Hildebrand's boat and he was supposed to be at Enoch's house. Another piece of Deek's crazy puzzle was fitting into place. But Sam knew the best conspiracy theories were wound around a spindle of fact. The problem was, so was the truth.

5

Deek drove out to the resort and went to the ballroom. It had almost fully morphed into an exhibition hall for The Great American Boat Show. A week of standing in a boring booth, handing out leaflets and stickers. No one really cared about the Department of Transportation or what they did. They would only care if the department wasn't there.

A UPS guy arrived with a trolley load of boxes and Deek signed for them. He placed the boxes of brochures behind his curtained table and then erected the popup banners at the back of the space. There really wasn't a lot more to do. The corporate event would start the following day and the people around him looked so excited. They didn't know what Deek knew.

He was no use to anyone here. There was a terrorist on the loose and Deek was the only one committed enough to track him down. Şeytan was out there, boating around, scoping out the territory, blowing things up.

"To hell with this," said Deek. He ripped open a box of brochures and placed a stack on the table, then he did the same with the stickers. There was a box of beer koozies that he left under the table—they felt like hot commodities. Another box was marked pens, so he threw a stack of those out too, and put a couple in his pocket. You never knew when you might have to jot something down.

Deek looked around the exhibition hall, then he turned and walked out of the hotel and back to his car. He needed a boat. And he knew just where to get one.

Angler puttered down Pine Island Sound under the cover of a Tampa Bay Buccaneers ball cap and souvenir shop knockoff Ray-Bans. The day remained clear with a few clouds out over the Gulf, and the sparkle off the water made the sunglasses mandatory. He motored back toward the mouth of the river but this time instead of banking toward the resort, he eased the jon boat to starboard around Little Shell Island and made for Iona Cove.

He passed a peninsula with apartment-type buildings on it that his map told him was a retirement village and slowed before he reached the canal that cut into the naturally protected marina of the St. Charles Yacht Club.

After killing the motor, Angler slowly let out the anchor. It didn't go far. The depth could have been no more than six or seven feet. The water was a murky copper color but he wanted to know exactly what conditions were like under the surface.

Angler glanced around to see if anyone was watching but he had selected his position well. He was five hundred feet off the shore that was nothing more than mangrove scrub. He was sheltered from the view of the retirement village by the curvature of the cove and from eyes to the east by Iona Point.

He dropped his sunglasses in his hat and tucked them into the bow, pulled on some fins, and then hoisted the air cylinder onto his back. The harness was old and neither were much to look at, but Angler wasn't concerned. The dive shop on Pine Island where he had stolen it clearly kept their old gear in decent repair, and this was not deep-water diving. He checked the regulator and made sure everything was functional. The pressure gauge was ancient but he wasn't planning on being down for long, or any deeper than he could easily surface in one breath.

Angler pulled the mask over his head and then swiveled around into the water—he feared a back flip might hit bottom. His feet landed on the mud, and he stood with his shoulders out of the water, no more than four feet deep. The shallow water was warm enough to go without a wetsuit, and his chart suggested it wasn't going to get a lot deeper other than in the boating channel.

He didn't want to draw attention so he didn't use a diving flag, instead just finning down and away from the boat. Visibility was poor. He couldn't see his hands out in front, surrounded by dense brown atmosphere as alien as any far-flung planet. He had to work at staying low enough in the water for his tank to not protrude like a dorsal fin.

Twenty minutes in the murk told Angler that the sand banks and zero visibility would make it hard to navigate without breaking the surface. He cut across the cove toward a tight channel that led from the main river in toward the yacht club. He popped up and found the markers, and seeing no traffic eased into the channel.

It was deeper but narrow. Either side the depth dropped sharply from about four feet to fifteen. Visibility wasn't much better but he found he could use the channel walls to navigate. He made his way out into the main river and then came up at the edge of the channel when he heard the increasing hum of motorboats around him.

As his head broke the water he realized the channel took a crazy turn—perhaps around some underwater impediment—and he found himself toward the middle of the new section. He heard the sound of the speedboat and kicked around to see the white hull hurtling toward him. He had figured the speed limit would be low to no wake but this boat was planing across the water like he was on open water.

Straight at Angler.

His instinct was to not be seen so he didn't try to swim out of the way. He dove hard, kicking toward the channel floor. He pumped his legs and heard the outboard motor roar toward him. He was diving into darkness when the boat hit his fins. The hull clipped the tips and pushed his legs down out of the way of the prop, and for a moment Angler thanked his luck.

Then the wake hit him. The props caused more turmoil below water than they did above, and Angler was flipped over and tossed around as if in a washing machine. As the boat passed and the thrashing died down, Angler was disoriented. Was he facing up or facing down? He didn't know. He put his hand to his mouth to make sure the regulator was still in place and touched his lips. Then he realized he was holding his breath, the mouthpiece having been knocked out.

He didn't panic. He reached for his octopus and found it had unclipped from the harness. Both hoses were floating somewhere around him, possibly behind his head where they attached to his tank.

Angler could feel himself sinking. He had the sense that his kit was dragging him down. The brown atmosphere looked lighter in front of him, so he decided that was the surface. That was up. And he was done diving.

He unclipped his harness and slipped out of it, letting the cylinder drag the rest of the equipment to the bottom. A couple of quick pulses with his fins and he was headed up, and a couple of seconds later he broke from the copper-colored water into the bright blue of a Florida day.

He turned to look at the speedboat zooming away, the wide wake spreading across the cove. After a quick 360 to confirm there were no further boats and no watching eyes, Angler spotted his boat a couple hundred yards away. He kicked toward it, keeping his nose just above the surface like an alligator.

When he reached the jon boat he crawled into it, ripped off his T-shirt, and used a towel he had taken from the safehouse to dry.

Then he donned his ball cap and glasses and started the motor, thinking that the copper water made scuba no fun at all, but it also made him harder to find, provided he could stay below the surface. He eased onto the throttle and motored away, looking across the water toward the resort, his mind whirring with possibilities.

6

Deek drove to the marina on Pine Island. He parked near the marina store and went inside to find the woman he had met on the pontoon boat. She was behind the counter as he stepped into the well-stocked store. It was part 7-Eleven and part camping store, all with a nautical twist, and it had the musty aroma of old rope.

"Deek," said the woman.

"Hello," he replied.

"Chris Eastwind," she said.

"Yes, of course. I wanted to go and see Sam on the island, but I think she was bringing my rental boat back here."

"It's locked up down the end there." She tossed him a key. "Bring back the key, will you?"

"Sure thing."

Deek took the key and found his skiff locked up with a handful of others. He unlocked his boat and pulled the chain through, then locked the other boats again and returned the key.

He motored across the sound to Baskin Island and along the shoreline until he found the small beach with the stilt house. Sam's boat was anchored to the sand but she was nowhere to be found. Deek grabbed the bow and pulled his own boat up onto the sand.

As he did he saw a tender cruising out on the sound with a shirtless man at the tiller. He wore a ball cap and sunglasses, and bore what appeared to be a graying goatee. South Florida was full of interesting characters but Deek wondered how a shirtless man wouldn't burn to a crisp in this sun. This guy had weathered skin that stretched taut over a burly frame. As the boat headed northward, Deek felt there was something familiar about the man's build.

Deek watched the boat until the mangroves stole it from view, then he turned and walked along the sand path. Within seconds he had lost the path and wandered into scrubby foliage, but he figured the island wasn't that wide, so he pushed his way on, deeper into the trees.

Angler reached the small cove at the top end of the island and left his boat at the empty dock across from the small marina. He took his wet shirt and headed around back. A man in a turquoise polo and navy-blue shorts walked out of the marina office and met Angler on the path.

"That your boat?" he asked.

"Yeah."

"Can't leave it there. That's a private dock."

"Didn't know that. I'll grab a shirt and move it."

"You staying at the resort?"

"Yeah."

"You can leave it there."

"Will do." Angler nodded and kept walking. He headed up past the marina and then banked south in case the guy was watching. The resort was in a small inlet just south of the cove, although Angler felt calling it a resort was stretching the truth. It was more like a fishing camp with small efficiency huts overlooking a boardwalk where anglers could park their boats out front.

Angler walked into the resort and cut inland, then turned onto a sandy road that led back to the north. He walked through the streets, zigging and zagging along the sandy paths. There were few people around and those who were seemed to keep to themselves. In another life this could have been the sort of place that he settled down. As it was, only time would tell whether he would ever be able to show his face around these parts again.

He found the safehouse and picked his phone out from behind a royal palm. The house was still vacant so he went inside and found a Guy Harvey T-shirt that fit well enough. He looked out at the airfield and thought about his options.

Although there weren't that many people around, his encounter at the marina reminded him someone was always watching. That was why he was in this safehouse. The fewer people who knew his plans, the better. His last mission had gone awry because the plans were not completely within his control, and he had no intention of letting that happen again.

But he did have another option. He had been told about the houses at the south end of the island. There were four, and they would be vacant. But that wasn't the case. One house had a boat moored out the back, and Angler had seen people around. He had written it off, but now he reconsidered. It was worth checking out. The boat might come in useful, for getting in or getting out. He preferred to cultivate multiple options for every eventuality, and he might need somewhere other than this place.

He pulled on his ball cap and walked out. He took the direct route back to the jon boat, then headed out and away along the shoreline. He motored past a small beach with an isolated stilt house that might have been the ideal staging point, but two dinghies on the beach suggested it wasn't as vacant as it looked.

Angler continued on to the south end of the island. The mangroves gave way to four similar homes, clearly built as a job lot. Each had a dock in the sheltered water behind, but only one dock held a boat. Angler noted that the second house from the south had two boats on the dock when he passed earlier, but the smaller fishing boat was now gone.

He eased off the throttle and pulled into the northernmost dock, between the pier and the mangroves. After looping the bow line around a branch, he stepped up onto the dock and headed for the house.

When he got to the rear slider he cupped his hands. The interior looked quiet and dark. There were no glasses or coffee cups, no mail on the dining table or remotes in front of the TV. He glanced along the row of homes and saw no one. Not an ashtray on an outdoor table or a bathing suit hanging over a chair. Nothing but the boat two docks down. Angler moved around the far side of the house. It was time to take a look inside.

Deek's pants were scratched and torn by the time he broke from the trees and scrub, out onto the long beach. The sand was white and the azure water gleamed in the sun. It was a postcard. But he had no time for it. He was looking for the campsite, expecting to find Sam there, but instead he had thrashed through a jungle. He looked down the beach for something familiar. And found it.

Two people were beach fishing a hundred yards away. One of them was the man who looked like a bear who he had met at the pontoon boat bar. The other was Sam. He waved as he approached.

"Agent," said Sam with a sarcastic grin. "You remember my Uncle Herm."

"Yeah." Deek scratched at the sand. "Catch anything?"

"Fish," said Herm.

"Right."

"What brings you out here?" asked Sam.

"I think I saw Şeytan again. The guy I've been telling you about."

"Groucho Marx glasses this time?"

"No. And no beard."

"Of course not. You took his beard."

"He had a goatee."

"Oh, he went to the barbershop?"

"I'm telling you I saw him."

"Where?"

"In a boat. A tender. Same as before."

"Where?"

"Out there, on the sound."

"A lot people boat on the sound."

"He was headed in toward the island, up at the north end."

Sam reeled her line in and then stuck the rod in the sand. "If we go take a look and he's not around, or we find he's just some guy out fishing, will you stop bugging me about this?"

Deek shrugged. "I don't know."

"Not good enough, Deek."

"All right. I won't bug you."

They left Herm to his fishing and Sam led the way back along the path that now looked as wide as a freeway. They strode through the camp and out to the stilt house. Sam picked up her anchor and tossed it into her boat, then pushed the bow into the water.

"Should I come with you?" asked Deek.

Sam gave him a look that said *yes*.

Deek rushed into the water before Sam had the boat too deep and levered himself in. She jumped in and then started it up and headed north, directing them into the back bay and toward the marina. She pulled into the dock and as she stepped up onto the pier the guy in the turquoise polo approached.

"Sam," he said.

"Wes. You seen any strange folks around today?"

"This is Baskin Island, Sam."

"Anyone you don't know?" She looked at Deek. "You got a description?"

"Last I saw, he was in a ball cap and sunglasses. And shirtless, not young but well built."

Sam frowned. "That's what you're basing this on?"

Deek shrugged.

"Yeah, I saw that guy," said Wes.

"Seriously?" said Sam.

"Yeah. He stopped at the dock over the other side and I told him it was private, and he said he'd move to the resort."

"He's staying at the resort?"

"He walked off that way, but when he came back he was coming from the north, so who knows. He took the boat back down to the south, but he wasn't headed for the resort."

"When was that?"

"Maybe ten minutes ago. Fifteen, tops."

Sam jumped back into her boat and thanked Wes, then opened the throttle up and sped down the coastline. Deek played with the watch on his wrist as if it were a nervous tic. "If we can get to St. James City we might be able to see him on the water."

Sam opened the throttle fully and then came off a touch. She didn't need to cook her motor. They zoomed down to the south end of the island, both of them scanning the water ahead for any sign of the mystery man.

Then Sam banked suddenly and Deek nearly went overboard.

"What are you doing?" he yelled as Sam turned hard toward the houses.

"There," she said. "At the dock."

"That's Hildebrand's yacht. I told you."

"Not that one. The other dock, near the mangroves. That's a jon boat, and it doesn't belong there."

Laura Smythe stood in the kitchen as her phone buzzed. One of the security sensors had flagged movement. There were no pets or house staff and the installer was long gone. She stepped to the rear slider and saw a small boat headed toward the docks. There was a man at the bow who she didn't recognize. But she knew the woman at the tiller. It was the woman who claimed to know the owner of the houses. Now a sensor had flagged and she was speeding toward the docks. But it wasn't them who had triggered anything. She slipped her phone in her pocket and went to investigate.

Sam slowed as the boat reached the docks. She moved in between the dock and the mangroves that sheltered them, then she killed the motor, drifting in toward the boat that was already tied up there. Deek grabbed hold of a piling and threw a bow line around it.

"It's a rental," said Deek. "There might be a record."

"Or it might be innocent," said Sam, pulling the kill switch from the motor and climbing up onto the dock. "Stay behind me."

Deek nodded as if that was always his plan and followed Sam up the dock. She ran to the corner of the house and rested against the wall. Deek followed suit.

"Do you have a gun?" he asked.

"No, I'm British."

"But you're with the sheriff."

"I'm a community liaison. You're American. You don't have a gun?"

"No. I'm an economist."

"All right then." Sam swiveled around so she was in front of the sliding glass patio doors. She cupped her hands and peered inside. The place looked quiet and dark, as expected. Enoch Brookes only ever used the southernmost house, and Sam couldn't recall anyone ever being in this one. It was the closest to the mangroves so had the most limited views.

Deek edged in and cupped his hands on the glass, then Sam pulled on the door and found it locked. She glanced down the row of patios and saw nothing.

"Let's check the front."

Angler pushed himself against the wall in the hallway and watched the woman looking in the sliding glass doors. He found himself holding his breath, despite knowing she couldn't hear or see him in the darkened interior. She was a brunette, lean but quite short, maybe five-three. She turned to talk to someone, then a man cupped his hands against the glass. Angler had seen this guy before at the boat show. He had scruffy blond hair and a nose that wasn't quite straight, but the kind of soft face that suggested it didn't get that way in a fight. For a moment they looked into the dark house, then they stepped out of view. Angler glanced above his head where the stairs led to the second floor, then back toward the sliders. Things were getting a little too hot.

He pulled out his phone and hit call. "You awake?"

"Ready as ever."

"I'm on Baskin Island. South end."

"No problem. When?"

"Now."

Angler ended the call and turned toward the front door. Someone was there. He didn't know if that someone had access, so he opened the door behind him and slipped into the closet under the stairs.

The recipient of Angler's call was sitting in a bar called Harpoon Harry's in Port Charlotte. He wasn't partaking of the bar's best work. Instead he was sitting on a coffee, killing time the way he often did. He slipped a twenty under his mug and picked up his ball cap from the bar, then he stepped outside where his ride waited for him in the sunshine.

Sam pulled on the front door and found it locked. She stepped back and called out. "Hello, anyone home?"

There was no answer. Then Sam's phone rang from an unknown caller.

"Sam Waters."

"Sam, help." It was not much more than a whisper, but definitely a woman.

"Who is this?"

"It's Laura Smythe. I'm upstairs in the end house near the mangroves. I'm tied up."

"Is anyone with you?"

"No, but he might still be inside."

"I'll have to call the sheriff. I can't break the glass, it's hurricane proof."

"I know the front door code."

"You do? How?"

"I saw him enter it. Hurry."

"Give it to me."

Sam entered the code into the keypad on the door and a metallic click told her she was in. She pushed the door wide open but stayed against the jamb, then she slid along the wall in the hallway. After giving her eyes a moment to adjust, she moved further in. The house was quiet and immaculate. The furnishings looked expensive and unused. She heard the hum of the refrigerator but nothing more.

She glanced back. Deek was still at the door so she waved him in. "Stay against this wall. Watch the stairs for anyone."

Deek nodded and Sam slipped into the living room. The sun coming though the rear sliders made it considerably lighter. She turned into the kitchen and found it empty, then she did a quick sweep of the rooms finding no one. Perhaps the man was still upstairs, or perhaps he had fled.

Sam retraced her steps and then moved past Deek and up the stairs.

"Be careful," whispered Deek.

"No kidding."

Sam stayed against the wall as she moved up the steps until she was in a landing, where the house broke off into three directions. Sam checked the first bedroom on the island side and found it empty. Then she moved to a room on the water side.

Laura Smythe was sitting against a built-in wardrobe with her hands and feet bound by zip ties. Her phone was on the carpet beside her.

"What happened?" asked Sam, dropping to her knees.

"I saw a man at the house so I went to speak to him. Like I had with you. I thought he was just a lookie-guy."

"Lookie-loo," said Deek from the doorway.

"Deek, find some scissors or something," said Sam. Deek moved to a desk and started rummaging through the draws and Sam turned back to Laura. "So what happened?"

"He said he was staying there, and I said that must be a mistake and he invited me in to call the realtor. He knew the code and everything. Once he closed the door he grabbed me and tied me up."

"I need to check the house properly," said Sam. "He might still be here."

"He's not," said Deek.

"How do you know?"

"Because I can see him right now." Deek pointed out the window.

Sam stood and looked out toward the water. The man in the ball cap was running along the dock.

7

Angler waited until he heard the voices upstairs, then he slipped out of the closest with a clenched fist. No one was waiting, so he strode across the living room to the sliding door and flipped the latch, then stepped out onto the patio. He closed the door behind him and jogged across the small lawn toward the water.

His feet echoed on the wood slats until he reached the new boat tied up there. He unlooped the rope from the cleat and gave the hull a shove with his boot, pushing it out toward the sound. Then he stepped back to his own boat, got in and scrambled to the bow where he untied from the mangroves. He pulled the rope to start the motor, and reversed out from the tight space. As soon as he reached the end of the dock he cut a U through the water and clunked the throttle into forward.

Sam sprinted onto the dock watching the man in the ball cap motoring away. She knew before she even reached it that her own boat had been untied and was floating away. Stopping at the end of the dock she watched the man disappearing as Deek caught up to her.

"Now what?" he asked.

Sam didn't answer. Instead she dove into the water. It wasn't warm like the height of summer but she had grown up in the chilly waters around the Isle of Wight, so this was nothing. She swam fast, pumping hard until she reached her boat, then she dragged herself up over the side. She pulled the kill switch from her pocket, put it in place and started up the motor, then pulled the tiller hard to swing around to the end of the dock.

"Get in," she yelled.

Deek hesitated until she was almost past then he leaped into the boat, landing on Sam's lap. She pushed him down into the hull and twisted the throttle hard. The bow spiked into the air, sending Deek back into Sam's lap.

"Sorry," he said, clambering back onto a bench.

Sam sped out onto the sound and Deek pointed to the north. "There."

The other man was in a rental boat, one made for neither comfort nor speed. Sam's vessel, on the other hand, had been cobbled together from an old hull that had been discarded in a corner of Christine's marina and a secondhand outboard that could have powered a full-sized fishing boat. Sam had learned to be careful when opening the throttle lest she flip the darn thing. As she eased up to full throttle, skimming across the surface, it reminded Sam of her police days in the UK, shooting across the South Coast waters in a marine unit RIB. In those days they were fast enough to catch anything. She couldn't reach those speeds, but she was certainly going to catch the little putt-putt she was chasing.

Angler saw the boat coming after him, closing the distance rapidly. Pine Island Sound was a wide expanse of water so he was confident he could zig and zag long enough, should it come to that. They were going to find it tough to get an angle to ram him, and jumping from a moving boat onto another was the stuff of movies. Little girls didn't do that in real life. He looked north and saw plenty of water ahead. Then he smiled when he realized he wasn't going to need much time at all.

Sam felt good. The salt spray was whipping across her face, the sun was out, and there was nowhere she would rather be than chasing some guy who may or may not be a terrorist across the sound. Plus, she was gaining rapidly on him.

Then a frown crept across her brow. Sam saw the dot on the canvas sky morph into an aircraft as it swooped in low. "What the hell is that?"

"That's a de Havilland DHC-3 Otter," said Deek.

"How on earth do you know—" Sam's words caught in her throat as the aircraft dropped only ten feet over the boat in front but continued down toward the water. It was like a regular single-prop aircraft except the landing gear had been replaced by pontoons, which sent twin wakes out as the floats hit the water between the two boats, heading straight at Sam and Deek.

Sam figured she wouldn't win a game of chicken with a plane so she yanked on the tiller. As they careened away the seaplane bounced off the water and Sam caught sight of wheels embedded in the floats. She killed their speed to prevent capsizing and sent a spray high into the air. The boat spun in place and Deek was thrown around the boat like a discarded beer can.

When Sam looked back toward her quarry she saw that the man in the ball cap had pulled a 180 and was headed back after the aircraft. Sam hit the throttle again, tossing Deek once more, and took off after him.

The pilot wore a huge grin. Being a pilot inherently meant being a rule follower. There were preflight checklists and inflight procedures and a rule book thicker than a Gideon's bible. Despite all the rules, flying was still fun. But this was something else. He loved working for people who went by code names and paid in cash. They weren't so worried about the rules. And flying low, landing anywhere but a runway, and scaring the life out of boaters—now *that* was fun.

As he hit the water he eased back on the throttle. To the south he could see the Sanibel Causeway and although he was confident he had more than enough room for takeoff, he knew there was nothing obstructing his path to the north. He turned around, his inside float biting in the water, and headed back toward the small boat with the man waving his ball cap.

Angler waved his cap at the seaplane and then threw it in the air. He banked around to meet the seaplane as it reached him. When the aircraft got beside him the pilot slowed. Angler waited for him to stop but he didn't. He was going to have a word about that—Angler was getting too old for this movie star crap. But he couldn't talk to the pilot now. He eased in alongside the seaplane, matched its speed, then with his hull butting against the float, Angler grabbed a strut and jumped across.

Sam glanced back and saw the other boat turn so the seaplane would come between them. She followed the lead and banked around knowing that she was faster than the other boat but not faster than any kind of aircraft. She could try cutting off the pilot's take off zone but stumped up against the chicken game again, and she lacked the speed to come at them from behind.

"Six or out," she said.

"What?" asked Deek.

Sam shook her head and eased her boat out a couple of hundred yards ahead of the aircraft and matched its heading. She turned the throttle and burst away, as if she was now the one being chased.

Angler clambered up into the cockpit and looked at the pilot grinning like an idiot. A man should enjoy his work but this guy was something else. Still, Angler envied the look on the man's face. For a second he tried to recall the last time he had enjoyed his work that much.

"Should I take her out?" asked the pilot.

Angler scanned the water ahead and saw the boat with the woman at the helm. Running her down would certainly put her out of the hunt, but Angler wasn't a fan of unnecessary casualties. And bodies on the water would bring the kind of attention that an unauthorized amphibious craft landing would not.

"No. We've got somewhere to be."

"You're the boss."

The pilot pushed throttle and the seaplane accelerated.

Deek watched the aircraft behind them as it powered up, the roar from the props telling him a takeoff was imminent. Sam eased her heading to bring the aircraft close by, then called to him.

"Take the tiller."

Deek hesitated.

"Come here, now!" she yelled.

Deek clambered over the bench seat and across the hull, keeping low, wanting anything but to fall into the water. When he reached the back bench he sat beside Sam, who directed his attention to the tiller.

"Keep it steady. Bring us in close."

She didn't say close to what, but once Deek had his hand on the control she scrambled to the side of the boat and leaned out toward the rapidly approaching seaplane. Deek was about to ask what she was doing but it was as apparent as it was crazy. She was going to try to jump onto a moving aircraft from a moving boat. It was completely insane and without a doubt the most exciting day of Deek's entire life.

The aircraft reached them and Sam waved for Deek to get closer to the nearest float. The boat bounced across the water, faster than was sensible but still slower than the accelerating aircraft. As Deek brought them into the path of the seaplane, Sam knew she would have to time it perfectly, and as she got into a sprinter's starting position, she wondered what her mother would think of what she was doing.

The tip of the float reached them, moving faster than Sam had appreciated, and a good two feet away. It was all too far and too fast. Then with a yank, Deek pulled the little boat hard into the float. The aircraft's cabin door flashed by and Sam saw nothing but wake behind the seaplane, so she pushed hard at the imaginary starter's pistol and launched herself out of the boat toward the speeding aircraft.

8

Sam had grown up around boats and had learned at a very young age that there were few surfaces that weren't hard. Wood, fiberglass, steel. Lots of places to bang yourself up. Even the cushioned bench seats tended to be on the firm side. Sam had every expectation that an aircraft was the same, but the impact with the float still sent a shockwave through her body as she wrapped her arms around the strut. Her feet hit the water and bounced up, ripping her shoes off and nearly pulling her from the pontoon.

She dragged herself onto the float and tried to regain her breath, but the aircraft was pounding up and down on the water, vibrating so violently she couldn't fathom how it stayed in one piece. Sea spray whipped her arms and face. She knew the seaplane could take off at any moment, but as she dragged herself up every movement seemed to take an eternity.

Sam willed herself forward from the back strut to the forward one, and then tried to reach for the cabin door. She couldn't hold on and open the door at the same time. It was a one or the other proposition. To get the door open, she was going to have to let go.

Then the cabin door opened. Sam locked eyes with the man inside. He was older than she had figured him to be, but not someone she would describe as an old man. The arm holding the door was muscular and a tattoo peeked from under the shirt sleeve. He wore a crew cut like an army guy, and his face was taut across his cheekbones. But it was his eyes that stuck with Sam. They were piercing and intelligent, not unhinged or afraid. He looked as calm as a golfer. He appeared to mouth words that Sam couldn't hear, then he raised one eyebrow as if to say, *them's the breaks*, and he thrust his boot at Sam's face.

This was no meek little girl. Angler opened the cabin door to find her hanging off the float strut. She was getting pummeled by the spray shooting up from the front, but she looked determined as all hell. She had guts, and for a moment Angler wondered why it was so hard to find crew like that.

"Sorry, kid. Some days you're the windshield, some days you're the bug."

Angler shoved his boot to push her off the float but she spun around the strut and he hit nothing but metal. He kicked out again and again but didn't dislodge her. She was holding onto the forward strut so Angler had to kick underneath the cabin door, which physics wanted to close on his leg. She was like an annoying mosquito, and he was trying to figure how to squish her when he felt the vibration of the aircraft change. If he couldn't dislodge her now, then they'd get rid of her once they were well in the air.

Angler resettled in the cabin and let the wind slam the door shut.

Everything changed. The sea spray stopped hurting and the vibrating eased. For a second Sam felt good about all that. Then the realization kicked in that the aircraft was taking off. She was drenched to the bone and her hands were cramping. She had no idea where the seaplane would go or how long it would be in the air, but she figured it didn't matter. She couldn't hold on for long, even assuming they didn't try banking to dislodge her, which they surely would. And if that happened thousands of feet in the air... Sam was so confident in the water that people often asked if she was part fish. But no one had ever asked if she was part bird.

As she felt the float lift out of the water she let go of the strut and pushed away with her bare feet. Then she curled into a ball and waited for the impact.

Deek saw the seaplane launch into the air but his focus was on the ball that bounced across the water like a dam-busting bomb. He lurched through the wake of the aircraft until he saw the ball unravel and then begin to sink.

The impact was percussive and knocked every gasp of air out of Sam's body. She was flung across the surface of the water, slamming against her back, then her shoulder, then as she opened up, her face smashed into the unforgiving water. When her momentum stopped she was face down, or maybe face up but underwater. She couldn't see light and wasn't even sure her eyes were working. Water surrounded her and she fought the compulsion to breathe. She was winded and dazed, and despite all her training, the programming to swim to the surface didn't kick in. Sam lived on the water, and she knew that panic was what killed most people. But she didn't feel panic. It was like being a little drunk, still aware but content to just go with the flow, even if the flow was down to the bottom of the sea.

Then she felt her body jerk and her orientation invert, and suddenly her face broke the surface and the wide blue sky blinded her. She felt herself get dragged against something hard, and she looked up to see a man holding her against the hull of a boat.

"Can you breathe?" he said.

Breathe? What a splendid idea. The application wasn't so much fun. Sam choked as salt water burned her throat, then she spat the brine out in a series of retches before something akin to air began taking the water's place in her lungs. She took a few shallow breaths to clear the fog and then looked around again. She was in the water, being held against the boat. The man wasn't trying to pull her in. Instead he was just letting her come to, and making sure she didn't disappear underneath the choppy surface.

She glanced up at him again. "Deek."

"You're okay," he said. "I got you." Then he looked up to the sky and Sam followed his gaze. An aircraft roared across the sky, banking hard to the west, out toward the wide expanse of the Gulf of Mexico. She watched the seaplane fly away until it disappeared behind the trees on Baskin Island, then she looked up at Deek.

"I'm sorry."

Deek shook his head. "Don't be. No one's gotten that close to Şeytan before. And you got a look at him, didn't you?"

"A good look."

"So now we know what he looks like."

"But not where's he's gone. He could end up anywhere."

Deek smiled. "I got the Otter's tail number."

"He's not going to ask for permission to land at an airport, Deek."

"No, he's not. But there's a lot of people out there who watch aircraft movements, especially interesting craft like seaplanes."

"But how will you know if someone sees it?"

Deek winked. "I've got an app for that."

9

"Where we goin' boss? Still Marathon?"

"After that little stunt, eyes will be on all of the major airports and marinas. We need to put down some place a lot quieter."

Angler listened to the drone of the engine for longer than his patience allowed.

"I know the perfect spot," the pilot finally revealed. "You need to get to Key West anyway, right? There are so many spoil islands in that area, it'll be easy to dip behind one, drop you, and run. They'll never find you."

"Sounds perfect."

"Ten-four, boss. Setting a heading towards the lower Keys. We should be there in about an hour."

"Did you bring the gear?"

"Of course. All the way back."

As the plane leveled off and headed south, Angler climbed between the seats and tugged a small duffel bag from under the back bench where it lay beside some dive gear and a pile of random engine parts atop an old blue tarp. He stripped off his T-shirt, wet and sticky from seawater and sweat, and donned a lightweight long-sleeved shirt favored by the fishermen in the sunny islands.

He ran his fingers through his stiff hair. He preferred a tighter cut, but he always let it grow longer—along with the goatee that grew in a little grayer each time—before an operation. Easier to trim and shave to change his appearance on the fly. He hadn't expected to need that step this early. But too many people had seen him already, and he still had too much to do.

He felt solid about the location. Plenty of options. Backups to the backups. Contingencies galore for every step. But he wasn't used to tapping into them this early. The little float-jumping spitfire and her doofus boyfriend gave him pause. Under any other circumstance, she was the type of number he liked to have in his back pocket. Guts. Determination. You don't find that often enough these days.

He balled up the soiled shirt, tucked it into the bottom of the bag. His hand brushed against cold steel, and he slipped the heavy item into the pocket of his cargo shorts.

"Chick was crazy! Think she bit it, boss?"

He glanced up at the seaplane pilot. The man had come when called. That was a plus. But as Angler slid behind the copilot's yoke, scanning the instrument panel out of habit rather than interest, he assessed the man with a team leader's eyes. Too much joy in the chase. Glee in the thought that the little blonde might not have survived the fall. Angler saw the residual adrenaline rush in the way the pilot's body still trembled and the corner of his lip turned up in a sneering grin. Angler's own thoughts on the matter were a little more complicated. The woman had locked eyes with him. She was close enough to see him.

But who was she?

"Hard to say. But neither option is great for us. Either she makes it and can identify us, or she doesn't and there's a body tied to your tail number. And the boyfriend is a witness regardless. We have some loose ends to tie up."

"*Au contraire, mon frère.* You think I'd fly a gig like this with a real N-number?"

Angler leveled his gaze to the left seat. Maybe he'd misjudged this guy after all?

"Tail number and all the colors are temporary decals. Peel right off. Everything but the model changes in under five minutes. Not my first rodeo, brother."

"And how many DHC-3 Otters fly around these parts?"

"Enough that no one has found me yet. You worry too much, boss." He ducked his head toward the instrumentation, looked past the glowing autopilot indicator, and pointed to the main GPS screen. "We'll be there in about thirty minutes. If you're wanting to disappear, your best spots will be here or here. I can be down and back up in under two minutes without anyone noticing, then I'll tuck into one of my many hidey-holes, change the numbers, and be on my way. No problemo and nice doing business with you."

Sounded good on paper. But blue stripes or orange, an Otter was an Otter, not a Cessna.

"But you should have kept her hanging on 'til I had a little more altitude. Hard splat, problem solved."

While the pilot had a valid point, Angler couldn't get past the glint in his eye as he rhapsodized about killing the woman. And on any other operation, a touch of crazy might be useful. But today? This week? Details mattered. Control was king. And this guy was out of control.

Angler pulled a deep breath through his lungs and slowly released it, his gaze focused on the horizon. Then he pulled the compact SIG Sauer from his cargo pocket, and in one smooth motion, pressed it against the pilot's temple and fired.

"That tail number you gave me? It's a dud. Registered to a twin Comanche that was decommissioned in 1988."

Deek wrapped his fingers tighter around the steering wheel and stared across the endless swamp that stretched to the horizon on both sides of the arrow-straight highway. His buddy Pete's voice echoed through the rental car's speakers.

"What else can you tell me? Model? Time it took off? Initial heading?"

Deek exhaled. "DHC-3 Otter. Seaplane. White with blue pin striping. Touched down on Pine Island Sound about forty minutes ago, then headed due south. I need to find that plane."

"Roger that."

Without the clacking of a keyboard, punctuated by grunts and the occasional profanity, Deek might have thought the call had dropped as he sped through nowhere significantly faster than the state troopers allowed.

"Not a twin? Couple of those in the vicinity."

"Nope."

Clack, clack, sigh. Pause. Clack, clack.

Deek almost jumped out of his skin when a ringtone burst through the speakers and a number popped up on the display.

Two-oh-two. The boss.

Deek hit decline and the sound of Pete's keyboard resumed. A moment later his voice burst into the passenger cabin.

"Hoo, doggie. This is interesting. So listen. I'm not seeing any single-prop Otters live in the area. But what I do have is a crop duster out of Palatka in the middle of the damn Gulf. But it's *also* in the air over a field three miles from the airstrip in Palatka. Looks like maybe your guy has tampered with his transponder. And if it had a different fake tail number, it's probably a guy you don't want to mess with, Deek. Want I should call the tower in Key West?"

Deek weighed his choice quickly. The first person to take him seriously was a buddy from his office geek Dungeons and Dragons group. Maybe he could get someone to bring this guy in. It might throw a wrench in whatever he's planning. But what were the chances of someone getting to him and then actually holding him, and on what charges? Şeytan was a pro. He'd surely disappear faster than a fart in a hurricane.

"No, I think better to watch him. See where he puts down."

"Gotcha. I'll call you back if anything changes."

The call ended and the sound of Eric Stone's latest single blasted over the Bluetooth. One Zac Brown and one Jimmy Buffett later, the station ID for Pyrate Radio was interrupted by an old-school ringtone. Deek checked his watch, then poked "Answer Call" on the rental's display screen.

"Your boy is ten miles south of Boca Chica and coming back around to the north. I'll keep watching, but if he's trying to be sneaky, it looks like he's gonna end up landing somewhere in the mid-lower Keys."

Deek glanced at the map. Key West was less than a hundred miles as the seagull flies, but the only road went through Miami. As he hit the red button, REM's distinctive guitar riff echoed Deek's thoughts.

You can't get there from here.

But he hit the accelerator anyway.

Thank Zeus for autopilot.

Angler had spent the last twenty minutes scrounging the small cargo space behind the seats for anything he could use as ballast. He pulled the dive weights from an old set of scuba gear, and raided a toolbox, finding several large crescent wrenches. The tarp he'd found was tattered and torn, but that made it perfect for Angler's needs. A few bungee straps and some duct tape, and the pilot's body was wrapped, weighted, and lying in the aisle between the passenger seats.

He briefly considered how, under different circumstances, he might even enjoy this jaunt as he passed over a narrow string of islands that cut an almost straight east-west line through the turquoise water below. But Angler needed to get over deep water, dump his unwanted cargo, and get his operation back on track.

Below him, just where the water faded from pale green to deep blue, the reef was dotted with boats. He needed to work fast.

Angler hauled, dragged, and shoved the corpse until it was awkwardly perched in the right seat, then climbed over the tarp into the left seat, completely out of breath. He flipped off the plane's automatic navigation, and began a slow descent, continuing three miles past the reef, then banking around. He reduced his airspeed and set a heading to take him through a wide gap between two of the boats moored along the reef. Far enough for no one to take note of a seaplane out on a nice little sightseeing tour.

Yawing the plane to the right to reduce the pressure, Angler reached over the body, unlatched the door, then rolled the plane hard to starboard, watching his hefty package flop into the door opening with a rush of wind blasting inside the plane. The corpse should have been flying through the sky by now. Nice and simple.

But today was not Angler's day.

He looked ahead and saw he was rapidly approaching the reef. He was about to lose his deep water. Throttling back to slow the plane further, he waggled the wings, hoping to jog the load loose. The body remained stubbornly wedged in the doorway, halfway out.

He just needed a little more.

As the reef and the turquoise water neared, Angler slowed the plane until he was sure he was flirting with stall speed, then rolled even harder to the right. Gravity won and the body lurched, shoving the door open wider, then disappeared, bouncing off the right float before tumbling to the surface where it made a huge splash.

Inside the reef.

"It is what it is." Angler muttered as he jammed the throttle forward, rolled the plane to the left with the wind slamming the door closed, then aimed for the shallow water and spoil islands north of the highway.

10

Kate Kingsbury listened to the soft hiss of air through her regulator then the gentle gurgle of bubbles as her breath passed out of her lungs. She'd been breathing underwater for years, teaching others to do it for nearly as long, yet it still felt like a wonder. And the sound of her breath in the still of the deep water was a meditation for her.

No matter the weather—and today's left a bit to be desired—bottom time was a holy experience for her. The reef that stretched the length of the Florida Keys, marking the south edge of the archipelago before the shelf dropped off to the depths of the Florida Strait, was a delicate ecosystem that had been fighting for survival in recent years. Humans had claimed it as their own, as they had with nearly everything they could reach and a few things they couldn't. Part of Kate's mission as a dive instructor was to teach her students to respect and protect the reef and the aquatic creatures who called it home. Every dive briefing she gave covered not only the dive profile and landscape they'd be covering, but a lesson on the micro-habitats they'd see, the fish and invertebrates they were likely to meet, and how the delicate balance of life could thrive or be destroyed from the actions of each diver.

Today, she was lucky. Her clients listened carefully and had spent the first dive of the day practicing their buoyancy and carefully avoiding contact with the corals struggling to survive at the edge of the deep. They'd been rewarded with glimpses of two spotted eels and an eagle ray soaring through the water above them.

Now, on their second dive of the afternoon, the light was fading and the four divers in the group explored the exterior of a small tugboat resting on the bottom at sixty feet. The *Katherine K* had torn apart and sunk during a hurricane a century before. Several years later, Tommy Miller, a former gangster from Chicago, hid a massive cache of stolen gold and jewels in the *Katherine K*'s hull. And not nearly as long ago, Kate had helped her landlord Chuck Miller, Tommy's grandson, find and recover the treasure.

The site was now a favorite of history buffs and treasure seekers alike, and Kate loved the taste of the saltwater that leaked through her wide grin every time one of her divers uncovered a stray coin or gem from the site.

The clang of metal tapping a tank pulled her from her reverie. She scanned across the aft deck of the *Katherine K*. A man in bright yellow fins waved to her, then pointed to a spot just east of the port hull. Kate finned over the wreck and eased over the encrusted gunwale to see a huge green turtle resting her fins on the silty bottom beside the tug.

She grinned, then rose a few feet in the water and signaled the other divers, pressing one hand on top of the other, waggling her thumbs in the dive sign for "turtle." Then she eased away to give the group plenty of space to take their photos without crowding the gentle giant.

As each member of the group floated away from the turtle, Kate checked in, flashing the "OK" sign and waving her air pressure gauge to get their readings. The turtle-finder glanced at his watch and frowned, then waggled seven fingers at Kate. She nodded, then pointed toward the mooring pin anchored into the bottom a few yards north, flashed the buddy-up sign, then gave him a thumbs-up.

Ascend.

She eased her way to the bow and gathered the other divers, signaling them that their time was up and to make their way up the line.

Looking toward the surface, she could just make out a darker shadow of the *Island Hopper Too*, the dive boat that she ran, waiting for the group to surface. Justin would help the divers out and have warm towels and fresh fruit and water bottles waiting for them, so Kate took her time making one more pass around her namesake before following her divers through their safety stop and then up to the boat.

Her head burst through the surface, and the noise of the wind and surf broke over the hiss and pop as she surged air into her buoyancy vest. Across the water, she heard shouts from the *Hopper*'s stern.

"Kate, check it out!"

She kicked around and followed Justin's arm to see the setting sun glint off the fuselage of a seaplane in the distance to the east, flying low over the coast, its wings just a bit unsteady.

"Shit."

Angler surveyed the shallows as the plane drifted closer to the choppy surface. The wind blew across the water from the east, and he hadn't figured on how rough the surface would be. He could fly just about anything. But landing? He hadn't put a seaplane down on the water in a long time. And even then, it had been on a calm day in a protected cove.

He scanned the water ahead and finally spotted a stretch of water protected by a little spoil island with a wide cove just north of the single highway connecting the string of islands to mainland Florida. He banked the plane, lined up, then eased back the throttle.

The checklist made its way from the depths of his memory. Gears up. Flaps down. Water rudders up. AOA in the green. Angler hated checklists. But checklists would keep him alive.

The lower he dropped, the rougher the water looked. He glanced at the mess splattered across the window to his left. Finding an airstrip was out of the question. He gently eased the plane lower until it was skimming just a few meters above the surface.

Nudge the throttle up. Ease the yoke back.

Like the push and pull of a clutch, but not like it at all. A mistake wouldn't be a simple stall at a traffic light. A mistake here and the plane would flip, roll, and rip apart. He might not die, but if he whiffed this landing, everything he'd worked for in the last few months would be for nothing.

No, everything was riding on him getting this right. And if he didn't get it down now, he'd run out of water.

Nudge. Ease.

The floats hit the chop with a rhythmic thud, the resistance jostling the plane, tugging it down. Angler gave the throttle a smooth nudge forward, maintaining power until the floats fully caught the water.

As he began to ease off the power, the plane jerked hard to starboard, smashing his temple against the window. Angler fought the yoke steady, resisting the instinct to pull off the power too quickly, carefully slowing the aircraft until it settled down fully onto the floats, rocking heavily and listing to the right as he guided it across the cove toward the spoil island. Finally, he revved it and ran the plane up onto the rocky beach, then killed the engine.

In the silence, he swore he could hear his heart pounding. But he didn't have time to indulge in rest. He quickly unsnapped his seat belt and scrambled to the cargo hold, peeking out the hatch at the damaged strut on the way. He scanned the area around the pilot's seat, looking for any sign of blood. Finding none on the cockpit window, windshield, or control surfaces, he congratulated himself on having had the hollow-points in the SIG—the bullet hadn't exited the man's skull. There was a bit of clean-up to do from his disposal of the pilot, and Angler did the best he could with some gauze and alcohol from a first aid kit. Next, he pulled a small inflatable raft from its compartment, unfolded its collapsible oars, and pulled the inflation pin as he tossed it out the hatch and its tether unfurled. Almost home free.

Angler scrambled down into the little craft and swiftly paddled out of the cove and began the arduous row against the crosswind. He pulled with his considerable strength, but each stroke seemed to take him farther from shore rather than closer. He looked over the side and into the crystal-clear saltwater. The weeds swayed in the current, nearly flattened against the hard bottom. Ebb tide.

Shit.

In water this shallow, the outgoing tide rushed in a current so strong he'd never be able to fight it all the way to shore. But he needed to get some distance between himself and the plane. And he couldn't stay out here forever. He had contractors to meet. Details to confirm. And despite all his careful planning, he sensed more contingency plans to execute.

No plan survives first contact. But this one hadn't even made it that far.

He scrambled the boat back into the cove where he had shelter from both the wind and the tide, tying it to the bent float strut. He flopped into the rear seat, panting from the hard and pointless row, and pulled out his phone.

"Exfil and repair."

"Hello to you, too." The voice on the other end of the phone sounded amused.

Angler rattled off a set of coordinates.

"How soon?"

"Yesterday."

He heard a sigh. No longer amused.

"Triple rate."

Over the sound of the wind, Angler heard the hum of an outboard motor rounding into the cove. "Fine. I'll call you tomorrow." He ended the call and tucked the phone back into his pocket beside the trusty little pistol.

11

A white center console boat rounded the point and made directly for the shoreline where Angler paced beside the crippled airplane. The captain, if a tiny runabout like that had what you could call a captain, was a short, barrel-chested man wearing the coastal uniform: a long-sleeved cotton shirt, cargo shorts, a tattered baseball cap, and, despite the sun quickly setting behind him, wraparound sunglasses.

"Ahoy, there, friend!" The captain's voice sounded like his entire throat was made of number four gravel. As the craft floated toward the shore, the man gave a quick reverse burst and it stopped just short of the shore as if it had brakes. The man waved to a tool chest resting in front of the console. "Need a hand?"

Angler glanced at his Timex. Triple rate or no, his guy wouldn't be here for hours, and Angler needed to get some distance from the Otter. He waved his phone in the air. "I got a buddy on the way to fix her leg, here, but I wouldn't turn down a lift to town."

Angler waded into the gin-clear water and climbed over the gunwale near the idling motor.

The captain stretched a hand out. "Chuck Miller. Welcome aboard."

He brought the little boat around and nudged her out into the center of the cove, then guided the boat back out into the rolling chop.

"You'll want to get low. Gonna get rough, but we're not heading far."

As Angler made a seat on the sturdy tool chest, the man punched it, and the little boat climbed up on plane and zoomed toward the fading orange remnants of sunset and a string of lights at the edge of the horizon.

They sped past thick mangrove clusters, pelicans perched atop channel markers, and random sticks poking barely above the surface to mark the poachers' traps scattered throughout the shallow waters. Angler had done enough business in the lower Keys. In contrast to the mercenary, every-man-for-himself culture on the mainland, the Keys felt like stepping back in time. With only one road in and the same road out, these folks had learned to rely on what they had, to watch each other's backs, and to not depend too much on the underpaid and understaffed public servants of the sprawling county. With more than fifteen hundred islands stretching over a hundred miles, a fair share of his associates had called the Keys home for a stretch of their careers. It was the perfect place to set both his muscle and motor into motion. He had rendezvous scheduled with both.

As the plans formed in his mind, the boat approached a long, low spit of land stretching from the highway to meet them. Its eastern coast was dotted with flickering orange fires and twinkling lights draped around decks and awnings, offering just enough brightness in the twilight to see a string of campers stretched almost the length of the island.

"Welcome to Shark Key Campground and Marina." The captain eased the throttle back and the boat settled back down into the water and drifted toward a sturdy aluminum dock. A few slips down, several people were climbing off another larger boat, carrying dive gear. Their excited chatter echoed across the water even with the strong breeze.

"That turtle was beautiful. So huge!"

"Did you see the two eels?"

"I saw three. There was another over by that really big coral head on the east side."

The divers filed up the dock and onto the island. Angler took note of the dive boat's slip, and watched as the crew of two began to clean and stow equipment. Always good to know where extra gear might be found.

"—get that looked at?" The captain's voice tugged Angler back to the moment.

"Sorry, what?"

"I said, it looks like you got a bit of a knock to your noggin, there."

Angler reached to his left temple. His fingers yanked away like a hot stove from where a tender knot had grown. He realized his head was pounding. He'd thought it was just the constant thunk of the boat's hull against the choppy surface. And when he looked at his fingertips, they were coated with a mixture of fresh and dried flakes of blood.

"Mm, yeah. I think I must have knocked it. I came down pretty hard into that chop."

"Hospital ain't but a few miles up the road. Be happy to drive you there, if you'd like."

Angler brushed the knot, testing it. "I don't think that's necessary. It's just a bump."

The captain tied the stern line to a cleat as a huge German shepherd raced down the dock, its tail wagging. Halfway down, it stopped short, frozen, its stare fixed on Angler. The hair on its back stood up and its lips curled up into a snarl.

"Whiskey! Down. Where are your manners, boy?" A short blonde poked her head through a gap in the seagrape hedge and recalled the dog. "Sorry about that. He's usually better with new people."

Angler followed the captain up the dock. Beyond the hedge, a crushed gravel parking lot stretched out to the left, bordered by another thick seagrape hedge on the opposite site. To the right, a low concrete cottage painted a bright yellow sat beside a big shop that reminded Angler of the old 1950s service stations, with a small general store and office in the front and service bays in the back. Beyond them, another stacked block building was surrounded by a massive deck, dotted with tables and chairs. And people.

As they walked toward the crowded deck, Angler spotted the dog, sitting at the edge with his attention locked on the men. He stumbled, skimming his fingers across the knot at his temple. "You know, maybe it's not such a bad idea to get this checked out."

The man who'd called himself Chuck waved toward an ancient, wood-sided Jeep Wagoneer. "Hop in."

Ten minutes later, the truck eased through the emergency entrance of Lower Keys Medical Center.

"Would you like me to wait with you? Got a place to stay tonight?"

This guy was a regular Mother Teresa. Angler waved him off, adopting a casual ease he did not feel. "I'll be fine. You've lost enough time on me already. Go enjoy your evening, and thanks for the rescue."

"Well, you take care then, and come back anytime. Whether it's for a day or forever, Shark Key's always there when you need her."

Angler forced a smile and waited in front of the glass doors of the emergency entrance, waving as the Wagoneer turned onto the ring road that circled the north side of Stock Island. As soon as its taillights disappeared, Angler walked away from the hospital's parking lot, across the highway, and into the first dive bar he found.

The last diver eased her car down the lane. Kate waved, then spun and ruffled the fur on Whiskey's head. He'd spent the last half hour sitting at the edge of the deck like a statue, staring at the parking lot without even seeming to blink.

"What's up with you tonight, boy?"

As a highly trained police K-9 retired after a traumatic attack, Whiskey sometimes had an overactive threat response, perceiving every iguana and squirrel as a hardened criminal and chasing them down with about as much mercy. But he'd been on permanent leave for years now. These days, he was usually content to curl up on the deck and take pets from anyone who'd give them.

Kate slid into a chair across from her friend and neighbor, Michelle Jenkins. "What's his deal? Has he been like this all day?"

"No. He was pretty normal until maybe an hour before you guys came in. Spent most of the day curled up in the shade in front of the kitchen door. Tripped Babette a couple times before she banished him to the end of the bar. But then a seaplane came across low and put down just the other side of O'Hara. Chuck went out to see if he could help, and then... this started." She dipped her chin at the dog, staring across the lot at the headlights coming up the lane.

"Typical male. Thinks we need him to protect our fragile selves..."

"Fragile? Who's fragile around here?" A woman built like a linebacker and dressed for the New York club scene dropped into the chair between Kate and Michelle. Whiskey finally left his post at the edge of the deck and rubbed up against the newcomer's bare leg. He was rewarded with a strong scratch to his ears, responding with a deeply satisfied groan.

"Hey, Kara." Kate shook her head at her blissed-out dog. "Apparently, we are. Or at least he thinks so. He's been guarding the women since the last man left. Speaking of which..."

The red brake lights of Chuck's Jeep lit up their faces as he parked in the scrubby grass in front of his cottage, then sauntered up and scratched the dog. "Good boy. Thanks for watching the place for me."

"You know you have humans to do that for you?"

"Just cutting out the middleman. Or middlewomen as the case may be. You watch the place, he watches you. Or he just watches the place. Simpler that way." Chuck laughed, deepening the wrinkles around his eyes, then reached behind the bar and filled a bucket with beer and ice and dropped it on the table.

"I'm pretending to be classy tonight." Michelle waved her wine glass at him, while Kara pulled a beer from the bucket and twisted the cap off with her bare hands and passed it to Kate with a wide grin.

"So what's the story with the seaplane guy?"

Chuck grabbed himself a beer and frowned. "Not much of a talker, that one. Clearly came down hard. Float strut collapsed in the landing and he took a bonk to the side of his head, so I ran him over to the ER. Said he has a guy coming to tow the plane out to repair it, but beyond that, I didn't get a word out of him. Not even a name."

Kate set her bottle on the table and swiped at the condensation forming around it. "He came across really wobbly maybe a mile to our east as we were surfacing from our last dive. Justin pointed it out. Said he saw something fall from the plane, but I didn't see it. Gotta be the same guy, right? Bigger plane, single prop, blue stripes?"

"Yeah, that's the one," Chuck confirmed with a nod.

"De Havilland Beaver. Or maybe an Otter."

Three heads turned to face Michelle, eyebrows raised.

"You don't stay married to a plane freak without learning a thing or two about them. William was looking at one a few years back after I sold my first app. Took all I had to talk him out of it. So of course that's when he bought the Cirrus instead."

"Boys and their toys..." Kara groaned.

"You're one to talk. What's your wig and shoe and purse collection looking like these days?"

"That's all for work. Every last Balenciaga. Ask my tax guy. He'll tell you."

"As long as he tells the IRS." Chuck drained the bottle, then pushed up out of the chair with a groan. "Anyway, I'm gonna check in on the kitchen, pop some ibuprofen, and turn in early. This old bag of bones can't take the chop like it used to."

The women raised their bottles and glass as he made his way back to the bar with Whiskey on his heels.

Deek flicked his brights on just in time to see a pair of glowing eyes. He slammed the brakes, instinctively glancing in the rental car's mirror. The car skidded to a stop a few yards before a small deer, roughly the size of a Labrador retriever, who stood frozen in the center of the road.

The animal stared at Deek.

Deek stared back.

His phone's ringtone startled him back to attention as the little deer broke the stare and meandered off the shoulder and into the tall grass beside the highway. Deek tapped the answer button.

"Good news and bad news, my friend."

Story of my life.

"Give me the bad." Deek knew it was always best to know the worst.

"Bad news, your plane-that's-not-the-plane has gone ghost. No signal."

"And the good?"

"Looks like they put down on an uninhabited island in the middle of nowhere. No roads in. Too far out to row the life raft to shore. If it even has a life raft."

"That's the good news?"

"Well, it's good from the right perspective. It means these guys can't have gotten too far. They're probably stuck on that little clump of trees waiting for first light."

Deek eased the rental car back onto the road and continued west. "Where are they at? What's the closest... anything?"

"You're in luck. There's a narrow little island called Shark Key. It's a campground and marina, and your guys took a path directly over it right before they went down. It's definitely the closest point of civilization. I'll text you the number."

"Thanks, man. I owe you one."

"Yes, you do. Remember that next time I'm getting overrun by orcs and you want to turn tail and run."

Deek rolled his eyes and hit the end call button. A few seconds later, his phone beeped with an incoming text. A three-oh-five phone number. He tapped the number and the ringing filled the car's speakers.

"Shark Key Campground and Marina. This is Chuck Miller."

"Hi, Mr. Miller. My name is Deek Morrison. I'm looking for a place to stay tonight, but I'm still an hour or so out. How late will you be open?"

Deek could hear the man's smile bouncing from cell tower to satellite to cell tower and into his vehicle. "We're always here. Just knock at the little yellow house at the end of the road if you're late. I'll leave the light on."

12

A sharp orange glow stretched across the window, chasing the midnight blue out the top of the frame when Deek peeled his eyelids open. He tugged the blanket tighter around his bare shoulders against the chill. Winter in Florida was a damn sight better than winter in DC, but it still wasn't shirtless weather when you didn't have heat.

He climbed out of the bunk, strapped his watch on, then stumbled forward in search of a toothbrush and coffee, not necessarily in that order. The guy from the yellow house—what was his name? Chad? Chet? No...—had shown him around the little camper the night before. He kept three trailers set up as temporary rentals, and he said Deek could find everything he would at a hotel, plus a sunrise to blow his mind.

Coffee cup in hand, Deek pushed the camper door open and stepped out into the cool morning.

Wow.

The man had not lied. Twenty feet behind the small Airstream, a low hedge lined the rocky shore. Beyond it, soft mist rose from water still as a mirror, reflecting the vibrant color in a sky that seemed so close Deek might be able to touch it if he just stretched a little.

In the few minutes it had taken to make coffee and brush his teeth, the colors had changed. Brightened. Deek wiped the dew from a sturdy Adirondack chair and allowed himself five minutes of indulgence to watch nature's light show. Then, as Sol peeked above the horizon and a light breeze rippled the surface of the Gulf, Deek peeled himself from the chair and headed to the outdoor restaurant at the north point of the island.

As he climbed the steps to the wide deck, a huge German shepherd trotted over to him, tail wagging and tongue lolling out in what could only be described as a grin. The dog gave Deek's hand a cursory sniff, then it sat and ducked its nose under his hand, demanding pets.

"Well, you're a friendly thing. How could I refuse you?" Deek laughed as he scratched the dog's neck and realized he hadn't felt this light in a few days. Then the heavy feeling crept back into the center of his chest.

This was not a vacation.

"Whiskey, come. Give the man some space." A blond woman in a gray hoodie, cargo pants, and flip-flops rose from a table along the railing then snapped her fingers at the dog. He shot up, spun, and returned to his owner in a single fluid motion.

"He's okay, really. I love dogs."

"Well, he clearly loves humans. Especially ones that will pet him," the woman laughed. "That's Whiskey. I'm Kate. You're new."

He met her halfway across the deck and took the hand she offered. Despite her small size, her handshake was firm and quick.

"I'm Deek. Got in late last night."

Kate nodded to the other woman sitting at her table. "That's Michelle. Would you like to join us for some coffee? The kitchen will be opening for breakfast in a little bit and this place'll start to get busy."

He settled at their table, his fingers wrapped around a cup of the best coffee he'd tasted in a while. Then he braced for the inevitable question.

"So, Deek, what bring you to the Keys?" Michelle's voice sounded like the coffee in his cup. Warm and dark and soft like a fuzzy blanket on a cold morning.

"I'm looking for a guy."

The comment surprised him as much as it did the women at the table. "I mean, not like—wait, not that there's anything wrong with —oh, let me start over." He felt flustered, almost like these women were sirens, calling him from his path and leading him to crash his ship into the rocks. But he also couldn't stop himself from spilling it all.

"I'm an agent with the Department of Transportation. Maritime Administration. I'm looking for a man who might be involved in planning something… not good." He'd started strong, but the longer the sentence got, the dumber it sounded. At least the two women weren't laughing. Yet. He pushed his fingers through his mop of hair and tried to get his story back on track. "Until yesterday, everything I had was circumstantial. Lots of hints pointing the same direction, nothing concrete. But yesterday, I chased him across Pine Island Sound and he escaped in a seaplane, which I tracked to a little island just east of here."

He paused for a gulp of coffee, waiting for them to dismiss him as a lunatic. But they traded a glance, and Deek thought he detected a subtle shrug from the blonde, Kate, as her friend's lips tightened. He felt the breeze against his eyeballs as he waited, unblinking, for their response. Finally, Michelle broke the silence.

"Pine Island. That's up off Fort Myers. We moored up there to wait out a storm last time we went up north." She turned back to Kate. "The boat show is this weekend, isn't it? William and Tony are supposed to meet up there before they head back home."

Kate nodded. "Yeah. But wait, a seaplane? Was it an Otter with blue striping? Pilot a graying guy maybe late fifties?"

Deek's cup slipped to the table with a thud.

"That's my guy. But he's not the pilot."

Kate's head tilted. "Only one guy was on that plane."

"How do you—"

"It came in really shaky right before sunset… the wind was pretty strong yesterday. Put it down just past that island over there. Chuck ran out in the skiff to help, and… Hey, Chuck! Ears burning?"

The man who'd checked him in last night limped up to the table with a carafe of coffee. "You talking about our seaplane friend?"

Deek nodded. "He's the reason I'm here. I'm with the Maritime Administration and I have a few questions for him."

Yeah. That sounded official. Legit.

"I dropped him off at the ER in town last night. He had a pretty good knot on his head, but I don't think it was a concussion, so I doubt they kept him. What's he into?"

"Well, first problem, there were two men on the plane when it left Fort Myers."

Chuck grimaced. "He was the only guy I saw, but I didn't search the plane. Didn't see a reason, just tried to help a pilot in distress."

Kate blanched. "Justin said he saw something fall out of the plane when we saw it comin' across the reef. Something big. I blew him off." She grabbed her phone and began to pace the deck, the device pressed to her ear.

A moment later she returned to the table. "This guy is on Fish's radar, too. His words: 'Pretty plane. Ugly pilot.' He'll be here in five."

Chuck rubbed the back of his neck, then pointed to Kate. "I'll get the skiff ready, but my back can't take the flats today, so Fish can have the honors. You prep the *Hopper*. I think we'll all be going out for a dive when they get back."

"Both homes are comparably equipped and stocked. Familiarize yourselves with what you have on hand." Laura Smythe led the two young women into the kitchen. "You'll be responsible to attend to their requests, and you're expected to maintain order and cleanliness at all times."

The rapid tapping of her lacquered fingernails on the counter echoed through the open space. While the concierges peeked into cabinets and drawers, Laura ticked through her own task list. A meeting like this succeeded or failed on the details.

Planning, down to the smallest detail, was in her blood. And planning those details for Harold Hildebrand was her mission.

She'd carefully chosen her role as his executive assistant—as the right-hand woman to a power broker positioned to change the world. She'd cultivated the right connections and made herself into the perfect candidate. And when the position opened up a few months earlier, she had provided him with unassailable references, though she doubted he'd called even one. The names had been enough for even a man like him, who called CEOs and MPs, to think twice about picking up the phone.

Despite the little hiccup from the day before, Laura Smythe was living her dream. Planning for all the details of such a momentous event came naturally to her—much more so than trusting the people hired to execute those same details.

She lifted her hand and snapped her fingers above her head.

The two young women jerked their heads out of a cabinet and snapped to attention. "Yes, ma'am?"

"I cannot repeat often enough how important it is that these delegates be comfortable. The nature of the meetings is confidential. I am not at liberty to even tell you their names or nationalities. Those details are irrelevant to you. But you must understand the importance of this summit.

"These men hold the future of your homelands in their hands. If they succeed, your families will have gas to heat their homes and cook their meals. They'll have grain to make their bread and feed their livestock. They'll drive cars to factories that are not shuttered for lack of electricity.

"If they fail, your families will go hungry. Your men will be unemployed. Your markets will be empty. The fate of your countrymen and many, many others are in the hands of these men. And the attitudes of these men are in your hands. Make your work count."

The young blond woman, Katya or Kata or something like that, stared with rapt attention. The brunette—Elenna? Amina?—picked at her cuticle.

Laura settled her gaze where Amina's eyes should have been and waited. When the girl finally looked up, she found herself trapped in Laura's cold stare.

"Is this information boring to you? Have you something more engaging to do? I—"

Laura broke off at the distinctive ding from her phone. She'd have disregarded any other notification, but regardless of one's current occupation, Harold Hildebrand was never ignored.

She held a single finger up to the women, then used it to swipe open the secure text app.

I've just left Teterboro. I expect everything to be in order when we arrive this afternoon.

She allowed herself one deep breath, releasing it slowly through her pursed lips before she typed her reply:

Yes, sir. Of course, sir. I'm briefing the concierges now, sir.

The app informed her that Harold Hildebrand was typing a reply.

And when Harold Hildebrand was typing, she waited as long as it took. Finally, the bubble appeared on her screen.

Be certain to explain the stakes to them.

She began to type a reply. She erased it and started over.

Yes, sir. Everything will be ready for you.

She tapped the send button and dropped her phone back into her pocket. It hadn't taken very long working for Hildebrand to learn his attention span was short with The Help, even those at her level. As soon as he saw her begin typing, he'd assume compliance and move on. Once, she'd timed it. It had taken him ninety-three minutes to come back around and read her reply.

But another time, he'd pinged while she was in the loo. She'd waited until she'd washed her hands. Three minutes, tops.

"I'd fire you this instant if I could," had been his response.

But she was living the dream. There was too much riding on this summit. And she wasn't about to let pet peeves stand between her and the mission.

Laura turned back to the helpers and resumed the briefing.

Angler jolted awake at the sound of a TV blaring. He rolled off the couch, landing on crusty shag carpet the color of a baby's diaper. The single-wide trailer and its primary occupant had both seen better days, but beggars couldn't be choosers. It was a roof that cost him nothing more than a little attention and the price of a condom.

But it sounded like he'd outstayed his welcome.

The bump on his head throbbed in time with the screaming trash on the television. He'd missed the intro, but in the few lines he'd picked up between the screeching and bitch-slapping, it appeared that a mother and a daughter were both pregnant by the same meth dealer.

Angler glanced around the trailer again and counted his blessings. Then he tugged his pants on and ambled out the door and up Maloney Avenue without so much as a goodbye.

He'd seen the neighborhood last night through the orange sodium lights and it held true in the full color of daylight. Key West was the ideal destination for vacationers and snowbirds, where money could buy happiness in the form of a flamingo pink golf cart. Stock Island was where joy went to die.

Maloney Avenue was lined with ramshackle single-wides that were too mean to die in one of the many hurricanes that had passed across the string of islands. The park owners were old-timers too stubborn to give up their paid-off postage stamp of rental income to the greedy developers who were undoubtedly salivating to turn this little clump of rock into Key West East a quarter of an acre at a time.

He made his way up the sidewalk, dodging clumps of dead palm fronds and pine needles, listening to the sound of the wind rustling the trees and the rumble of work trucks hauling debris to the transfer station a few blocks down. He'd been here once before and it clearly hadn't changed. He grinned, knowing he'd find exactly what he needed here.

When he reached Highway 1, he passed the tidy, new CVS and made his way on to Dion's for a coffee, three new burner phones, and a backup plan. He nodded to a shriveled man sitting beside the door in a sliver of shade, lips folded in over his gums where his teeth should have been. Angler bought an airplane bottle of rum and an extra cup of coffee and handed them to the man as he crouched in the shade beside him, his gaze fixed on the four lanes of vehicles creeping up and down the pavement.

"Know where a guy might find a boat around these parts?"

From the corner of his eye, Angler saw the man nod and take a sip of the coffee.

"Lots o' boats 'round here." Another sip. "Anything in particular you looking for?"

"Fast. Long range. Crew that keeps to themselves."

The man held a gnarled brown hand out. Angler dropped one of the burner phones into it.

Ten minutes later, three calls made and the SIM separated from the phone, Angler ambled halfway across the Cow Key bridge and flung the pieces over the railing.

13

As the little center console skimmed the surface, its nearly flat bow slapping every roll, Deek wondered if yoga had a monkey pose. If so, Deek had been holding it for the last ten minutes. Right hand holding his ball cap on top of his head. Left hand clutching the broken zipper on his borrowed windbreaker. Thighs clenched, knees bent, and feet planted wide in a valiant effort to keep his seat.

The man at the helm, who had called himself Fish, seemed content to let his jacket flap in the wind and he ignored his own cap with the confidence of a man who spent his days in craft just like this.

Deek let go long enough to check the GPS pin his friend had sent the night before, and his cap took its opportunity to fly free and find its own way in the world. For a guy with a career in Maritime Administration, Deek didn't do boats very well. Not well at all. He held his phone up for Fish to see. The man nodded, then eased the skiff into a wide arc to starboard as Deek's phone rang.

Boss again. Deek hadn't even taken the time to listen to yesterday's voicemail. No point, he knew what his boss wanted, and he didn't have a good answer yet. So he hit decline and watched as the little boat made a full lap around the spoil island without finding even the smallest part that could belong to a DHC-3 Otter. Until—

"Wait, there!" Deek shouted, his eye catching a flash of white tangled deep in a mangrove root.

Fish eased back on the throttle and the little boat settled down into the water. With the motor just above an idle, he nudged the bow around and motored toward the shore, stopping just short of the rocky beach.

"Here." He pulled his flip-flops off and handed them to Deek. Deek looked back, his eyebrows raised.

Fish pointed to Deek's loafers. "Can't get ashore in those. These'll keep your feet from getting shredded on the rocks. Go see what it is. It could just be trash—people dump anything and everything, and sometimes stuff just flies away like your hat just did. But it also could be something. See those fresh cuts on the stone over there? That's about the width of a float-plane's gear."

Deek rolled up the cuffs of his khakis then removed his socks and carefully tucked each one into its corresponding loafer. He had one thought as he slipped his size ten feet into the size thirteen flip-flops.

He was not prepared for this.

But prepared or not, he was here. He had people who were taking his hunch seriously. Now wasn't the time to let a little water—

Damn!

Everything shriveled and crowded up into his body as his feet dropped over the side of the boat and onto the rocky bottom.

"I thought the tropical waters were supposed to be warm?"

Fish laughed as he nudged the boat's throttle to hold it in place. "Contrary to popular belief, it does get cold down here. This water's so shallow, it gets cold too. Now, if you were here in August, it'd be as warm as a hot tub. But it's not August. And you're not on vacation. Now go get that trash so we can see what we're looking at."

Deek shuffled the flip-flops along the hard bottom and stumbled his way across the shore. He leaned over, gripping the mangrove root for balance, then jerked back, staring at his hand.

"Oh, yeah, I should have warned you. Those roots'll cut a man. Might want to avoid scraping against them."

Crouching as close to the tree roots as he could without touching them, Deek stretched into the cluster of roots and pulled out a wad of sticky white vinyl. He peeled back a corner of a narrow piece and spotted a bright blue stripe.

He stumbled backward, landing his tailbone against a pointed stone. Taking the vinyl in his left hand, Deek gingerly pushed up off the inhospitable little island and waded back toward the skiff. As he inched forward, he peeled another wider swath away from the bundle, where he spotted a very clear, large letter "N."

"Fake tail number." Fish concurred as he pulled Deek back over the gunwale.

Deek settled on a padded fish locker and peeled the vinyl apart as Fish guided the skiff back out to the channel. "This is definitely the same plane that attacked us in Fort Myers. My buddy tracked the transponder, but he said it went dark here last night. He told me he'd contact me if it came back online and I haven't heard anything, so I'm assuming someone towed it… somewhere?"

"Unfortunately, that happens a lot around here. Sheriff's putting a BOLO on the plane, but with as much coastline and as many islands as we have around here, we just don't have the manpower to keep tabs on all the little guys who can zip in and out of here before our systems can throw up a flag and we can scramble a team."

"We?"

"I'm with the Navy. I serve on a special border patrol task force. We watch guys like this, but with more coast than capacity, we have to focus on the big rocks." He pushed the throttle up, and the little boat leapt to the surface like it was born to fly. Fish shouted over the wind and the motor. "This guy is on our list, but not at the top of it. But the weird thing is that the description of the guy you and

Chuck and Kate all saw does not match the one we have for this plane's pilot."

"What do you think that means?" Deek dreaded the answer.

"We're gonna need a bigger boat."

Angler eased his stolen scooter beside a stack of empty pineapple crates near the end of the boatyard. Hulls in various states of disrepair sat on blocks all around. Workers climbed up and down ladders, spraying and scraping and painting. Captains and owners drifted in and out of the little office trailer, checking on progress or making payments.

They say they're cleaning up Stock Island. You sure as hell couldn't afford to buy a home there anymore. But there were still plenty of spots to do business if you knew what you were looking for. No security cameras. Enough people milling around that three more wouldn't be noticed. Multiple ways out if a man didn't mind getting wet.

Miami was a far better place to pick up a crew. Miami had air conditioning. He winced, brushing the knot on his head as he wiped a bead of sweat from his temple before it got lost in the stubble hiding his face. For this job, though, Miami was about the worst place to recruit a team. No, it was impossible to keep a contract quiet around there. They'd all go to their graves before they'd rat a guy out—well, most of them anyway—but talk amongst themselves? It was a small world. Despite every assurance, operational security lost the race to gossip and ego. No one wanted the routine gigs. Everyone talked about the big ones. Bragged they were on them. Shit-talked if they weren't.

So here he was, in hell's armpit.

He glanced at his watch then back up the wide lane that stretched the length of the facility. Thick seagrape bushes lined the west side of the drive. Angler could smell the shallow, briny marsh beyond it. To the east, a deep channel split Cow Key in two and led to a basin lined with marinas and dive bars. Across the channel, a web of power lines and massive storage tanks lined the seawall. Emblazoned on each tank was a wide logo, branding them all as property of Hildebrand Energy.

Angler bristled.

Most of his career, he'd worked for the highest bidder. Built a name for himself as objective, reliable, and most of all, discreet. He'd never gone in for the "true believer" stuff—emotions just clouded your judgment, and ops like his needed clear heads and balls of steel. But this job was different. Wasn't even a job at all. This time, it mattered.

Angler was ready to trade it all in. This was a young man's game, and as he massaged out the soreness that was creeping up his neck, he had to admit he wasn't young anymore. Thankfully, he'd found some deep, albeit faceless, pockets to foot the bill.

Up the lane, he finally spotted them. He'd done enough past business with the man on the left. Solid. Reliable. Adapted well in fluid situations. But on the right? A lanky form ambled toward him with an unsteady gait. If this was his horse, he had a problem. Late, and lame.

No, this wasn't going to do.

Angler could have just flipped his cap backward, climbed on his scooter, and gone for Plan B, but something about this kid made the hair on his neck stand up. He pulled Grady Foster behind the hulking hull of a sailboat resting in a cradle. "This some kind of joke?"

Foster pressed his lips into a flat line and shook his head.

"He's not what we discussed."

"The guy we discussed is no longer available."

Angler growled. "I pay you to make people available."

"You pay me to get a job done."

"A two-man job. Two men I know. Two reliable men."

"You threw money at me, and I got the charges you wanted. I got the detonation system you wanted. But no amount of money's gonna solve this one, sir, so I had to pivot. You wanted me to get you a guy who could work under water. This is who I got. He'll follow orders. Take him or leave him."

Angler peered around the keel as a stack of pineapple crates crashed to the ground. The kid bounced beside the mess, rubbing his nose and looking around nervously.

"He's not coming with us."

"He's paid up."

"Whatever. Look at his pupils. He's higher than Mount Everest. He's not coming."

"Copy that." Foster strode toward the kid, then pulled him behind a dumpster. Angler heard a distinctive pop, then a thud. Four seconds later, the man strode back toward the sailboat, counting a wad of cash. "It's our lucky day. Managed to get a refund."

If he had more time, Angler would have been tempted to add a second body to the pile, history be damned. But unlike money, he couldn't make a phone call to get more time. He had to work with what he was given.

Snatching the money from Foster's fist, he pointed back to the rusting steel container. "Take care of that. We're too close to let mistakes like this put the operation at risk."

The man saluted. "Yes, sir. On it, sir." Then he turned as he adjusted his shirttail to cover the lump at his waistband.

Angler glared at his back, then climbed onto his stolen scooter, and rolled up Shrimp Road before he could change his mind.

Deek left Fish to tie up the skiff and leapt onto the sturdy dock. He jogged over to the *Island Hopper Too*'s slip.

"Ahoy!" He waved as Kate popped her head out from inside a gear locker. "That's what you're supposed to say to a captain, right?"

Her wide grin fell as Deek stepped onto the *Hopper*'s deck. "Followed by asking the captain permission to board before you set foot on her ship."

His eyes bulged until he spotted the twitch in her cheek. He wasn't always good at reading when people were teasing him, but this time, he figured it out quickly and decided to play along. He scrambled back up to the dock, snapped to attention, and shouted "Permission to come aboard, *sir!*"

"Granted," she laughed as Deek stumbled onto the deck, misjudging the gentle roll of the hull. "For a Maritime Administration agent, you don't seem to have the best sea legs."

"Economist. Cursed to live out my life as a basement-dwelling desk jockey. Closest I get to water in my daily life is the retaining pond in front of my apartment complex, and my experience with boats is limited to writing apps to track their movement. In related news, college freshmen should never be allowed to make life choices, full stop."

"You write apps? You should definitely talk to Michelle—she's a developer, too." Kate stepped over Whiskey's sleeping bulk, then slipped a faded BCD over a green and yellow tank and snapped its strap tight. "I think she's up on the deck. I'll be ready to roll in about fifteen minutes. Can you pop up there and check on the cooler Chuck was packing for us?"

"Ten-four, Cap'n." Deek saluted, then clambered back up to the dock. He found Michelle sitting with her laptop in the shade of the outdoor bar. He slid into the chair opposite her. "So I hear you write apps."

The woman grinned, her perfect white teeth glowing against her dark skin. "I dabble."

Chuck passed their table towing a large cooler on wheels. "Don't let her fool you. This one sold her last creation to that crazy spaceman for forty mil. Ask me, she should have held out for more."

Michelle's eyes dropped and she shrugged off Chuck's praise. "It wasn't even MVP, and it was more important for me to see their development roadmap than to get more money. I got more than I can spend anyway."

Chuck patted her shoulder. "William'll spend it for you fast enough. He's going to the boat show this weekend, isn't he?"

"The *Knot* is our home. He'd never." She blanched. "At least not without me there."

"The *Knot*?"

Michelle turned to Deek. "We live aboard our catamaran, the *Knot Dead Yet*. We bought it after I sold my first app. William thought the name was a clever nod to both our early retirement and his love of Monty Python. I spend every first conversation explaining it. Maybe it is time for something new, but I'm terrified he'll come up with an even worse name for her."

"Shut your mouth, woman. You love the boat, the name, and the man. Probably in that order." Chuck winked at her and dragged the cooler off toward the *Hopper*.

"So, you *dabble*, eh? Dabbling is what I do, messing around with my little yacht-tracker because I like watching the traffic. Sounds more like serial entrepreneurship is your game."

"I just get ideas. And when I can't shake one, I make it. Some of them have been total duds. A few have had more potential than I can realize on my own. So when some rich mogul sees that and can afford to put a team on it..." Michelle shrugged. "Now tell me about this hunch you have. You think something is gonna go down at the boat show?"

Deek leaned forward. "How much do you know about the ongoing conflict between Armenia and Azerbaijan?"

"Are you referring to the border disputes or the problems the Azeri are experiencing with their pipeline through Georgia?"

Deek's eyebrows shot up.

"We had a little run-in a while back with the CEO of a Chinese energy conglomerate. I'm good at research."

"Well, that makes this conversation exponentially easier. And you're the first person to even take me seriously enough to have it, so thank you."

"Happy to oblige."

"Okay, so yeah. The Azeri are, in fact, looking for backup plans, and I believe that Harold Hildebrand is arranging a private meeting with the Armenians to try to broker an arrangement."

"But Hildebrand has been transporting LNG from here into Europe to make up for the disruptions. Why would he cut off his business?"

"Why, indeed? Especially when he's building a fleet of new tanker ships so he can carry more?"

Michelle sighed. "Of course. Optics."

Deek tapped his index finger to the end of his nose. "Exactly. He harbors no illusion that these guys could agree on what to have for dinner, let alone to negotiate and then actually build and manage a pipeline together, no matter how good the deal could be for both their countries. The bad blood runs generations deep, but the political capital he gets for trying to make it work would be priceless. Harold Hildebrand, statesman. Has the type of ring to it that guys like him crave."

"And you think someone wants to… what?"

"I think he wants to have his cake and eat it, too. A guy like him has contingencies for his contingencies. An attack would be nothing but good for him."

"And regardless of what he's thinking, an operation like that can't come cheap. So, we follow the money. Good thing I've got an app for that." Michelle winked at Deek, then turned to her laptop and started tapping.

14

"So, we'll start here, a little ways west of where Justin thinks the Otter came across." Kate tapped her rough drawing on the whiteboard, then nodded at Justin, who stood at the helm, his sandy dreadlocks bouncing from the wind and waves.

She had enough search and recovery successes under her belt to know that if something was there, she'd find it. It's what she did. But two guys left Fort Myers. One guy arrived in the flats. She dreaded what she expected to find and for a split second, she wished her innate gift for finding things would fail her, just for today.

Kate had seen more dead bodies than the average divemaster, starting with her husband and ending with a crew of kidnapping Colombian gem-smugglers. But it had been a while, and if she had her choice, it'd be a while longer.

Her problem, though, was that she didn't really have a choice today. If what Deek suspected was true, they needed to find this guy. And finding what—or whom—he'd ditched was the first step.

She turned back to her briefing. Even though Deek would be staying topside, he'd need to know their plan, follow their bubbles, and be there when they surfaced.

"We're looking okay on viz today; divers out this morning were reporting sixty to eighty feet on the reef, which is pretty good considering how windy it's been. So to conserve bottom time and cover the widest search area, Justin and I will level off at thirty feet and swim parallel courses about fifty feet apart, maybe a bit closer if we lose some viz. As long as we don't have to dip deeper, we'll go 'til we find something or when the first one of us is down to three hundred pounds. We're both pretty competitive, so don't freak out if we're down there for an hour and a half. Just keep our bubbles ahead of you. When they stop moving, we're on our way up."

She led Deek up toward the helm, stepping over Whiskey. "He will curl up and sleep wherever it's the most inconvenient for you, but if you stay on the wheel, he probably won't trip you. And both of you stay in the shade so you don't get burned. That wind might feel cold, but the sun is still a killer."

Fifteen minutes later, Kate wriggled into a three-mil wetsuit and clipped into her faded BCD. She buddy-checked Justin, waited for him to do the same for her, then they left Deek and Whiskey on the *Hopper* and backrolled into the chilly Florida Strait.

She pulled a deep breath through her regulator as her body gently sank through the salty blue. When her watch showed the target depth, she popped a little burst of air into her BCD, quickly found neutral buoyancy, and then rolled onto her side to spot Justin.

He tapped his head in a giant "OK" signal, and she repeated the gesture back. At this distance, they'd have to work to keep together, but Kate had a clear view of a wide swath of the reef and the bottom forty feet below. She waved her arms ahead of her in an exaggerated "Swim" signal, and the two of them set off along the reef.

Every few minutes, Kate executed a lazy barrel roll, checking Justin's position, then confirming that the *Hopper*'s hull still hung behind them. As she relaxed into her rhythm, drifting through the quiet ocean without worrying about novice divers or keeping to a timetable, she remembered why she'd taken to the water in the first place. Diving provided a deeper sense of mindfulness and focus on the now than she'd ever found in meditation or yoga. In the months after Danny's death, the only peace she found was beneath the surface. And, in time, she'd found that peace above the water, too, thanks, in no small part, to the community of friends at Shark Key.

As she finned east, she made a mental list of the many people and things she had to be grateful for. And as she was thanking God or the Universe or whomever for the time she'd had with Danny, pledging to always love him even as she moved forward into new relationships, she spotted an unnaturally square corner of something dark flapping in the current on the south edge of the reef.

As Angler reached the end of Maloney Avenue and passed through the gate into Key Vista Resort and Yacht Club, he felt like he'd crossed from the slums of Calcutta into the fanciest neighborhood in Dubai.

He took it all in with disdain. Everything looked like a movie set, from the tidy, weedless brick pavement to the buildings freshly painted in every cliché tropical color. Key Lime Pie. Tangerine Twist. Flamingo Pink. Probably painted by the same folks living twelve to a single-wide trailer up the street where he'd abandoned the scooter between a dumpster and a minivan on blocks.

Several guests milled around a tiki bar at the end of the quay. They wore the uniforms of the elite, the women in pressed white sleeveless tennis dresses with colorful sweaters that matched the resort's architecture tied around their shoulders. The men all wore sharply pressed khaki pants and even more sharply pressed Tommy Bahama printed shirts.

Angler looked down at his own attire, more suitable for the boatyard he'd just come from than for the yacht club he was entering. A string of boutique shops lined the path down to the charter docks, offering everything from beachwear to sailing gear. He dipped into a shop. He was ready with a story that he was a workman checking the lightbulbs along the canal, but he didn't need it. The clerk chatted on her phone while fixing a chipped nail —his stained shirt and cargo pants rendering him invisible to her. Rather than bothering to catch her attention, he slipped out with a Hawaiian shirt tucked under his T-shirt.

Ducking behind an oversized vending machine filled with slices of rainbow-colored cake, Angler tugged off the tags and slouched into the designer shirt, buttoning it halfway up to cover the spots on the gray crewneck beneath. He adjusted his sunglasses and ambled back out onto the pier, acting every bit the part.

The wide, polished-concrete dock was inlaid with pale decking, artificially aged to the color of bleached beach sand, bordered by concrete benches and planters overflowing with tropical flowers. At the end, short docks stretched into the harbor, each slip home to a luxurious yacht or ketch or sportfisher, all bobbing gently in the protected water. Gentle waves splashed against the quay, sparkling in the sunlight. But beneath it all, a hint of motor oil and the dockmaster's cigar reminded him that this was all a manufactured paradise.

Angler ordered a grilled lionfish sandwich, then settled onto a concrete bench in the shade of the snack shop's awning. He adjusted his cap as a man walked towards him, wearing a navy-blue blazer and crisp white trousers. Angler thought of the millionaire from Gilligan's Island, believing his position in the posh crowd that belonged at the exclusive yacht club insulated him from danger. But anyone was just a three-hour-tour away from disaster. He stifled a derisive laugh when the man stepped a stiff new deck shoe in a pile of seagull droppings that the resort staff hadn't been quick enough to remove.

A moment later, exactly on time, a sturdy stranger in a white visor wearing a white short-sleeved button-down shirt with epaulets on the shoulders leaned his elbows on the railing, his gaze resting on the first row of boats along the channel. Angler's contact had vouched for the man and arranged the transaction, but nothing could be taken for granted now. He ambled up beside the captain and listened to the breeze rustling in the tall palms.

Finally, the man spoke. "I hear you need a boat."

"Maybe. Depends on what you've got."

"Whatever you need, I can get."

"Speed. Range. Stealth."

"You're not asking for a lot, are you?"

Angler snorted. "Pretty standard stuff, really."

The man nodded to a white sportfisher tied to the first slip, *Beeracuda* emblazoned across her stern. "She can do it. This weekend, right?"

"This weekend. Boat show. Lee County."

"How many?"

"One. Maybe two."

"Destination?"

"South of here."

To Angler's surprise, the man didn't flinch. "Not a problem for me, but it's not going to be cheap. The right guy gets paid to be the right guy. And I'm the right guy. Plus, I'll need a mate."

"Your crew, your problem." Angler shrugged. "Money's not an object. Just tell me where to wire it. Half up front. Half on completion."

"Cash. All up front, or no ride."

"Cash? No one pays cash anymore."

"They do if they want to stay as under the radar as you want."

"If you want that kind of cash, I need time." The small wad of cash in Angler's pocket was nowhere close to the price for the right guy. He held the man's gaze in a game of financial chicken.

"Fine. Half before we leave. Half when I drop you in Cuba." The man reached in his pocket and pulled out a business card, its edges ragged like the cheap, perforated cardstock you can get at an office supply store. The only printing on the card was an email address. "Details go there. Use a VPN."

"Not my first rodeo."

"Good." The man stepped away without ever meeting Angler's eyes. "I'll see you in Fort Myers."

Deek winced as Whiskey dropped the slobbery tennis ball in his lap.

For the past thirty minutes, he'd been keeping the lumbering boat's nose into the waves, nudging it forward, and keeping the two sets of bubbles off either side of the bow. And for the past thirty minutes, this supposedly professional working dog had been dropping the ball into Deek's lap, then pecking his hip with its wet nose until Deek tossed the ball across the deck to be fetched and the cycle started all over again.

"Whiskey, man, give me a break." Deek checked for Kate and Justin's bubbles, then dropped the boat into neutral. He tossed the ball toward the stern and Whiskey scrambled after it as Deek pulled a water bottle out of the big cooler and cracked it open. He turned back and squinted through the windscreen, his right hand lazily resting on the throttle. When he didn't see bubbles ahead, he glanced at his watch. He had only taken his eyes off the surface for a few seconds. Thirty at most.

His heart raced. He promised Kate he'd keep an eye on them. Be here for them when they surfaced.

Whiskey jammed his nose against Deek's hip.

"No, boy. Not now."

The dog whined.

"Whiskey, sit." Deek tried to keep the panic from his voice, and Whiskey's tail hit the deck, his ears ticked forward and his eyes clear. At least he knew when a human meant business.

Deek scanned the water ahead of the boat three times, then expanded his search around the starboard gunwale. Finally, he spotted a concentrated spot of bubbles not far off the stern. He scrambled to the rail and peered over into the water. About halfway to the bottom, he saw his two divers, buddied up and hovering together above the reef.

Deek pushed out a breath he hadn't realized he was holding, then he jogged back to the helm and brought the boat about, holding it steady about twenty yards east of Kate's position. A minute later, a bright orange safety sausage broke through the surface.

They were coming up.

Justin's head broke the surface first, and he swam hard for the stern. Deek killed the engine then ran back to the transom to pull Justin's gear out as he climbed aboard. They strapped Justin's tank into a cradle, then Justin threw a line forward to Kate, who bobbed on the surface in a fully inflated BCD, her phone already in her hand.

She tapped the screen, then let it dangle on its wrist tether. Justin reeled her in like a marlin, then grabbed her fins and BCD. As soon as she was stable on the swim platform, she whipped her phone out of the underwater housing and dialed.

"Fish? We found it. I marked the spot below, but didn't touch anything. I'm sending you a pin. I'll be ready to go down again as soon as you get here."

Deek stared as Justin made for the nearest mooring ball to the east. It wasn't that long ago that no one believed him. Hell, he almost didn't believe him. But now, shit was about to get real.

15

"Can't swing a cat in this town..." Angler muttered under his breath as he strolled past another dive bar packed with sunburned tourists. The stench of coconut oil with an undertone of stale beer and sweat poured out onto the sidewalk with the crowd. The men all wore low-cut tanks and board shorts. The women's string bikinis barely held in the assets they'd paid their plastic surgeons so dearly for. Everyone held their cell phones over their heads, capturing a moment they were too distracted by filming to participate in. Far cry from the yacht club crowd, yet with a common thread of excess and subtle desperation.

Angler caught himself humming along with the Jimmy Buffett cover band blaring over the din of the crowd. Sometimes a cliché is a cliché for a reason. But he was here for business, and even though his stroll through Key West's Old Town was meant more for operational security—he needed to move around like a tourist, use the credit cards and phone attributed to his cover identity—he needed to stay focused.

He tapped the screen of his burner phone and fired up his Virtual Private Network—VPN—app. The final number was in his secure inbox. To a civilian, the number would have been eyewatering. To Angler, it confirmed he'd chosen well. He tapped again. Still no news out of Fort Myers. And to Angler, no news was good news. Plans were coming together.

He ducked into a quiet alley and made the call.

"Account numbers?" The androgynous digital voice at the other end was disconcerting. Angler had become accustomed to it, but he'd be glad when this operation was behind him.

"Risk profile?"

"Anonymous. Clear numbers, unmarked vessel. Crew of two, expendable. Cash up front."

A rooster ambled up the alley, stopping to peck at scraps of trash dropped by the drunken passengers of the cruise ship that loomed over the town. Angler kicked at it, expecting it to scurry away. But these feral animals were almost as holy as a cow in India. The rooster didn't just hold his ground, the little bastard attacked, pecking at Angler's feet until he danced back to the street and ceded the alley to the foul fowl.

"It's too much."

"The right guy gets paid to be the right guy." Angler repeated the captain's line, almost regretting he wouldn't have a chance to use it for his own benefit.

"Half up front means half price."

Angler swore. He hadn't really expected to get away with the final payment for himself, but it was always worth a try. "Even at full price, this op is a bargain."

"Are you expecting a parade?"

Angler smirked. "I'd settle for a bonus."

"Your fee has already been established. And I might add that it's quite generous, considering the personal nature of this operation."

"Point taken."

Angler waited through another lengthy period of dead air, checking the screen to be sure the call hadn't dropped. Finally, the dead voice returned.

"Cayman International Bank and Trust. Grand Cayman. Mrs. Montgomery-Trottman will expect you tomorrow."

Angler bristled. "I need to pick it up in Miami." But when he looked down at the screen, the call had already ended.

The shallow waters of the Gulf of Mexico sparkled under the late-afternoon sun as Harold Hildebrand's private tender glided towards the dock extending from the south end of Baskin Island, its engine's low rumble humming beneath the calls from a colony of gulls off the starboard gunwale. The billionaire slipped his phone away and stood at the bow, anticipation racing through his veins as the coastal breeze tousled his thinning hair. The weight of the impending summit bore heavily upon his shoulders. Three steps behind him, Barbeau Roux gripped the tender's rail while the captain tied the small craft a few yards astern from Hildebrand's motor yacht *Aeolus*.

His security chief had been a reliable, steady gravitational force in his organization for years. Roux's vigilance had saved him from threats ranging from tree-hugging green energy protestors to shopping bag-laden gold diggers. But those were nothing compared to the challenge facing them this weekend.

The two delegations had decades of mistrust between them. And if Harold Hildebrand had his way, this weekend would be remembered for decades to come.

Striding up the thick buffalo turf lawn, he surveyed the four identical houses standing side by side in a row. Directly ahead of him, the southernmost house was his friend Enoch Brookes's personal home. It boasted the longest and deepest dock for *Aeolus*. Brookes had generously offered the other three houses for the weekend, and Hildebrand intended to use them to their fullest.

He'd left detailed instructions for his new assistant to prepare each of the homes. Looking up toward the second house, he spotted several new security cameras dangling like monkeys from its deep eaves. He glanced back to Roux and then pointed up to one of the offending devices.

"I'll have it corrected immediately, sir. They'll be hidden before the delegations arrive. You have my word."

He swept through the French doors of the third house. He had directed that it be configured to host a welcome reception following the first day's meetings, provided both delegations could set aside their differences and focus on their common interests.

Behind him, Roux's quickened steps across the polished tiles stopped abruptly, followed by a thud and clatter. Hildebrand stopped short and spun around just in time to avoid crushing the cell phone sliding across the floor.

"Sir. You've arrived, sir." Laura Smythe extricated herself from Roux's grip, then scrambled to collect her phone from beneath the toe of his custom Italian shoe.

Roux glared at her with one eyebrow raised as she clambered to her feet and smoothed the fabric of her slim black skirt.

Hildebrand stepped back and summoned the patience of Job as he waited for her to collect herself before she finally spoke.

"We're ahead of schedule and fully ready for the delegations to arrive the day after tomorrow, sir. The CCTV contractor is on the way to finish installing the housings around the exterior cameras, and the catering order is due to be delivered at ten tomorrow morning. *Aeolus* was catered this morning and is ready for you to board at your leisure. The captain and crew are expecting you."

She turned to the security chief. "Monseiur Roux, after Mr. Hildebrand settles in, I'd appreciate a moment of your time to review a small concern?"

Roux glanced toward Hildebrand, his eyebrows ticked upward.

Hildebrand filled his lungs with a deep, salty breath. "Miss Smythe, this summit is of the utmost priority. If you have a security concern, I'd like to hear about it firsthand."

Her cheeks flushed at the admonishment. "I'm sure it's nothing, sir. Not worth your attention."

He tightened his jaw. "No detail is beneath my attention this weekend, Laura. Please do go on."

She waved him toward a pair of white leather couches. He remained standing. Finally, she spoke.

"We had an intruder yesterday, sir. A number of contractors had been in and out, and a young woman who works with the local sheriff was here with a federal agent. They chased him away in a small fishing boat. The alarm systems have been reset and armed, and I don't expect any further problems, sir."

"This intruder. He was alone?" Roux's bicep twitched as he pulled his hand into a fist, then released it.

"He was. He—" Her head shook slightly, then she squared her shoulders and looked back to Hildebrand. "I believe he was simply a vagrant searching for an empty house, and he stumbled into more than he bargained for, sir. I just wanted to make Mr. Roux aware of the incident. That's all, sir."

Hildebrand nodded towards Roux, then glanced down at his watch. "I'll be aboard *Aeolus*. Text me any additional updates. And Miss Smythe? No more mistakes. There's too much at stake."

Deek sat atop a padded locker and dangled over the transom of the *Island Hopper Too*, his hair flopping across his eyes. Piloting the boat, he'd been okay. Not fine, but okay. But as soon as they hooked to the mooring ball and killed the engine, Deek's stomach started doing Olympic-level backflips. Deek's embarrassment deepened the greener he turned.

"Maritime Administration, my ass," Justin had joked, pointing him toward the locker and handing him a tattered bucket.

He'd chosen the most downwind spot on the craft, with a clear path over the transom for when the inevitable happened.

Over the starboard gunwale, a military rigid-hull inflatable was tied to the cleats of the larger *Hopper*. Fish had raced there directly from the naval base, and was in the water less than five minutes after he'd rafted up. After setting up a perimeter of buoys above their site, Fish and Kate had descended on the reef.

For the past fifteen minutes, Deek had tried to calm himself by tossing Whiskey's ball, making small talk with Justin, and staring anywhere except the unmoving pad of bubbles in the center of the zone. If asked, he couldn't have answered if his digestive gymnastics were a result of the choppy seas or the idea that a human being was most likely wrapped in that tarp sixty feet below.

"Probably both."

Deek looked up and his stomach pirouetted. "Did I say that out loud?"

"Dude, you've been mumbling over here since they went down. I get it. Normal people don't usually have to deal with chasing bad guys and finding what they leave behind. You're doing great, considering the circumstances." Justin handed Deek a soda. A single chunk of ice clung to the bright red can, slowly losing its battle with gravity. "This'll help. The sugar will settle your stomach. And stare at the horizon line. Don't take your eyes off it."

Deek lifted his gaze to the sharp, straight line where blue met blue. Around the edges of his vision, waves rolled by and collided against the buoys off the *Hopper*'s stern. Whiskey had nudged his ball into Justin's hand when Justin's ringtone pulled Deek's eyes from the horizon to the man sitting in the shade.

Deek snapped his focus back to the horizon a moment too late.

Here, fishie, fishie, fishie.

"...out on the reef right now."

Deek looked up as Justin absently tossed the ball and continued his conversation. Even though he knew his mother would have slapped him in the back of the head and whispered, "Mind your own business, boy," Deek needed something other than his floating breakfast to think about. And to see.

"...no, I'm free this weekend... Cash? That's fire, dude... three o'clock. Got it. I'll be there." Justin stuffed his phone into his pocket as the boat rocked and Whiskey's ball rolled. The highly trained dog scrambled back and forth after it, his long legs splayed in all directions.

Deek took a tentative sip from the soda can and was delighted to find his stomach accepting the syrupy liquid. And the more he sipped, the better he felt. Just when he thought he might be able to hold down a cracker, two heads burst through the surface just off the swim platform.

Kate tossed her fins up and started to roll out of her BCD. But Fish floated in the water a few feet away with his phone's waterproof housing already pressed to his ear.

16

"Can you run me through this one more time?"

Kate pulled a bottle of water from a cooler and handed it to the deputy. She'd heard Deek's theory a few times through, and if she hadn't seen the foot poking out from the bundled tarp, she might not have believed any of it either. She still wasn't completely sure how much of it made sense and how much of it was an overblown conspiracy theory.

She leaned across the *Hopper*'s starboard gunwale. Fish balanced at the helm of his RIB. "They have everything they need, so they should release you pretty soon. Get him back to shore and get some food in him. He looks like he's about to lose more than his lunch."

Kate glanced over at Whiskey lying in the shade beside Deek, who clutched a tattered bucket between his knees as he repeated the chain of unusual events to the sheriff's deputy and tried to explain the connections between them. "I need to fuel up, so we'll stop at Key Vista's marina on the way in. They make a great lionfish sandwich that should hit the spot."

Fish untied the RIB from *Hopper*'s cleat and pushed away, firing up the little boat's powerful outboards as it drifted free. "Call me when you get back in. I'll see what I can dig up."

Kate waved as Fish punched the throttle forward and the RIB climbed up on the chop and zoomed north. She turned back to the dive deck where the deputy continued taking notes.

"...on the lookout, right? A middle-aged white guy. Average height. Average build. Blond or grayish hair. That narrows it down to half the population."

Deek cast his eyes down to the deck. "I'm sorry I can't give you more."

With a single eyebrow raised, the deputy dug in his breast pocket and pulled out a business card. "If you think of anything else, please give us a call. Any detail could be important."

After the deputy untied from the *Hopper*'s port side and pushed away, Kate nudged the dive boat forward and unhooked from the mooring ball, then set a course away from the cluster of sheriff's boats.

Fifteen minutes later, Kate eased up to the fuel dock at the new resort marina, then led Deek up to the small snack shop with Whiskey on their heels.

"You need to eat."

Deek's head shook, then frantically looked around the open patio, his face turning greener by the second. "Bathroom? Where's the…"

Kate pointed across the quay, and Deek took off at a dead run.

"Is your friend okay?"

Kate turned back to the young woman in a pale blue polo running the snack counter. Her makeup was perfectly contoured and her hair was tied back in a sleek ponytail. The Key Vista logo was embroidered on her shirt. Far cry from the casual come-as-you-are vibe at Shark Key.

"He just doesn't have his sea legs yet." Kate shrugged. "Can I get two grilled lionfish baskets to go, please?"

Whiskey whined beside her.

"Make that three."

"Fries okay with that?"

"Yep, perfect." Kate pulled a debit card from her front pocket and tapped the reader on the counter, then leaned against the brightly painted siding to wait.

Deek gripped the sparkling chrome grab bar and pulled himself to his feet. He tugged a length of soft two-ply from the roll, blew his nose a final time, then flushed the tissue away. He glanced around the roomy stall. The bathroom smelled like a fresh ocean breeze with a hint of pineapple. The stall walls and doors were full height and solid, with real hardware and locks, and an automatic hand sanitizer dispenser was mounted on the wall beside the door.

This was not your average Joe's marina.

Deek rubbed a bit of the sanitizer on his hands, then shuffled out to the sinks and waved his hand under the faucet. As he bent to splash water on his face, he sensed another man make his way to the urinals mounted on the opposite wall.

In all the hurry to calm his stomach, Deek realized he'd been neglecting his other needs. He turned toward the three porcelain vessels separated by thick partitions. The stranger stood at the middle urinal, a Tampa Bay Rays ball cap perched backwards on his head.

Deek made his way across the room and started to unzip at the left compartment, keeping his eyes down. Over the soft acoustic version of "Margaritaville" drifting through the ceiling speakers, he heard the other man's breath catch. Steady stream… stopped. The distinctive sound of a hurried zipper tug.

Deek had lived his entire life by the "never look another man in the eye at the urinals" code. But today, he looked up just in time to see Şeytan Taciri bolt out of the bathroom without washing his hands.

Angler hurried his steps. Tried to add some distance between himself and the disheveled man shouting after him.

What were the odds?

Angler tried to reason with himself. Paranoia always began to creep in during the days before any op. Angler tried to calm his mind. It couldn't be the same guy from Baskin Island. The guy from the sound. This had to be his brain playing tricks on him.

"Wait up!"

Angler scurried around a corner and found himself ten feet from the woman from the marina. He stopped short as her dog rose to its feet and planted itself in Angler's path.

Angler heeded the dog's deep growl. He spun, rounded the corner and sprinted down the quay.

Shouts of "Stop him!" And "Whiskey, go!" rang out behind him as Angler scanned the docks.

Angler raced along the dock, hoping in vain some foolish soul had left their keys in the ignition. But even if someone had, he didn't have enough time to get an unfamiliar boat started up, untied, and underway.

No, he needed another plan. And he spotted it just a few yards ahead at the fuel station. He fixed his eyes on the prize and pumped his legs as fast as he could.

But the dog was faster.

He heard the snarl a split second before he felt a hard tug on his left side. His body jerked and spun like a car with a blowout. He crashed down on the pavement, the snarling dog straddling his hips.

The big shepherd held the side of Angler's Hawaiian shirt in his jaws. Angler tried to roll away and pull his shirt out of the dog's mouth. The dog snarled and tightened its grip.

Angler rolled back toward the dog. Punched it on the nose.

The dog leaned back and tugged harder, dragging Angler along the brick pavers.

Time stood still as Angler noted each tooth's pressure against the surprisingly sturdy fabric. Angler finally froze, realizing that every struggle would cause the dog to grip tighter—a real-life Chinese finger puzzle.

He curled into a ball, hoping the dog would sense victory and release his jaws. The strategy paid partial dividends, as the dog eased the pressure on Angler's shirt, but still clung tight enough that Angler couldn't get away.

"Whiskey, off!"

The woman's voice echoed across the water in the basin as the dog immediately released Angler's shirt and dropped into a crouch beside him, daring him to run.

Which is exactly what Angler did.

Before the dog could react, Angler launched himself into a skiff that had been tied up behind a big dive boat. Its owner had been preparing to pull away from the fuel dock when he stopped to watch the commotion on the pier.

Angler shoved the man overboard and gunned the little boat away from the seawall. Ignoring the no wake signs, he blazed down the channel and then aimed the boat west, the throttle open as wide as it could go.

Three hours later, after dodging in and out of coves and channels along the coast as the sun set at his back, Angler ditched the stolen skiff under a bridge on the east side of Cudjoe Key and made his way up to the highway.

"Ice machine's broke, if that's what you're wantin'"

Angler ignored the clerk and crossed the narrow convenience store to the fountain soda machine. He tugged a thirty-two-ounce cup off the stack and filled it with RC Cola from a sputtering tap. He carefully pulled a lid up and snapped it onto the soda.

"Marlboro Reds. Box."

"It's your lucky day. Hard-pack is all we got anymore." As the clerk reached to the rack above the counter, the television behind him flashed images of sheriff's marine units floating under the bright lights of a Coast Guard cutter.

"A body found wrapped in a tarp on the reef just outside Key West this afternoon has resulted in widespread traffic snarls both on the Overseas Highway and in the waters surrounding the westernmost island in Monroe County. Local residents traveling up and down the Keys are advised to allow extra time to pass through the roadblocks through at least tomorrow morning." A pretty brunette in a bright red blazer appeared on the screen. "Officials have not released the identity of the victim or any additional details about the find. We will be following this story as more information is available, so stay tuned to WDLN for more details or follow us on social media for real-time updates."

The clerk tossed a box of cigarettes on the counter. Angler held his breath steady and his head down as he tossed a ten-dollar bill on the counter and took the smokes and soda and pushed out the door without waiting for his change.

His heart pounded, blood throbbing in his temple as he worked through contingency plans. No operation ever went smoothly. That's why backups to the backups were always in place. But Angler was not accustomed to tapping so many contingencies so early in an operation.

As he walked north across the brackish swampland toward his destination, Angler tapped the pack of cigarettes against his palm and took stock of his status.

There was no way to tie him to the body in the ocean.

There was no way to find a plane that didn't exist.

He had a team lined up where every detail was separate, and no one knew enough to be a security risk.

He needed to get to Grand Cayman by morning, then hightail it back.

Angler stepped off the barely paved back road and pressed through the thick foliage until the ground grew soggy and soft beneath his feet. He followed the waterline around to a thicket that rose from the flat shore, and he smiled, pulling the camouflaged netting away.

The DHC-3 Otter was standing tall at the edge of the water looking shiny with the wrap removed revealing red stripes on the white body, and a brand-new fictional tail number. The floats, struts, and landing gear all looked straight, and the fuel tank was full.

Finally, something had gone right.

Angler flung the still-sealed pack of Reds into the brush, then climbed inside the Otter. He was dog tired, and the continual barrage of problems had set him on edge. Messing with his head. A bad combination for flying an unfamiliar plane, especially a water takeoff... at night. With a deep sigh, he reassured himself that all was not lost, and the prudent decision was a decent night's sleep. At dawn, after resting, he could slip away from the Keys amongst the clutter of early morning air traffic, and with that thought in mind, he lay down and soon fell into a deep sleep.

"Sorry, man. If it's any consolation, they seem to be taking your story a little more seriously now. They're reviewing the security tapes from the resort, sending the photo out, and setting up a roadblock on the bridge at North Key Largo. He won't get off the islands if they can do anything about it."

Deek looked across the table at Fish and shook his head. "He's already gone. Şeytan Taciri isn't stopped by roadblocks. Even Whiskey here couldn't keep a hold of him."

The big shepherd rested his head in Deek's lap with a soft whimper. It was almost as if he knew Deek needed an apology.

"Eh, that plane wasn't goin' nowhere, and between the sheriff and the Coast Guard, he's not getting out by car or boat either." Chuck dropped a bucket of water bottles and beer in ice on the table. "We'll figure it out."

Deek reached for a bottle. As he twisted the cap off, a dark hand reached over his shoulder, took the beer and slapped a water bottle into its place.

"You'll thank me for that, because you're heading for the airport, my friend." Michelle dropped down into a chair beside

Deek, set her laptop on the table, and took a long swig from his bottle.

"Okay, I'll bite. What did you find?" Deek cracked the water bottle open, poured some into Whiskey's bowl, then drank for himself.

"Well, it's less what did I find and more what my crack algorithm rooted out. I can only take the credit of a proud computer mama." She grinned and leveled her gaze at Chuck. "Do you remember how they got Al Capone?"

"Of course." Chuck turned to Deek. "My granddaddy worked for Capone back in the day. I shouldn't be proud of it, but I also wouldn't have this place if it wasn't for him. Gramps knew the feds had him, so the day Capone was convicted, Gramps and his girl snuck crates and crates of loot out of Capone's vault and made a run for it. Drove south 'til the road ran out, and they ended up here."

Deek was fascinated, but his heart beat faster as he watched Michelle fire up her laptop.

"It's always the money," Michelle began. "And people always think they're more clever than they really are. I told the algorithm to start looking for transfer patterns that coincided with attacks attributed to Taciri. Then I pointed it at banking activity in the past few months. It took a few tries, but then things got interesting."

She turned the screen around and pointed at a window that looked more like the web of a drunken spider than a series of bank transfers.

"No human could have found this. But my little baby here found a pattern. A series of transfers that look unrelated, except that a percent and a half of each transfer makes its way through four different banks before it lands in one of three numbered accounts in Switzerland. So then I told it to look for the origin of everything that had landed in those accounts.

"It churned for so long, I thought maybe it was going to either spit back every bank account ever opened or just error out. But then it came back with a series of transfers highlighted that match the pattern it found before the last two attacks by Taciri. Transfers that coalesce at one time. In one place. A bank in Grand Cayman. Tomorrow."

"So I'm going to Grand Cayman?"

Michelle grinned. "I haven't told you the best part yet. It tracked back through shell company inside shell company until it found a single name." She raised an eyebrow and took another sip of her beer.

Deek's heart pounded. Finally, the trail he'd been looking for. The true name behind the legend, Şeytan Taciri. He nodded.

"Harold Hildebrand. We've got him."

"Yes!" Deek pumped his fist in the air, then froze. "Wait. So I was right, but I was also wrong. If Harold Hildebrand is Şeytan Taciri, then who have I been chasing?"

"I don't know," Kate said, "but the part you were right about is that this guy is up to something big. He nearly killed you and your friend. He's already killed at least one other person. You can't let him get away."

17

How many more things could go wrong? Angler had fallen asleep with that question on his mind, and woken the next morning still wishing he knew the answer. Being in control of his own destiny had sounded a lot better than it was turning out to be. A restless few hours of sleep, crammed between the seats in the back of the plane, hadn't done much to ease his mind, but he hung to the hope that things would be smooth sailing from here. They had to be. This would be his highest paying gig in a long and tumultuous career—the one which finally enabled him to call it quits... and that meant he had to make it work, regardless of the challenges.

It was still dark outside, but with a long flight ahead, he hauled his tired body to the open cabin door, and relieved himself into the water below. His flight time would be half if he flew over Cuba, but then he'd be obliged to have his transponder on from the beginning and get their permission, unless he wanted a MIG up his ass. No, he'd take the long way around the western tip as though he was flying to the Yucatan peninsula, then cut back east to the Cayman Islands. At that point he'd turn on the real ADS-B Out transponder for the plane and request permission to land in the waters off Grand Cayman.

He'd stop long enough to refuel and run to the bank, then be floats up within an hour or two. That would put him touching down in Key West before dark, and God knows, he didn't want to be landing the seaplane in the dark. Angler had plenty of hours in his logbook, and some of them were actually legitimate flights he'd recorded, but many weren't. Very few were at the controls of a seaplane, which didn't make a bit of difference once in the air, but the takeoffs and landings made his rear end clench.

For a moment, he regretted shooting the pilot. His original plan had been to get rid of the guy after they'd returned, but the man had made him uneasy. Like that idiot Grady Foster had brought with him. There was far too much riding on his retirement gig for loose ends.

Angler yawned and double-checked the cabin. He had a six-pack of energy drinks, a urinal jug he'd found on board, a large bottle of water, and a selection of candy bars and other snacks. Everything a man could want for a five-and-a-half-hour flight in a small plane. With autopilot, he'd be able to leave the pilot's seat for a while, but in the cramped cabin, it wasn't like he could stand up and stretch his legs.

Ten minutes later, with the lines cleared, pre-check done, and the hint of dawn on the horizon, Angler idled the seaplane away from the tiny uninhabited island lost amongst a myriad of other uninhabited islands. Lining up on a straight run he'd planned out between the sandbars and islands, Angler eased the throttle forward, and once he felt the floats lift from the drag of the water, skimming across the surface, he pulled back on the stick, and took to the air.

Deek woke with a start, Strauss's *Also sprach Zarathustra* ringtone blasting from his phone as he banged his head on the side of the trailer and knocked a lamp from the nightstand. Finally locating his cell phone in the dark, he answered the call with a groan.

"Morrison! Where the hell are you?" came his boss's angry voice.

Deek tried to sit upright and swing his legs out of bed, but the covers wrapped him up like a burrito and he slipped—sheets, blanket, and all—to the floor with a thud.

"Sir," he managed to gasp. "Key West, sir."

"Why the hell are you in Key West when the boat show opens today hundreds of miles from there! Huh?" he roared, not giving his analyst time to respond. "I sent you down there to man the booth, not waltz around in women's underwear in some perverted street parade in Key West!"

"Women's underwear?" Deek muttered, double-checking he still had his tighty-whities on. He'd had a couple of drinks in the Shark Key bar, but he was sure he'd remember if he'd been involved in a parade.

"So, Morrison?" his boss fumed.

"I'm in my own underwear, sir..."

"I don't give a damn about your underwear, Morrison! Why are you in Key West? And if you're about to tell me you followed a lead on this ridiculous wild goose chase theory of yours, don't bother!"

Deek found the lamp on the floor, picked it and set it back on the nightstand, then switched it on. He wasn't sure how to respond.

"Well, damn it?!"

"Sir, you said not to bother if I was here..."

"I knew it!" the man interrupted. "You understand I have to sign off on your expenses, Morrison? Well guess what? I'm not approving any of this completely unnecessary, unapproved, and un..."

"Helpful, sir? Unhelpful?"

"Damn it, Morrison! Don't smart-mouth me."

Deek let his head drop back onto the bed and groaned. The line went quiet and just as he thought his boss had hung up, he spoke again, his voice somewhat calmer.

"We're economic analysts, Morrison, not agents or officers. We analyze and pass our findings along to professionals who do the investigations, if, and only if, they deem the analysis worthy of pursuing. So, please explain to me why one of my analysts is in Key West instead of the boat show in Fort Myers?"

"I can tell you but you're not going to like it, sir."

"We've covered the part about me not liking it, Morrison. We're now to the part where you offer up your ludicrous reasoning for not following my clear and explicit instructions. Go ahead, please."

"Well, sir, I tracked a seaplane to Key West which brought the man I believed to be Şeytan Taciri on board."

"How do you know he was on board?"

"Because we saw him, sir."

"You saw the man?"

"Well, I didn't see him clearly as I was driving the boat alongside the seaplane while it was trying to take off, but the woman, Sam, from the sheriff's department got a good look before she was thrown off the float as the plane took off."

The line went silent.

"Sir?"

"I'm processing, Morrison."

"Let me know when I should continue, sir."

"There's more?"

"Oh, yes, sir."

Deek heard a long sigh.

"Continue."

"Thank you, sir. So after arriving in Key West a body was kicked out of the seaplane over the reef which we were able to dive and recover, and we believe he was the pilot."

"You were scuba diving?"

"No, sir, that was Kate and her friend, I drove the boat, sir."

"You're driving a lot of boats, Morrison."

"Yes, sir. We are the Maritime Administration, sir."

"Let me ask you something, Morrison. If I was to administer a random drug test on you right now, what would the result be?"

Deek looked at the phone in his hand. His thoughts were racing on how best to relay everything he'd learned over the past few days, and his boss was asking about drug tests?

"Oh, you're thinking I may have taken an illegal narcotic of some description at a street parade in Key West, sir?"

"Either that or you morphed into James Bond since leaving the office, Morrison."

"I assure you, sir, I'm not on drugs, and I'm not James Bond."

"I know that, Morrison."

Deek breathed a sigh of relief. "You had me there, sir, I thought you were really worried about the drug thing."

"I am. I meant I know you're not James Bond."

"Oh. Right. Well, anyway, sir. We found the stickers to the seaplane that the man I believed to be Şeytan Taciri had removed to reveal the true tail number underneath, and he and the plane are now missing again. But Michelle tracked…"

"Wait, wait, wait," his boss interrupted once more. "First of all, twice now you've said *believed* in reference to Şeytan Taciri, as in past tense. So the man you were sure was this mythical tyrant, is no longer who you thought?"

"Correct, sir. I believe the man I've been tracking is in fact working for Şeytan Taciri, who I'm now convinced is Harold Hildebrand."

His boss laughed, but Deek couldn't hear much humor in his voice.

"Morrison, let me be crystal clear. If you're not behind the counter of our booth when the boat show opens at midday today, you will no longer be employed by the Maritime Administration."

"Sir?" Deek mumbled in disbelief. "No one gets fired from the Maritime Administration, sir. I don't understand?"

"If you don't get your conspiracy-theoried ass to the boat show by noon, you will be the second person shit-canned under my watch!" his boss shouted before calming himself again. "The first didn't show up for work for forty-seven consecutive days, in case you were wondering."

"I'm so close, sir," Deek pleaded. "I truly believe people are in danger at the boat show."

"Then why are you in Key West, Morrison?"

"Because I tracked the man in the seaplane here, sir, and now we've tracked the money to the Cayman Islands."

His boss scoffed. "Seriously? Now you want to saunter over to the Cayman Islands?"

"I would, sir."

Once more, the line fell silent, and Deek wasn't sure what to say or do.

"Here's what we're going to do, Morrison. You're going to drive back to Fort Myers and stand behind our counter when the show opens."

Deek realized his boss was expecting him to fill the subsequent pause with a response.

"Yes, sir."

"I am going to reach out to a friend of mine with the FBI..."

"Really, sir?!" Deek blurted.

"May I finish, Morrison?"

"Of course, sir. I apologize."

"I am going to reach out to a friend of mine with the FBI, and mention some of your mad ramblings to him. If he feels there's anything worth further discussion—which I strongly doubt—then I'll leave it with him to pursue as he sees fit."

"Can I talk to him, sir?"

"No. Are you driving yet?"

"I'm talking to you, sir."

"I'm hanging up, and you will proceed directly to Fort Myers, Morrison. Do not pass go, do not collect $200."

"Sir?"

Deek looked down at his silent phone. His boss had hung up.

Twenty minutes later, having hurriedly written a thank you note to the Shark Key crew who had helped him so much, Deek started the long drive north on Overseas Highway. Two hours after that, with an extra-large gas station coffee making him squirm in his seat, Deek's phone rang again. This time he checked the caller ID and answered once he saw it was his buddy, Pete.

"Guess what?"

Deek sighed. "There's FBI agents going through my desk?"

"Huh?"

"Never mind. What do you have?"

"A de Havilland Canada DHC-3 Otter just pinged from the Caribbean Sea."

"Okay… but our guy was pinging as a crop duster yesterday, right?"

"Sure, but you found the stickers he stripped from the plane, so perhaps he's now using the real tail number and real transponder."

Deek thought for a moment as he crossed one of the multitude of bridges between the Keys. A sign informed him he was now in Islamorada.

"Can you tell where the plane came from?" he asked.

"That's what makes this weird," Pete replied. "There's no trace of this transponder anywhere else today. It's like he fell out of the sky southwest of Cuba."

"Meaning, he turned on the transponder."

"That would be my guess."

"And where's he heading?" Deek asked.

"I'd say Jamaica, but depending on where he took off from, that might be pushing his range in an Otter. Of course, he could refuel in Grand Cayman on the way. He'll fly right over the Cayman Islands."

Deek barely hung on to the coffee in his bladder. "Grand Cayman?"

"Whoa! Do you think that's where he's going?" Pete asked.

Deek looked at his watch, the Omega Seamaster his parents had bought him when he graduated college and joined the Maritime

Administration. They'd told him the model seemed appropriate, and he shouldn't go to his new job wearing his ancient Casio calculator watch. It was now 8:30 a.m.

"When's the next flight to Grand Cayman out of Miami?" he asked, and while his friend tapped away on his keyboard, Deek ran through all the reasons why he should continue to Fort Myers and forget about chasing ghosts. There were all the obvious ones, like keeping his job, but the one reason that made his heart sink was the fact that he didn't have any money. His personal card was maxed, and his boss had made it clear that he wouldn't reimburse any of the reservation expenses. He had twenty-six dollars in his pocket, and checks which would either bounce like a space hopper or cause his rent to do the same, depending on the timing.

"There's a 10:57 a.m. on American," Pete replied. "The boss will lose his shit if you fly to the Cayman Islands, Deek. You can't be seriously considering this?"

Deek began to shake his head until he spotted a bright yellow sign above a blue roofed building on the right. *Keys Pawn—Luxury Jewelry and Watches.*

18

Angler relaxed his hands on the controls and tried to settle his nerves. Taking off in the seaplane was tricky, but landing was far more treacherous. He'd been given an approach which would allow him to taxi into a harbor—which looked more like a small bay—where he could tie up and refuel, as well as clear immigration. Now, as he skimmed the water, watching for any boat traffic that might cross his path, Angler tried not to look at the large cruise ship anchored off his starboard side, or the concrete wall of the commercial dock up ahead to port.

The floats grazed the light chop and he eased back the throttle until the floats skipped across a few peaks before settling into the calm waters. The sudden drag threw him forward into the belts, but his path was clear of traffic and he was able to gently slow the plane until he coasted into the harbor.

There was no quiet way of landing a seaplane in the waters off Grand Cayman. No islands to hide behind, or large uninhabited stretches to touch down away from curious eyes. Angler taxied alongside the guest dock where a man stood waiting to begin refueling from the barrel of avgas he'd ordered brought from the airport. Looking toward town, he noticed a crowd of curious onlookers lining the harbor front, cell phones aimed his way. He pulled the ball cap down a little tighter, shading his face, and shut the engine down while the dockmaster secured the Otter.

Striding down to meet him as he stepped to the dock, Angler extended a hand to the immigration official. He'd selected a Canadian passport for this trip, one he'd used several times in the past without issue, but had changed his mind at the last minute and gave the man a US passport instead. They chatted amiably as the officer looked over the plane's paperwork. The pilot had the registration through a Florida LLC then leased the plane to himself with a contract, the copy of which Angler had discarded mid-flight, along with his SIG Sauer. He told the official he'd been contracted by the LLC to fly the trip to Cayman.

The whole process took under ten minutes, including a cursory inspection of the plane. Once complete, Angler handed the dockmaster most of his remaining cash to cover the fuel, and grabbed a Glock 19 the pilot had foolishly disclosed his secret location for. In a dive shop by the narrow frontage road running through the waterfront of Grand Cayman's capital, George Town, Angler picked out a good-sized waterproof duffel bag with shoulder straps, then set off on foot for the bank.

Deek's foot tapped like a courthouse stenographer's fingers as the Boeing 737 MAX touched down at Owen Roberts International Airport, turned around on the runway, and taxied back to the terminal. He impatiently hopped from one foot to the other in the immigration line, running through all the scenarios and obstacles before him. He had the name of a bank, the possibility that the man he'd been following had flown the seaplane to the island, and just about nothing else. Well, nothing else. There was no *just about* involved.

The immigration officer raised an eyebrow as Deek nervously fidgeted before him.

"Where you staying, sir?" the officer asked in the musical accent of the island.

"I'm not sure yet," he replied honestly. "I'm only here for one night. Do you have hostels?"

The officer stared at Deek. "No, we don't. What's the purpose of your visit?"

"I'm..." Deek began then quickly reeled himself in. He took a business card from his wallet and handed it over. "I'm here on business."

"Maritime Administration. Economic Analyst," the officer read aloud. "You're here on business for one night, according to your return ticket, wit nowhere to stay? Who's da business wit?"

"Cayman International Bank and Trust," Deek replied. "I'm investigating an individual's connection to a potential threat on US soil," he added with confidence that surprised himself.

He nodded to the man, one national official to another, proud of the line he'd rehearsed on the plane for a moment such as this.

"Do you have da authority and permission to conduct an investigation in da Cayman Islands, sir?" the officer asked, and all Deek's confidence blew away like a feather in the wind.

"I'm really here to ask a few questions at the bank," he stammered. "Investigation is probably a stronger term than I should have used."

The officer looked him over once more, adjusted the date on his stamp, found an empty page in Deek's passport—which was the first page as he'd never travelled anywhere of consequence in his life—and smacked the stamp down, making Deek jump.

"You're approved to stay for forty-eight hours. Try da Sunshine Suites, dey sometimes have last-minute rooms, if not Eldemire Guest House. Welcome to da Cayman Islands, Mr. Morrison."

Deek snatched his passport from the man, scurried through to the baggage claim area where he had nothing to collect, and on to customs where another officer took his entry form from him.

On the other side of customs, Deek was greeted by a dizzying array of signs held by an assortment of people from a variety of tour companies and resorts.

"Taxi, my friend?" another asked.

Deek was about to accept, until he remembered his perpetual state of poverty. The pawn shop had given him $1,100 for his $4,000 watch, and American Airlines had relieved him of $860 for his middle seat air ticket. He had $240 left which he needed to cover a roof over his head, food, plus the airport parking fee on his return to Miami.

"Is there public transportation here?" he asked the man.

"Sure ting. Take a taxi into town, den da buses run up and down, George Town to West Bay. Just wave, den dey stop."

The man turned to lead him to a waiting taxi in the blazing sunshine beyond the sliding doors.

"Sir, is there a hotel in George Town?" he asked, having no idea where West Bay was or what route the man meant.

"No, sir. Dey all along da Seven Mile Beach. Now follow along and I'll get you to da beach."

Deek trailed the man outside where the fierce heat and bright sun made him catch his breath and squint. Rolling towards him was a minibus with Marriott Grand Cayman Resort emblazoned down the side. Below in smaller letters were the words Seven Mile Beach. Deek's hand shot in the air, and he practically ran out in front of the bus, causing the driver to stomp on the brakes.

"Come at me like a chicken dere, sir," the driver said, hopping out and opening the side door. "No luggage?" he asked, looking around expectantly.

"Traveling light," he replied, stepping into the minibus, joining a handful of tourists who shuffled over to make room. The driver closed the door as Deek waved a feeble apology to the taxi man who glared back at him.

Ten minutes later, they reached a palm tree-lined parking lot leading to the covered front entrance of the resort, and Deek released his grip on the back of the front seat. The whole way he'd been thrown for a loop as the driver sat on the wrong side of the bus, like a postal delivery van, and then drove on the wrong side of the road. The numerous roundabouts were especially vexing to a man who didn't spend much time away from the office, let alone overseas.

The passengers filed out and gathered at the back of the bus to collect their luggage. Deek took the opportunity to slink away, scurrying back to the road running past the hotel. He hoped this was the road the taxi man had referred to. Unsure which direction led to George Town where he knew the bank to be, he walked clear of the entrance so the Marriott staff couldn't see him and watched for a public bus.

Deek didn't know what to expect. Everyone knew about the red double-decker buses in England, and as this was a British Overseas Territory, he assumed they'd have something similar. Two public transport buses went by before he realized they were not much bigger than a minivan with a yellow stripe above the front window. The bold black lettering stating it was a *Public Bus* should have tipped him off sooner had he not been looking past them in search of a double-decker. After flagging down the third passing bus, he crammed himself in amongst several locals with their weekly grocery bags, and decided shipping double-decker buses to a Caribbean Island probably didn't make financial sense.

After stopping twice more to pick up people, everyone had grocery bags on their laps when the bus pulled up in front of a sheltered waiting area signed as the Bus Station. People got out, bags were sorted, and pretty soon Deek was left alone wondering where the address he had might be. He turned on his cell data, deciding he wouldn't have to face that charge for another month in which time he'd be unemployed and bumming off his parents.

Instinctively, he glanced at his watch to check the time and sighed at the slightly paler band of skin where his watch once rested. He didn't know how, but he hoped he'd be able to buy it back before it went out front for sale in the pawn shop, although the job loss thing would certainly hamper that plan.

He checked his cell phone. It was 12:31 p.m. He quickly typed the bank's address into the maps app and a few moments later, a red line zigzagged across the screen, telling him he had a one-minute drive, or a three-minute walk. Deek set off, rehearsing the speech he planned to give at the bank.

Angler waited with his bag on his lap, watching the people come and go in the bank. The Cayman Islands had strict gun laws so he'd stashed the Glock outside in a shrub before he'd entered, which had been fortunate as the lone security guard had checked his bag. The man raised his eyebrows at the cell phone collection, but the extra passports were stuffed in his back pocket to avoid scrutiny.

He'd almost shown the bank manager the Canadian passport, quickly grabbing the one he'd used to enter the country with. It would have been a tough mistake to back out of, but he'd remembered in time to use the US passport he'd been saving for a very long time. It was the one he'd originally used to open the account. His own.

After what felt like an agonizing amount of time, Angler was invited into a private room, where the stack of cash he'd been promised sat in neat piles on the table. One and a half million dollars didn't look like much until he stared at the individual slivers of hundred-dollar bills.

"Take your time, sir," the manager offered, before opening the door to leave.

"Wait," he said, and she paused.

He picked up one of the bound stacks and slowly flickered them with his thumb.

"Your machine counts better than my old eyes. We're good."

"Are you sure, sir?" she asked. "There's no rush."

"Maybe not for you," he said under his breath. "We're good," he added, louder so she could hear.

"Then knock when you're ready, and our security man will escort you out."

Angler shook his head. "Tell him to pay no attention to me at all. Nothing screams cash in the bag like a uniform walking with me."

"As you wish, sir," she responded, and left the room, closing the door.

Two minutes later, Angler opened the door, pausing for a moment to scan the other customers in the bank, before heading for the entrance. The security guard watched him from the corner of his eye like the amateur he was, Angler noted, then the man held the door open and wished him a good day.

Outside in the bright sunshine with the ocean breeze blocked by the buildings, beads of sweat formed on his forehead. He quickly moved to the shrub, retrieved the Glock, and glanced at his watch. 12:36 p.m. If he hurried, he'd be floats up not long after one o'clock and touching down in Key West long before dark. Finally, something was going right.

Deek was sweating like Cool Hand Luke eating eggs by the time he marched into the Cayman International Bank and Trust. He owed half of his perspiration to the balmy climate of a tropical island, and the other half to the fact he had no idea what to say. He looked at his watch, which of course wasn't there, so he checked the clock on his phone. It was 12:37 p.m.

The security guard welcomed him while looking him over suspiciously. Great start, Deek thought to himself. Walking over to an open window, he nervously wiped the sweat from his brow.

"Hello, I wonder if I may have a word with the manager?"

"Do you have an appointment, sir?" the young lady asked.

"Oh... I'm afraid I don't, but it's an urgent matter," he explained as firmly as he could muster. "I'm a government employee from the United States."

That didn't sound as dauntingly official as he'd hoped.

"May I ask what this is in regard to, sir?"

"Umm... I'd say it's best I explain to the manager if you don't mind, ma'am," Deek said, sliding a business card under the thick Perspex.

His business cards had sat in his desk since they'd been given to him a week after he started at the Maritime Administration, the first ten being handed out to family members. He was now dishing them out like candy and was in danger of running out of the few he'd brought with him. The cards were one color black print on the cheapest white stock available. The most unimpressive kind you could buy online for $9.99 a box.

The young lady looked at the card, flipped it over expectantly, and finding nothing, pushed her chair back. "One moment, sir."

Deek waited anxiously, drumming his fingers on the counter and trying not to look at the security guard who was watching him carefully. He wiped his brow once more and realized his clothes were beginning to smell like clothes a man had sweated in for two days straight with seawater tossed in for good measure.

"How may I help you, Mr. Morrison?" a lady said, making him jump.

She was behind the counter but didn't take the bank teller's seat as though she wasn't expecting their discussion to take long.

"Is there somewhere private we could talk?" he asked.

She glanced around the empty reception area of the bank, then back at Deek. "Perhaps you can give me an idea what this might be about, sir?"

"Yes, of course," he bumbled. "Has a man been here this morning, ma'am?"

"A multitude of men have been here this morning, Mr. Morrison," she responded, looking at him like he was the idiot he currently felt.

"Of course, I'm sorry. This man is late forties, maybe early fifties, close cropped hair, stern, and I'm guessing he either brought you or withdrew a large amount of cash. Perhaps in the thousands..."

Deek let the last part hang as though a bank in the Cayman Islands had never seen such a sum before.

"I'm afraid I'm not at liberty to discuss our clients with you, Mr. Morrison," she responded, her eyes momentarily looking past him. "Perhaps if you wouldn't mind explaining why you're here and under whose authority, I may be of further assistance."

"Nobody believes me," Deek mumbled, looking down at the counter.

"If you'd like to come back with a member of local law enforcement, Mr. Morrison, who have jurisdiction here, I may be able to assist you."

"We don't have that kind of time, ma'am," he said, shaking his head. "I followed the money trail here and I have reason to believe a dangerous man flew here this morning in a seaplane, and it's all about a secret meeting at a boat show in Fort Myers this weekend, so time is not on our side. Lives are at stake, ma'am."

Deek heard the front door open and close followed by a man's friendly voice with an English accent. "Afternoon, Dorothy."

The woman smiled over Deek's shoulder. "Morning, Henry. How was last night's crowd?"

"Can't complain, my dear, can't complain at all," the man said, his enthusiastic voice trailing off at the end.

Deek turned the man's way, and noticed the security guard was ushering him away.

"Sir, I'd like to see some ID please," came a female voice beside him, and Deek whipped around.

A tall, slender Nordic-looking woman stood before him in a Royal Cayman Islands Police Service uniform. One hand rested on a Taser and the other she held out, expecting a document.

Deek glanced at the bank manager. "You called the police?"

"Standard procedure in situations like this, sir," she replied.

"Situations like what? I'm trying to stop a major catastrophe, and everyone thinks I'm crazy," he said, his voice tired and defeated.

"Are you?" the policewoman asked, and he noticed she even had a Scandinavian accent.

"Crazy? No! I'm an Economic Analyst, and I have a theory if you'll just hear me out... Officer Sommer," he said, reading her badge.

"*Constable* Sommer," she responded. "And you already sound nutty as a *kransekage* to me," she added, staring at him without an ounce of humor in her eyes.

19

Angler double-checked his cargo, which didn't take long. All he had on board the Otter was a set of dive gear and his waterproof bag full of cash, passports, phones, and papers. Settling into the pilot's seat, he began his preflight checks and the tedious task of clearing for takeoff from the water. Directed by the air traffic control tower at Owen Roberts International, he would taxi out into open water, before turning and taking off into the easterly wind, which would aim him back at the island.

As he idled from the harbor, Angler keenly watched the boat traffic for potential obstacles. His mood had lightened since all went well at the bank, but this was no time to let his guard down. Hell, he hadn't even started the op yet—this was all logistics and preparation. The cruise ship hadn't moved, and a tender looked to be delivering a handful of people back to the behemoth at anchor. Beyond that, he spotted a local fisherman's skiff motoring into the harbor and not much else except for a few sailboats anchored to the north.

By the time Angler turned the Otter to face the harbor, he was over a half mile offshore. He had more than twice the water he needed to get airborne, and the control tower had given him permission to take off, then vector over the North Sound for his departure from the island. Easing into the throttle, the seaplane bumped and rolled over the heavier chop of the open water. The wrap around swell from the southwest tip of the island created following seas despite heading into the wind, so the plane glided over the peaks and eased down the troughs.

His palms were sweaty from the heat and a few jitters, if he was honest with himself. The landing had been nerve wracking, but the takeoff was no walk in the park either. As the Otter picked up speed, the floats began to rise in the water, planing across the ocean, jerking slightly from one side to the other as the floats dug into the tops of the waves he was overtaking.

Angler quickly checked out both side windows before returning his attention to the front as he felt the seaplane begin to pitter-patter across the water, reaching takeoff speed. He squinted as the next trough came into view. *What the hell is that?*

Everything happened at once. He recognized the profile of a man paddling a large kayak just as he was about to pull back on the stick.

"Idiot!" Angler yelled at the exact moment he felt and heard the crash of the starboard float hitting the hefty plastic vessel.

Thrown forward into the belts like he'd been hit by a train, Angler sensed the seaplane lifting into the air, yet all he could see out the window was water. The roar of the engine abruptly stopped, replaced with the sound of ripping metal and water thundering against the Otter. Though the crash was over in a matter of seconds, it felt like it went on forever. Every thump, jolt, and wallop feeling like the last he'd ever know. Just as quickly as the impact had started, all became still, and Angler slumped against the belts.

Water slurping in and splashing his face revived his senses, and he looked around him. He could barely see the ocean surface through the top left corner of the windshield, as the rest was under water. A large tear in the roof above him where the right wing had been ripped away was letting the ocean in at an alarming rate, and he instantly knew he had little time.

Unclipping his belts, Angler wriggled free of the pilot's seat and staggered in the swaying cabin, clutching at seat backs to pull himself up the slope. He turned and looked at the windshield. It was solid blue water. Grabbing the waterproof duffel, he slung it along the floor of the cabin towards the rear door before hauling himself the few steps to the cabin exit. He reached for the handle, and paused. The door opened outwards, which meant he'd either let more water in, or he wouldn't be able to open it at all.

"Damn it," he muttered and twisted the lever, shoving the door.

Water poured in through the crack he'd opened, then the pressure slammed the door closed once more.

He was trapped inside until the plane completely sank and the pressure equalized on either side of the door. Angler had no clue how deep the seafloor was where he'd crashed, but he knew the island was an underwater mountain which barely peeked above the ocean. You didn't have to go far from the coast before the famous walls dropped to thousands of feet. The thought of plunging to the depths sent a shiver through his whole body.

Around him, the seaplane creaked, and the ocean slapped against the sides while the raucous sound of rushing water echoed around the quickly filling cabin. At some point the water weight would drag the nose down and the air pocket in the tail would dangle the Otter like a toy on a string. When or how the plane would finally sink all the way was beyond Angler's comprehension, but he knew the fuselage was tipping at a steeper and steeper angle, and he wanted the hell out.

Next to him, something shifted and clattered against the back of the final pair of seats. The dive rig! Just as he reached for the BCD, the seaplane began swinging nose down, and clutching to the seats, Angler watched in horror as the water level rose quickly up the passenger windows, slowing one short of the exit door. When the movement settled, he was bobbing waist deep in seawater, his feet touching seat backs. The rushing of water had stopped, but the level outside the windows was still rising and his ears popped as the pressure inside the cabin increased.

Forcing down the urge to panic, Angler dragged the dive rig toward him, letting it splash into the water. He made sure to crank the tank valve open, then shoved an arm though a shoulder strap and fought to pull the BCD on all the way. There simply wasn't enough room between the seats in the cramped, upright cabin. The water level now reached his chest, floating the dive rig and making it even harder.

Angler grabbed the door handle again and twisted. The door flew open without any resistance, taking him by surprise. Of course! He figured, the tail was in the air and the door just above the surface. To confirm his theory, seawater lapped over the edge of the opening. He let go and the door dropped closed. Angler scooped up the duffel, and opened the roll top. Crushing as much air as possible from the bag, he rolled it tightly once more and clipped it closed. Shoving the door open again with one hand, he wedged the bag in the opening then watched more water lap over the edge.

The trickle instantly turned into a raging torrent as the base of the door dipped below the surface. He'd just uncorked the bottle and the plane would be heading for the depths in a matter of seconds. Clambering and clawing at the seats, Angler shoved his body into the door opening, sending the duffel bag floating away.

"No! Come back!" he yelled, as though his bag of money were a Labrador he could command to heel.

The BCD and tank were still looped over one shoulder and now smacked against the side of the cabin, refusing to fit through the sideways door. Angler barely had his face above the water and flapped around like a wounded bird until he realized he had to drop back inside. Taking a deep breath, he pulled himself backwards into the sinking seaplane, and yanked his arm free of the BCD. It was getting darker inside the cabin and his vision was blurry through the water which stung his eyes.

Taking hold of the tank, he rammed it through the door opening which was now fully immersed. The rig left his grip and began slowly floating towards the surface trailing the regulator and pressure gauge hoses like tentacles. The regulator he needed to breathe from.

Angler felt no sensation of sinking. Instead, it appeared like the light through the door which now held itself wide open against the fuselage was slowly fading above him. Grabbing the sides of the door opening, he wriggled himself through, and used his feet to push away and up.

He surfaced with a spluttering gasp, staring at the tail sticking straight up beside him. The dive rig bobbed a few feet away, so he pulled it to him and wrestled his arms through one strap, then rolled on his back to secure the other one. Now he could finally cinch the cummerbund and find the regulator with a sweeping arm motion in the water.

The white tail with a red stripe was rapidly sinking, and the last evidence of the seaplane was about to leave him exposed on the surface. *The bag!* Everything was in that duffle. The money for the operation, half his fee, and all his passports he'd use to disappear into blissful retirement. He swung around, searching the bright blue warm water and spotted the bag, bobbing five yards away toward the shore. In a few strokes he reached the duffle and turned to see the last four feet of the tail about to disappear—just like he needed to do.

Shoving the reg in his mouth, Angler lifted the dump valve above his head and pressed the release button. He heard a short *pssst* sound, then nothing happened. Weights! He realized he'd used the dive weights to sink the pilot's body, and now didn't have any ballast weight to counteract his own buoyancy, and that of the remaining air in the duffle. He was trapped, bobbing on the surface like a plastic duck in a bathtub. If he was rescued, there'd be far too many questions, and digging around in a bag which contained one and a half million dollars cash to find the right passport would certainly invite further scrutiny.

He'd figured he'd deal with the mask and fins once he was out of sight, but needing propulsion, he unclipped the mask, which was hanging from the BCD, and quickly slipped it over his head.

Dipping his face in the water, he reached down and untied, then removed his tennis shoes, letting them drift away. Desperately fumbling, Angler unclipped the full-foot fins, slipped them on, one at a time, then used the same carabiner on the BCD to secure the duffle strap. Now, with both hands free, he ducked his head, inverted, and tried kicking his finned feet. Splashing and floundering on the surface, he finally managed to drag himself below, then kicked like crazy for the bottom.

As the water pressure increased with depth, his buoyancy lessened, and when he leveled off at fifty feet under, Angler was finally able to catch his breath. Below, at what he guessed to be 20-feet deeper, sat the Otter, now forlornly resting on the sandy seafloor, with one wing missing. Slightly overwhelmed by the fact he'd just survived a plane crash, Angler turned toward shore, and smoothly kicked away.

20

AJ Bailey had her Mermaid Divers 36-foot Newton custom dive boat up on plane and aimed for where she last saw the seaplane before it slipped below the surface. Her best point of reference was the large section of wing still floating nearby.

With six customers aboard, she'd slowed to an idle for them all to watch the seaplane take off, intending to cross behind its path on her way south to the Nicholson wreck off Sunset House. That was the plan, until the single-engine seaplane hit something, and cartwheeled to a stop in spectacular fashion.

Her first mate and sole full-time employee, local man Thomas Bodden, franticly called in the accident over the marine radio as she held *Hazel's Odyssey*'s throttles to the stops.

"My gear's already set up," AJ shouted to Thomas, with the wind carrying her soft English accent. "You'll have to stay aboard as the boat will be live."

"I ain't seen nobody in da water," Thomas fretted, his voice uncommonly sullen. "Doubt anyone survive dat crash, Boss."

AJ let out a long sigh, her shoulder-length purple-streaked blond hair blowing in the wind. "Gotta look, right? Maybe there's an air pocket or something."

Easing back on the throttles, the boat immediately slowed, coming off plane and dropping lower into the water.

"Over there!" AJ shouted, pointing to a man clinging to a piece of wreckage a hundred yards off their starboard side.

"No way," Thomas muttered in amazement. "I tink dat fella's still alive. But dat can't be da pilot."

"Here, take over, Thomas," AJ said, stepping back from the flybridge helm. "As soon as I splash, pick that guy up, okay?"

"Got it, Boss," he said, taking her place.

AJ peeled off her long-sleeved Mermaid Divers sunshirt and tossed it on the boat's dash as she headed to the ladder.

"Be careful," Thomas added, before she slid down the ladder without using the steps.

On the spacious aft deck, she quickly weaved past the customers to the stern where her gear was already mounted to a tank. There was no time to don a wetsuit, so her bathing suit would have to do, her toned arms decorated in beautiful underwater scene tattoos. Questions flew her way from the customers, and as she pulled on her fins and slipped into her BCD, she spoke firmly and loudly.

"Doug, aren't you a doctor?"

The group quieted and a large man in glasses nodded. "I'm an anesthesiologist, actually," he replied in a southern American accent.

"Close enough," AJ replied. "Everyone, please stay on the boat. I'm going in to check the wreck, then Thomas will pick up the guy we spotted in the water. Help Thomas, but please follow his directions." She looked at the doctor as she pulled her mask in place. "Do what you can for the guy, doc, help will be here soon."

AJ stood, shuffled to the swim step, and took a giant stride off the stern, dropping under, and with no air in her BCD, continued down. Above, she heard the engine note pick up as Thomas left to help the guy on the surface.

Deek was beside himself. Once again, he was left trying to convince someone that he wasn't a lunatic, and that the guy he'd been following was working for Şeytan Taciri and planning a terrorist attack at the Great American Boat Show in Fort Myers. Constable Sommer's expression hadn't changed at any point during his rambling tale as she escorted him from the bank.

She'd been about to send him on his way when they'd both heard it. A low drone to which he hadn't really paid any attention to had abruptly stopped, followed by a cacophony of loud voices drowning out the sounds of traffic on the frontage road.

"Don't cause any more trouble," the constable said, as she took off in a sprint toward the harbor front.

Deek immediately followed, although he soon discovered he couldn't keep up with her long, athletic legs. He was unsure exactly why he was choosing to stick with the policewoman who didn't seem the least bit interested in his plight, but he sensed the commotion they'd heard was important.

A mixture of locals and tourists crowded along the railing of the harbor, many with cell phone cameras raised in the air, filming something over the water. Deek reached the edge of the crowd as Constable Sommer was quizzing an older man over the incident.

"Bloody awful," the man said in an English accent which reminded Deek of the presenters on BBC America's news shows. "He was taking off towards us, then all of a sudden the plane flipped into the air and hit the water with an almighty thump!"

"A seaplane?!" Deek blurted, pushing people aside to get to the railing.

"Of course it was a seaplane," the man said, frowning at him. "How else would it be taking off from the water?"

"Where is it?" Deek asked, looking at the people next to him.

"It sunk," a young woman said excitedly. "Got the whole thing on my camera, too. Already uploaded to my Insta."

"That dive boat raced over," the old man added. "I saw a diver jump in, then the boat went looking for something. Survivors I expect."

"He hit a kayaker," another man shouted. "That's what flipped the plane!"

Sirens wailed in the background and local accented voices streamed from Constable Sommer's handheld radio on her belt. To their left, a Joint Marine Unit police boat shot away from the dock with its lights flashing.

Deek whipped around. "See! That has to be the sea…"

The blond constable was already walking away, so Deek jogged after here. "Wait up! Don't you see? This has to be the plane belonging to the guy I've been following."

"Just because you saw a seaplane in the harbor this morning and added it to your story, doesn't make you any more believable," she said, marching toward the dock where the police boat had departed from.

"What if I could tell you the tail number?" Deek said, still half jogging to keep up.

The young policewoman rolled her eyes.

"Right, I could have seen that this morning too," he muttered. "What if I put you in touch with a woman from the sheriff's office in Fort Myers? She's the one who was hanging from the pontoon thingy of the same seaplane. Although it had a different tail number then, because they peeled the stickers off like I told you…"

"Look, are you reporting a crime here on the island?" she asked sternly without slowing.

Deek thought for a moment and dodged around a light pole just in time to avoid running into it. "I bet you'll find money on that plane!"

"Do you have money in your wallet?"

"Not much," Deek scoffed.

"Should I arrest you for having money in your wallet?"

Deek groaned and trotted to catch up again. "Of course not. I'm saying, I bet the pilot was just in the bank, took out a bunch of cash, and you'll find it on the plane."

They reached a group of other policemen and women who'd

gathered by the dock, where a tall, slender man in a suit was directing them. The constable stopped and turned to Deek.

"Still no crime committed," she said. "Besides, he's probably dead, so you won't have to worry about your terrorist anymore."

Deek looked out across the water where several more boats had now gathered. *She had a point.*

The seaplane sat upright in the sand, tilted on its port side, leaning against the tip of the remaining wing. The water had already cleared from the wafting sand that would have billowed from the wreck when it settled on the bottom at 65 feet. AJ was one of the local divers on call when the police required them, so this wasn't her first crash site, although she'd usually have a dive buddy with her.

She finned straight for the cockpit and shone her dive light through the front window. Her body tingled in nervous anticipation, and AJ held her breath, waiting to be startled by the vision of the dead pilot.

Seeing no one, she kicked along the starboard side, noting the twisted struts and wrinkled float beneath her. The cabin door was ajar, and she eased it open, reeling backwards as something leapt at her from inside. AJ caught her breath once more and cursed into her regulator as she watched the seat cushion ascend towards the surface.

Playing her light beam around inside, the cabin appeared undisturbed and intact, beyond several more cushions pinned to the ceiling where a thin air pocket remained trapped. There was no sign of a body, and certainly no one gasping at the last traces of air, but she still considered going inside. *Could a body be caught, out of sight behind a seat? Maybe.* Instead of penetrating the wreck, AJ moved along the side of the plane, aiming her light through the series of round windows, checking each row. Nothing. No luggage, no cargo, no body.

She finned away from the wreck and looked up. She'd heard more motors, and could see the hulls of three boats above her. She needed more divers to organize a proper body search, but she'd take a quick look around the immediate perimeter. The pilot wasn't inside, and the cabin door was open, so he must have left the plane at some point. She hadn't heard a metallic banging from the surface which would be the diver recall signal, so she presumed he hadn't been spotted floating up top either. That left the seafloor. If he'd managed to escape the plane but ran out of breath on his way up, the chances were he'd have sunk to the bottom with his lungs full of water.

It took a couple of minutes to make her first lap around the wreck, keeping the plane at the edge of her visibility so she didn't miss anything in between. At ten feet off the seafloor, the remnants of stirred up sand made that distance about 40 feet, resulting in 80 feet of coverage as she checked to her left and right.

With no body in sight, AJ slowly ascended and used the automatic countdown on her Shearwater Teric dive computer watch to perform her three-minute safety stop at 15 feet.

Angler gathered several rocks from the seafloor as he kicked toward shore. He needed the ballast as the depth shallowed and the surrounding water pressure diminished, or he'd pop to the top like a cork. Between the depth lessening and a reading on the compass hanging from his BCD, he knew he was heading toward the island instead of deeper water, but exactly where, he had no clue. Running into the side of the cruise ship wouldn't help his already unravelling cause, and neither would surfacing amongst a sea of law enforcement vessels that would surely be on the water by now.

As the depth on his gauge showed 25 feet, the duffel bag felt like a balloon tugging against his BCD, keeping him rolled over on one side. He'd run out of places to stash rocks and hands to carry them. Below him was now mostly ancient dead coral forming a pitted and jagged rock formation called ironshore, and he knew he must be nearing the coastline. His next problem would be waltzing out of the water in scuba gear, wearing jeans, a polo shirt, and carrying the bag. With people's attention already focused on the water from the plane crash, he feared too many eyes would be watching from the shore.

At 15 feet, Angler couldn't stay down any longer, and rose to the surface like a breaching submarine. Clutching the bag to his chest, he rotated upright, letting his head innocently pop above the surface. To his right, a hundred feet away, was a small parking lot and a business signed Eden Rock Dive Center. A few people stood by the seawall looking over his head toward the crash site. To his left, about the same distance away, was a house, and straight ahead was an empty lot.

Angler waited, thinking. If he was spotted emerging from the water in civilian clothes, he'd be reported in some manner at some point when it became clear the pilot of the plane was missing. Jeans and a big duffel bag weren't standards in the warm water recreational diving world. He looked over at the people in the parking lot. Two families, he guessed, by the adult to children head count. Probably there to rent snorkeling gear from the dive shop, until a seaplane cartwheeled across the sea and sank.

Beyond the people, at the seawall in front of the shop, a set of steps with a metal railing led into the water. Bobbing on the surface nearby were snorkelers in bright orange vests and two divers, surface swimming away to deeper water.

"Damn it," he muttered, and unzipped his jeans.

Cramming the bag between two larger rocks at the edge of the empty lot, Angler swam toward the steps, hoping his boxer shorts looked enough like board shorts for no one to pay attention. Two minutes later, keeping his dive mask in place to obscure his face, and fins in hand, he walked up Eden Rock Dive Center's steps, and out of the water. A bench with tank racks offered him a place to sit and remove his gear, before snatching someone's towel they'd left nearby and wrapping it around his waist.

The hot asphalt of the parking lot burned his feet as he slipped behind the cars, looking in the back windows as he passed by. Stopping at an SUV, he prayed his luck would change, and tried the tailgate. He stepped back and almost let out a cheer when it opened. The divers had changed into their wetsuits, leaving behind their shirts and dry shorts for when they came out of the water.

Fitting in easily with the beach vibe in board shorts, Hawaiian shirt, and flip-flops, Angler retrieved his bag from the water's edge. The two families had lost interest and moved on, so he paused to take a look across the ocean. He felt a mixture of despair and elation. The unending obstacles that seemed to be constantly thrown in his path were relentless, and yet he'd just survived a spectacular plane crash.

He looked away from the frenetic scene on the water and refocused himself. If he could find a private flight off the island, he could still get back on track and be in Fort Myers by Friday.

21

Deek loitered off to the side while the police milled around the harbor area taking statements from witnesses and having those who'd recorded cell phone footage of the accident send the files to the police department. The man he'd presumed to be the detective in charge had taken a smaller boat out to the crash site, and now returned after nearly an hour, on the larger police boat. With him was the female diver Deek had seen exit the water, before sending her own boat on its way to stick around and continue helping with the search.

What Deek hadn't seen was a body. Well, except for the unfortunate guy in the kayak the plane had hit. He'd been brought ashore and taken away by ambulance. Lucky to be alive, he'd sustained two badly broken legs according to the paramedic Deek had overheard telling Constable Sommer. Apparently the kayaker had been wearing wireless earbuds which explained his complete obliviousness to a large, noisy seaplane in the vicinity. Deek kept his thoughts to himself, but he was grateful for the man's ineptness as he may have inadvertently prevented a terrorist attack in Fort Myers.

The detective gathered a small group together on the dock and Deek moved closer to hear what was said.

"The site's yours, Bob," the detective told another man in a suit. "Let me know if you need our assistance from here out."

"Thanks, Roy," the second man replied. "Not much we can do until an official investigator arrives from the UK."

The detective nodded. "We've strung a buoy to the wreck, and between the Joint Marine Unit and the port authorities, we'll keep boaters and divers away until your investigator arrives."

Constable Sommer stood next to the shorter diver, who had a towel around her waist and a bikini top revealing colorful tattoos on her arms. The two seemed to know each other and Deek was dying to know what the diver had found on the wreck.

"Where should we look now for the pilot?" Constable Sommer asked, and Deek couldn't stand aside any longer.

"He's still missing?" he blurted, and all heads turned his way.

"Who are you, sir?" the detective asked.

"This is the conspiracy bloke I mentioned earlier, sir," the blond constable replied before Deek could say a word.

He was pleased he'd been brought up in their discussions, as that suggested she'd believed at least a part of his story, although "conspiracy bloke" didn't inspire confidence.

"Deek Morrison. I'm with the US Department of Transportation, Maritime Administration. I've been tracking that seaplane and its pilot for two days. He's a dangerous man."

The small group parted until Deek faced the detective who eyed him suspiciously.

"I'm Detective Whittaker with the Royal Cayman Islands Police Service. Can you tell me the pilot's name?"

Great, Deek thought. First question the man asks and of course he doesn't know the answer.

"I was working on the premise he's an international criminal known as Şeytan Taciri, but I've since come to the conclusion the pilot is his henchman. I don't have a name for you, Detective, but I can tell you we fished the original pilot's body out of the water in Key West yesterday."

"For what purpose do you think this man flew to Grand Cayman, Mr. Morrison?"

Deek ran his hand through his hair which he half expected to come out in clumps from the stress. "Money," he replied. "I was attempting to follow up with the Cayman International Bank and Trust to confirm that fact, when I..."—he paused a moment to consider his phrasing—"ran into your constable," he finished, nodding to the policewoman.

"He was freaking out the manager," she added, and Deek frowned her way. She was back to not helping his cause.

"The point is, if you didn't find a body then he might still be alive. Which means he's still a threat to attack the boat show in Fort Myers," Deek urged. "Was there money in the seaplane?" he asked, looking at the diver.

She shook her head. "I didn't see anything that didn't belong inside an aeroplane," she answered in an English accent, which surprised him.

He wasn't sure what he'd expected, but from the tattoos and purple-streaked hair, it wasn't a pleasant, well-spoken Englishwoman.

"Were there signs of trauma?" Deek persisted.

"Nothing obvious," the diver replied. "Windscreen was still intact. Found a pair of trainers floating nearby though."

"I'm sorry, you found what?" Deek asked.

"Trainers," she repeated. "You know, tennis shoes I think you call them."

"Oh," Deek mumbled. "But no one attached to them?"

"Were the laces undone?" Constable Sommer asked.

"Yeah, they were actually," the diver replied. "I remember the laces floating like little skinny arms."

Deek leaned over to the constable and whispered. "So he must have untied them, right?"

She shrugged her shoulders. "Possibly. Or he doesn't like tying his laces. Or they fell off a cruise ship tender."

"All right," Whittaker said, holding up his hands. "We will continue our underwater search for the body, but also comb through the video footage witnesses took during the accident and afterwards. Perhaps we'll find some clues."

"Do we have a picture of this guy?" Constable Sommer asked.

"We don't as he checked in with immigration here at the dock where they couldn't scan his passport. But we have his passport details, which gives us a name. Wayne Daniels. We'll run a search using the name and passport number."

"The bank would have CCTV," Constable Sommer suggested.

"That's true," the detective agreed. "Why don't you work on that, and I'll coordinate a continuing search, camera footage, and background checks. Once we have a usable picture of Mr. Daniels, we'll distribute it everywhere. The guy might have sustained a head injury and is wandering around the island. I'll warn the hospital to be on the lookout, too."

"Or he wasn't seriously injured at all and escaped," Deek offered. "In which case, he'll be trying to find another way off the island."

"We'll send his details to the airport security. He'll not be able to fly," Whittaker assured him.

"What time is it?" the diver asked, and Deek reflexively looked at his watch, then cursed under his breath at his bare wrist.

"Ten past three," Whittaker replied, glancing at his own watch. "That's a good point. Unless one has been delayed, our afternoon international flights have already left. Don't worry, Mr. Morrison, if the pilot is still alive, we'll find him."

The group began to disperse, leaving Deek standing alone on the dock.

"What should I do?" he asked, looking in the direction of the detective.

"When do you fly back?" Whittaker asked in return.

"Tomorrow's flight to Miami," Deek responded.

"Then the best thing will be to go to your hotel. Where are you staying? I'd like to know how to contact you if something comes up."

"Umm..." Deek mumbled, remembering he hadn't yet secured a roof over his head. "Not sure yet."

"Sounds like you might want to work on that then, Mr. Morrison," Whittaker said, with a pleasant smile. "Please give Constable Sommer your mobile number so we can reach you."

The policewoman was already halfway along the dock, but she paused and reluctantly turned around at the sound of her name.

"Why don't I stick with her?" Deek quickly suggested. "I might be able to help as I've been following this guy all over the Caribbean."

Whittaker looked dubious and the Scandinavian cop scowled at Deek. He looked back and forth between the two with his best version of an encouraging smile. The diver, who'd walked away with Constable Sommer, now had a grin on her face, which seemed odd to Deek.

"Proceed at your own peril, Mr. Morrison," the detective said. "And Nora," he added, looking at his constable, "please be nice."

Deek trotted to catch up with the two women who'd continued along the dock.

"I'm AJ," the diver said once he'd caught them. "I'm actually on your flight tomorrow. Meeting some friends and heading for the boat show you mentioned in Fort Myers."

"Then you have a vested interest in stopping this man," Deek pointed out. "I believe he's planning to assassinate several foreign ambassadors at the show."

"That doesn't sound good, but it's Nora you have to convince, mate," AJ said, nodding at the policewoman who was two steps ahead of them. "And don't feel special, she's a little icy with everyone at first, but once you win her over, she's a mega star."

Deek hurried to keep up and tried to think of a good way to break the thick ice with the Nordic policewoman. Social interactions had never been his strong suit.

"You're from Sweden, I assume?" he asked.

AJ laughed. "Top-notch, Deek. You're off to a bloody awful start."

Deek groaned. "Not Swedish, then? Dutch?"

AJ now roared with good-natured laughter. "Try sticking with Scandinavian countries, Deek."

"I'm Norwegian," Nora snapped, letting him off the hook before he dug himself a deeper hole.

"There you go," AJ grinned. "Ice broken."

"Really?" Deek said in surprise, pleased he'd made progress.

"No," AJ and Nora replied together.

Angler sat under the shade of a palm tree at a quiet cove called Smith's Barcadere, according to the sign. The rocky, ironshore coastline had a small break allowing a yellow sand beach to extend into the turquoise water. A couple of local mothers sat chatting on the rocks while their children played in the ocean. Finding a secluded spot had proven to be harder than he'd anticipated as the waterfront was shoulder to shoulder homes and condominium buildings. Any open real estate had new construction with too many workers around. After stealing an odd-looking scooter from behind the dive shop building, Angler had ridden away from town and finally spotted the cove. The two women had watched him pull in, then continued gossiping without paying him much attention.

Connecting through the secure VPN, Angler accessed the internet. Over the years, he'd built a wide net of connections to resourceful people around the world, and right now he'd need to call in a favor or two. In his circles, calling in a favor didn't usually mean a discount or freebie, but the knowledge he'd be taken care of with no questions asked. There was always a price.

As he messaged with one person after another with his request being handed along an underworld chain, Angler could feel his bag of money getting lighter. Last minute transportation off the island, under the radar both figuratively and physically, would not be cheap. The cash he had with him didn't represent his entire retirement funds, but it was certainly the additional amount that would make his plans possible. If he parted with too much of the cash, it would mean the inevitable "one more job."

Finally, after bouncing around between several contacts, Angler had a plan in place. All he had to do now was stay out of sight for a few hours, meet with a guy about the flight, and get to the Fixed-Base Operators section of the airport, or FBO as it was commonly called. It was where the private planes were based, and immigration and customs had a small office with officers on call as needed. They would not be requested or needed for a sunset flight around the sister islands.

Harold Hildebrand looked out the window beyond the dock to the water off Baskin Island, his jaw set and a scowl on his once square-jawed face. Age and fine dining had taken their toll over the years, and he simply didn't have the time for a regular exercise routine. His personal trainer sent him daily emails with a variety of innovative workouts, but so far, none of the emails had helped him slow the expansion of his waistline. Turned out, he needed to actually do the exercises for them to work.

In Hildebrand's diverse lines of work, he had a multitude of pings, alerts, and warnings which buzzed on his phone and computer. A few hours earlier, one which rarely popped up had sent him into a pacing rage he still hadn't calmed down from. "Seaplane crashes on takeoff in Grand Cayman."

He'd been called a control freak, behind his back of course, by many associates, employees, and clients, and he was proud to be seen that way. In his mind, details always made the difference, and while the dizzying scope of his interests meant relying on thousands of people to execute their roles correctly, some projects were simply too important not to handle himself. Which made this one all the more frustrating.

Hildebrand had personally chosen the operative from a cast of characters whose services he'd either used prior, or who'd come recommended to him by associates he trusted. The man had the perfect balance between experience and drive, a hard asset to find. The younger operatives had all the drive, determination, and bravery, without the tempering influence of experience. On the flip side, many of the older more experienced choices were overly cautious, knowing their longevity in the business had already defied the odds of being caught or eliminated.

The man, known simply as Angler, appeared to perfectly level the scales. He retained the foresight and prudence earned from years on the job, yet the drive to see the work through no matter what. One way or another, this would be the man's final mission. He would either be successful and quietly fade into retirement, or he'd fail, in which case it would be his last gig, period. No doubt, Angler was unaware of the consequence attached to failure on a Hildebrand personal project, but now it appeared to be irrelevant. The man had retired early by killing himself in a plane crash.

Hildebrand gripped his cell phone so hard he was lucky the plastic didn't explode, but instead it let out a quiet ping. He had another alert. This one was telling him a blog he followed had been updated.

"You never fail until you stop trying," Hildebrand read aloud.

The Albert Einstein quote from the blog page instantly relieved the tension from his brow, and he let out a long breath. The mission was still in play.

22

The Cayman International Bank and Trust had high-resolution CCTV from multiple angles inside, and two outside the building. Deek had seen the man he'd been chasing several times from varying distances, and Sam had given him a good description from seeing him in the cabin doorway of the seaplane. In the CCTV, he clearly matched the photograph Whittaker sent Nora after tracing Wayne Daniels's passport. The name also matched the bank account, and while Dorothy, the manager, couldn't share account details with the police without a court order, she verified his identity.

"Or this could be the name he's currently using," Deek pointed out as they left the bank.

Nora paused on the sidewalk and thought for a moment. AJ stood next to her, her hair still damp from the dive. She'd borrowed a T-shirt from her friend as they'd passed by Nora's beaten-up old Jeep, but was still barefoot and her bathing suit made damp patches through the shirt. Nora was supposed to be dropping AJ back at her dock, but currently the three looked like an odd sampling of life on an island.

"Fake passports aren't as easy to get as the movies make out,"

Nora finally said. "Especially ones which will stand up to inspection and scanning."

"These people have deep pockets and endless resources," Deek assured her. "If Hildebrand is really Şeytan Taciri, which I believe he is, then he's not only one of the wealthiest men in the world, he's one of the most ruthless and dangerous. This guy alters world politics to make money."

"Okay, assuming you're right," Nora said, "then how would Daniels leave the island now?"

Deek thought for a moment, running through the options in his mind. Nora still didn't sound convinced, but was at least playing along, so he needed to win her over. Which meant being right.

"Boat's too slow, isn't it?" AJ said before he'd come up with a conclusion. "You said he needs to be in Florida in a day or two. That rules out going all the way by water."

Deek nodded. "That's true."

"Unless he uses a boat to get to another island, and then flies," Nora countered. "He could be in the Sister Islands, Jamaica, or Cuba by morning."

"How many airports are there on Grand Cayman?" Deek asked.

"One," Nora confirmed.

"So light aircraft, private jets, commercial, everything, fly from the one I arrived at?"

Both women nodded.

"I can track which planes come and go from the airport," Deek said, thoughtfully. "Maybe something will stand out."

"How will you do that?" AJ asked. "Stand at the fence and watch them all evening?"

"I have an app," he said, finally able to puff his chest out about something. "And a buddy with some cool tracking software."

According to the message from his contact, Angler needed to be at the airport by 6:00 p.m. for wheels-up by 6:30 p.m. Sunset would be around 7:00 p.m. at sea level, but a little later from altitude. Of course, he didn't give a hoot about a colorful horizon, but the ruse had to be perfectly timed.

With two hours to kill, he made a mental list of all the items he needed to accomplish before leaving the Cayman Islands. Top priority was finding different transportation. The scooter was no doubt reported stolen by now, and likely the clothes he was wearing too. There hadn't been a helmet with the bike and from the odd looks he'd been given in the short run to the cove, he guessed they had a helmet law on the island.

What Angler needed was a car no one would miss for a few hours, and a set of neutral-colored clothes that actually fit. The board shorts he'd taken were a size too small and were crushing parts of his anatomy he planned to use during his retirement. Studying the map on his phone, he found a thrift store between Smith's Barcadere and the airport. The direct route was back along South Church Street, the road to the dive shop and town, so he mapped out an alternative path, keeping him off the main roads—if the two-lane island streets could be called that.

Slinging the weighty duffel bag over his shoulder, Angler pulled the scooter out of the shade and fired it up. The two women were herding their kids to a car on the opposite side of the dirt lot, and one of them looked his way. She tapped a finger to her head and said something he couldn't hear, no doubt reminding him to wear a helmet. The last thing he needed was nosy mothers getting a good look at him, so he gave her a thumbs up and quickly pulled to the road.

He heard her shout a bit louder, but ignored her and accelerated down the street, looking for his turn. A car coming toward him in his lane reminded him he was supposed to be on the other side of the road and he quickly veered left, passing the car who honked his horn. Perfect, he thought, all he needed to do was slide by unnoticed for two hours, and so far he'd done nothing but draw attention to himself.

As excited as Deek had been to use his app once more, he was equally disappointed when it showed no planes of interest heading to Grand Cayman. They were now at Nora's Jeep, and after giving him a blank stare which he took as conveying something between disgruntled and ready to kill him, she announced they'd be running AJ to her dock. Deek clambered into the back seat of the lifted CJ-7 and was fumbling with the seat belt, which didn't appear to have anything to attach to, when Nora's handheld police radio came to life.

"All units be on the lookout for a white Honda scooter reported stolen from Eden Rock Dive Center."

The dispatcher continued with a license plate number, but Deek was still consumed with the seat belt and didn't pay any attention.

"Central, this is PC277. What time did the scooter go missing? Over." Nora asked, and Deek's shoulders dropped.

The one person who'd taken a hint of interest in his story was now moving on to petty theft crimes and playing taxi to her friend. He wondered how he could rent a car without a working credit card and nothing more than a handful of change in his pocket. Somehow, he needed to get to the airport.

"PC277, this is Central. Sometime after 12:30 p.m., but he can't be sure when. Over."

"Central, this is PC277. Got a picture? Over."

"PC277, this is Central. Sending now. Over."

"I know you have to do your police thing, but I must protest..." Deek started, but Nora held up her hand.

"Shut up."

He stopped talking and wondered what she'd be like if the detective hadn't told her to be nice.

Nora studied her cell phone for a moment, then handed it to AJ in the passenger seat, and pulled out from her parking spot.

"Got a few more minutes for a detour?" Nora asked.

"Sure," AJ replied. "That's a Honda Ruckus. They're pretty fun little bikes." She then handed Deek the phone.

On the screen was a picture of a young guy standing behind a weird-looking scooter. It was white with a low-slung motor just in front of the rear wheel and a tubular frame holding a red seat. It looked more like the production version of someone's home-built fun-bike project. He handed the phone back.

"Okay, so some kid's had his scooter stolen. How could this possibly take precedence over a potential terrorist attack?"

Nora was heading south out of the small waterfront downtown area of George Town. The road soon became lined on the right with oceanfront homes and condominium buildings, with smaller homes inland to the left. The Jeep's big off-road tires made a bunch of noise on the asphalt and the wind whipped over the vehicle, blowing AJ's hair in all directions. Deek was about to yell to be heard over the racket, when Nora slowed and turned into a parking lot on the right. Deek noted the sign on the accompanying building advertised "Eden Rock Dive Center." When they stopped, he stood up in the back of the Jeep, held onto the roll bar, and looked over the ocean. He could see the buoy marking the seaplane wreck bobbing in the water no more than three hundred yards to the north. He beamed like a kid hearing the ice cream truck music approaching the neighborhood.

"I like the way you're thinking, Nora!" he said, leaping from the Jeep and yelping as the drop was twice as far as he'd anticipated.

Heading east on Denham Thompson Way, Angler came to a T-junction with Walker Road. Across the street, surrounded by a tall chain-link fence, was the group of buildings he was looking for. According to his map, these were a variety of further education, conference centers, and administration offices attached to the local high school. He crossed over Walker and pulled into the parking lot, hiding the scooter behind a van.

Angler spotted a small, two-door Toyota with sun-faded silver paint which had both front windows down a few inches to vent the steamy tropical heat. He shook his head.

"Someone who trusted humanity enough to leave their windows down, deserves to get their car stolen," he scoffed to himself.

It had been a while since he'd hot-wired a vehicle, and now it had been two in one day. He told himself it was always good to keep the skills sharp, although after the boat show gig he hoped to leave all this behind. He was too old for petty shit like this.

The old Toyota sparked into life and Angler groaned. The little car sounded like the muffler had been left along the road somewhere, and the air vents blew nothing but warm air. He wound the driver's side window down, then reached over and managed to get the passenger side halfway down before the mechanism locked up.

He felt his blood pressure rising once more, and sat in the hot car visualizing the tropical beach he'd soon be resting his tired bones. He actually laughed as he realized he was on a beautiful tropical island dreaming about a beautiful tropical island. Still, he'd already worn out his welcome on this one, courtesy of an idiot in a kayak.

Backing out of the spot, he steered the little car toward the road and focused on which lane he'd use with the right-hand drive car. He promptly switched on the wipers instead of the turn signal and the crusty rubber blades screeched across the glass.

The young man whose scooter had been stolen was still at the dive shop, waiting on a ride home. He had no clue who'd taken his bike or any idea at what time, as he'd returned on the Honda from lunch at 12:30 p.m., then stepped out to leave at 4:00 p.m. One of his coworkers thought it was gone when they'd gone out back for a cigarette break around two, but they couldn't be sure.

He also said a couple of divers had come in the shop

complaining about clothes missing from the back of their car. Apparently, several bits of spare dive gear had been left untouched, but shorts, a shirt and a pair of flip-flops were missing.

By far the oddest mystery to the dive shop employees was the full set of dive gear in their bench rack by the steps. At first they'd guessed someone was coming back to dive again, but as they neared closing time, and the owner of the kit was yet to return, they'd begun scratching their heads.

"Sir, we believe the pilot made it to shore by Eden Rock," Nora explained over the phone, having called the Detective Whittaker. "He may have had dive gear in the plane. We've found a set here that no one knows where it came from. Can you send someone from SOCO to check it out?"

Deek couldn't hear the other end of the call, but from Nora's responses it sounded like they were taking the idea that the pilot had made it out alive and well quite seriously now.

"Okay, I'll look for private CCTV along South Church," Nora said, then hung up.

"I'm not crazy," Deek said as they jogged back to the Jeep and climbed in.

Nora started the CJ-7 and turned around. "Being right about this guy doesn't make you *not* crazy, Deek," she said, and AJ stifled a laugh.

Deek just grinned. Inside his heart was thumping. The gorgeous Scandinavian cop had remembered his name.

Nora pulled up to the road and while she was waiting for a gap in traffic, her phone buzzed. She handed it to AJ. "Read this for me."

AJ took the phone and looked at the text message. "Shit. It's Jazzy. She's had to stay late and is asking if you can pick her up. She says she tried my mobile, which of course is on the boat."

"*Faen*," Nora muttered, and Deek guessed it meant something unsavory in Norwegian. "Tell her yes. We can be there in a few minutes."

Deek was flung back in the seat as Nora took off up the road, then pulled himself forward and stuck his head between the two front seats. "Who's Jazzy?"

"Her teenager," AJ said, nodding at her friend.

Deek's mouth fell open but nothing came out. He'd guessed AJ was in her late twenties, maybe early thirties, but Nora looked to be ten years younger. *How on earth could she have a teenager?*

AJ grinned. "Don't worry, she didn't give birth at age six," she said, guessing what was rattling around Deek's mind. "She's Jazzy's foster home."

"*Temporary* foster home," Nora corrected, as she turned left and drove faster than seemed appropriate down a narrow lane.

"Don't you have to be, like… older to foster children?" Deek asked, hanging on tightly as Nora braked hard for a T-junction.

"Jazzy was living on the streets until Nora rescued her, so now Nora's the only person Jazzy trusts. The authorities have bent the rules a bit and let her stick around."

"Like chewing gum," Nora added, turning right and accelerating down at a street called Walkers Road.

AJ laughed then pointed ahead. "There she is."

Deek spotted a dark-skinned girl in a school uniform walking toward them. She had a huge mop of frizzy hair which she was busy tying back with a purple scrunchy. Nora slowed and stopped by the sidewalk.

"Jump in, I'm working," Nora said, and Jazzy peered into the Jeep.

"Who's this?" she asked, using the big rear tire to clamber in the back.

"I'm Deek Morrison," he said and held out his hand.

Before she could shake, Nora abruptly accelerated while turning hard right in front of an oncoming car which braked and honked loudly.

"Bloody hell, Nora," AJ gasped as everyone hung on to whatever they could grab. "We're not in that much of a hurry!"

"We are now," Nora replied, shifting gears as she pinned the gas pedal to the floor.

"Why?" AJ and Deek both shouted back.

"That's your guy in the car up there," she said, pointing to a silver Toyota two hundred yards ahead.

"But he stole a scooter!" Deek yelled. "Are you sure?"

The Toyota picked up speed ahead of them then suddenly whipped right onto a small residential street signed Windsor Park Road.

"I am now," Nora replied, and slid the Jeep through the right turn with its oversized off-road tires screeching in complaint.

23

Angler looked in his mirror. The big Jeep had aggressively made the turn leaving him in no doubt the driver was chasing him. He couldn't believe his luck; he'd stolen a car that a friend must have recognized and was now playing hero. But the driver looked... blond? *Was he being pursued by a pissed-off girlfriend?*

With his cell phone clutched in his left hand, he worked the wheel with his right as he flew down the narrow streets. A mixture of older and newer homes lined the first road before he made a sharp left by a small park and basketball court. Two dogs barked loudly as they joined the chase, and he heard the driver of the Jeep honking their horn to scare off the mutts. Following the route he'd planned out, Angler turned right between large homes, then another left where it was back to older dwellings with cars in the front yards in various states of disrepair.

Despite the lack of power in the worn-out Toyota, Angler was managing to stay a hundred yards ahead of the Jeep. For now. The relentless ninety-degree turns helped as the lifted Jeep looked in peril of rolling over each time, but if he came across a long, straight stretch, he knew he'd be overrun. On top of that, he couldn't go to the airport with a crazy woman on his tail.

Angler glanced at the map and saw the road he was now on, Anthony Drive, curved and twisted for a while before reaching a junction where he'd be turning right. At a roundabout, no doubt, as the island seemed to use too many of the damn things in place of traffic signals. Between driving on the left, and figuring out where he was supposed to be and which way to go around the roundabout, he knew he'd screw something up.

Anthony Drive made a hard left with a church on the outside of the street, and a small road going left shortly after the turn. Angler swung the little Toyota down the side road and watched his mirror as he accelerated away.

"Where the heck did he go?" AJ shouted as Nora braked for the roundabout.

"Here," Nora said, taking the opportunity to unclip her handheld radio from her belt and give it to AJ. "Call in the registration number."

"Oh, blimey," AJ groaned, taking the radio. "What do I say?"

Nora made a lap around the tiny roundabout which was little more than a circle of slightly raised paving stones. "Open the mic and hold it over here."

AJ did as instructed.

"Central, this is PC277. In pursuit of suspect from the seaplane. He's driving a silver Toyota…" Nora looked at AJ and shrugged her shoulders.

"I don't know!" AJ whispered back.

"Yaris," Deek shouted from the back. "It's a Toyota Yaris."

"Yaris, Central," Nora repeated. "It's a shitty-looking silver Toyota Yaris. Over."

"Language, PC277," the voice came back sternly.

"Sorry Central. Please put out a BOLO on the silver Yaris. Last seen near Anthony and Smith. Over."

"Copy. Over."

Nora took Smith Road east toward the airport slowing her pace and looking around the businesses and office building parking lots.

"I had one in college," Deek said absentmindedly.

AJ turned and grinned at him. "I can see that."

"So, what's goin' on?" Jazzy asked in her thick island accent, looking at Deek as the others were in the front. "Who da man we chasin'?"

"Did you hear about the seaplane that crashed earlier today?" Deek asked, watching for the Toyota as they kept moving.

"Yeah!" Jazzy replied excitedly. "Everybody talkin' 'bout it. Dey say da pilot missin'. Dat him?"

Deek nodded. "Nora thinks so, and he tried to outrun us, so it appears she's right."

"Tried, nuttin', mister. Look like he outrun us just fine," Jazzy said with a smirk. "In a Toyota *Yaris*," she added and shook the back of Nora's seat.

"*Ikke vær så oppstinasa*," Nora said sternly without turning around. "Help look, or I'll kick you out and you can hitchhike home from here."

Deek was taken aback until he saw the big grin on both Jazzy and AJ's faces as they shared a glance. Jazzy giggled as Nora slowed and found a break in traffic to turn around and head back the way they'd come. The local girl then joined the others in scanning the traffic for the silver Toyota.

AJ had been right, Deek figured; Nora played the Ice Queen with everybody, including the ones she clearly loved.

Angler slung the duffel bag over his shoulder and walked away from the piece of crap he wished he'd never stolen. Nestled amongst a bunch of other cars in the strip mall, he hoped he'd be in the wind before anyone discovered the Yaris. But now he was back to needing wheels again.

He noticed many of the businesses were medical clinics and

supply firms, and when he walked to Smith Road, he saw a sign to the hospital. Staying in the shadow of a building on the corner, he carefully looked both ways down the road. Not seeing any police vehicles, he was about to head left down the sidewalk when he spotted the old faded blue Jeep approaching the little roundabout. The driver was not only blond, but as she turned left, heading in the direction they'd chased him from, he could now see she was wearing a police uniform. Who the others in the vehicle were, he had no idea.

Once the Jeep had disappeared from view, he moved quickly along the sidewalk toward the hospital. Angler couldn't believe that on a job of this scale, he was reduced to jacking cars like a street thug. He also knew each petty crime carried as much or more risk of being busted as the big jobs. Although the penalty for stealing a car couldn't compare to what lay ahead if he was caught in Fort Myers.

In the back of the hospital parking lot, at the end of a row of vehicles, which varied from shiny Mercedes to sub-compacts even smaller than the Yaris, he found a white four-door sedan. Angler nonchalantly peeked in the window and saw with relief that it was left-hand drive. It was a newer model, which would be harder to break into and start, but had the benefit of looking like every other rental car roaming the island.

Five minutes later, after a fair amount of cursing under his breath and tangled wires behind the dash, Angler left the hospital parking lot, and drove down Smith Road toward the airport. The first junction was the little roundabout which instantly threw him into confusion. He was now in a left-hand drive car, driving on the left-hand side, with the sidewalk just outside his door. Instead of the driving world being mirrored, he was now on the wrong side of the car for driving on the wrong side of the road.

Whatever tropical island he landed on after this shit show is over, he told himself, it'll be one that damn well drives on the right. Like America. Fortunately, another car was in the roundabout which verified the correct direction of travel, and Angler breathed a sigh of relief once he was safely on the other side and could see the high fence surrounding the airport ahead.

Deek checked his wristwatch and swore once again. According to his cell phone, it was 5:30 p.m. He then checked the flight app on his phone one more time.

"I still don't see any private flights arriving here this evening," he said.

Nora had retraced their steps all the way back to the school, where she'd found the scooter and called it in over the radio. If there'd been any doubt that it was the missing pilot she'd spotted, they could now be certain. She drove slowly once more through the back streets where they'd chased the Yaris, knowing he'd be long gone, but unsure where to.

"Someone will surely spot the Toyota soon," AJ said. "If enough coppers are looking, right?"

"He's not in the Yaris anymore," Nora said flatly. "He will have switched."

"Already did once. Bound to do it again," Jazzy added.

"So if there's no private flights coming to get him, and he can't waltz through the commercial terminal without being stopped, how's he leaving the island?" AJ asked.

"Maybe he'll disguise himself," Jazzy offered, "and use a different name."

"I think we should consider that option," Deek agreed. "I'm telling you these people have the kind of resources and money to buy quality fake passports."

"Whittaker will have the commercial airport covered," Nora responded. "He just crashed a plane, and we've had the guy on the run, so I doubt he's had time to piece a workable disguise together. Your app only shows flights en route, right, or does it have anyone who has filed a flight plan?"

"Just en route, sort of," Deek said, leaning forward between the front seats again. "But I have a good friend who can access flights en route and even filed flight plans if we know where from."

"Probably South Florida or the Keys, yeah?" AJ suggested. "A fancy jet could be here in a few hours or less. We'd have a two-hour warning if your app picked them up."

"The airport closes at 9:00 p.m.," Nora pointed out. "No one is landing after that without an emergency, which would attract a lot of attention."

"What about another seaplane?" AJ asked.

"It'll still show up on Pete's software," Deek replied. "It's how I tracked him here."

"Unless they turn the transponder off," Nora said, now heading east on Smith Road.

"True," Deek admitted, thinking how the Otter had suddenly popped up on tracking halfway to Grand Cayman. "But seaplanes aren't easy to come by," he added.

"We know a bloke in Key West with three vintage seaplanes," AJ said. "But I doubt this bloke stole one of Buck Reilly's planes. Buck's a bad-arse, huh, Nora?"

The Norwegian nodded from the front seat.

"Buck has a crush on Nora," AJ said, turning to Deek with a grin.

"Buck Reilly has a crush on all women," Nora scoffed. "But especially Charity Styles."

AJ laughed and Deek wondered how the conversation had derailed into talking about people he'd never heard of. "This was a de Havilland Canada DHC-3 Otter," he said, trying to get back on track.

"Buck's are all named after birds, not mammals," AJ replied. "Gooses and the like."

"I'm pretty sure Wayne Daniels stole the one he crashed from a guy in mainland Florida," Deek explained.

"That bloke can't be happy," AJ chuckled. "Get your aeroplane nicked, then the wanker goes and crashes it for you."

"He's dead," Deek said. "We found his body, dumped from the plane in the waters off Key West."

"I guess he's not too worried about his plane after all then," AJ commented, and Jazzy chuckled. "Wait a sec," AJ continued, "are you saying Wayne Daniels killed the owner and pitched him out of his own plane?"

"That's exactly what I'm saying, and *have been* saying all day."

"So we not chasin' after a car thief," Jazzy said excitedly. "We huntin' a murderer?"

"I'm sure of it," Deek replied.

"Cool," Jazzy whispered.

"Not cool!" AJ and Nora said at the same time.

Jazzy rolled her eyes and grinned at Deek. "Be cool if we catch da man."

Deek nodded. "Yeah. That would be cool."

Angler would have preferred for the man not to see his face, but there was no other way of handling the situation. While he waited, cars came and went through the busy gas station down the street from the airport. He was pleased to see many of them were white four-door sedans, like the one he was in. Finally, a small red SUV pulled in and instead of going to the pumps, parked off to the side, two spots over. A man got out and looked around. He was late forties, maybe early fifties, with short graying hair and a solid build.

Getting out of the stolen car, Angler looked over and caught the man's attention, nodding for him to approach. They both got into Angler's vehicle and shook hands.

"Are the instructions for the flight clear?" Angler asked.

"Crystal," the man replied.

"Good. Here," Angler replied, handing over a wad of hundred-dollar bills. "Count it."

The man did as instructed, then tucked the cash away in his cargo shorts pocket.

"Six o'clock sharp," Angler said firmly.

"On the nose," the man replied, and got out.

Nora crossed over a busy intersection then made a left in front of one end of Owen Roberts International Airport's only runway. The road followed the perimeter fence to the right, then after a straight stretch, curved left around buildings where light aircraft could be seen on the apron. Making a right on Roberts Drive brought her to the FBO entrance between a pair of large buildings. Nora pulled into the parking lot where she saw the sign for Cayman Islands Customs & Border Control, and found a spot near the office entrance.

"Wait here," she said to the others, and hopped from the Jeep.

"I need to come with you," Deek urged, and scrambled out of the back seat, more carefully jumping to the ground this time.

"Why?" Nora asked, looking at him with the same stern expression she seemed to have frozen on her face.

"Because I..." Deek began, then trailed off.

He found conversing with people awkward enough already, but the tall and beautiful Norwegian with her abrupt manner completely threw him.

"You mean you *want* to come with me," she challenged.

"I suppose that's more accurate, yes..." he mumbled, although inside he felt an overwhelming *need* to pursue every possible lead.

"Then say that," she replied, and walked through the front door, holding it briefly for Deek to follow.

"We're keeping an eye out," a dark-skinned man in a Cayman Islands Customs and Border Control uniform greeted them, seeing Nora's police outfit. "Your Detective Whittaker has everyone on high alert. Nothing suspicious as of yet."

"Constable Sommer," Nora said extending a hand to the man.

"This is Deek Morrison. He's been tracking the suspect from America."

"Officer Jeffries," the man replied, shaking their hands in turn. "Is that where he's trying to get back to, America?"

"We believe so," Nora replied. "Florida."

"Okay, well like I said, we haven't seen anything worth reporting yet, so, how can I help you?"

"Do any planes take off without a flight plan?" Nora asked.

"No," Jeffries said with a shake of the head. "In Cayman, both IFR and VFR have to file a plan and get clearance."

"That's instrument flight rules…" Deek began explaining to Nora.

"I know what IFR is," she interrupted him with her attention still on Jeffries. "Anyone requesting a plan or clearance tonight?"

"I'm not sure," Jeffries replied. "That's handled by air traffic control. We're only notified if the plane is leaving the Cayman Islands."

"So, there's local flights that you don't have anything to do with?" Nora verified.

"Correct. We have several locals with light aircraft who'll fly around the island, or run over to the Sister Islands. Some have repetitive flight plans."

"We need to know who of them is asking for clearance," Nora said. "Where would they depart from?"

"Out here," Jeffries replied, throwing his thumb over his shoulder in the direction of the apron they'd seen driving in. "We can listen in to air traffic control or I can call and ask about requests."

"Call them," Nora quickly responded. "How do we get outside to where the planes are?"

24

Nora hurried through the building with Deek on her heels. Jeffries lagged behind as he called the air traffic control tower on his cell phone and spoke with someone as requested. Bursting through the offices, Nora shoved open the door leading outside, and ran down a roadway to the apron. As Deek followed, his own cell phone rang and he looked at the caller ID.

"Oh boy," he muttered, and answered. "Hello, sir."

"How's the show, Morrison?" his boss asked.

"Crazy, sir. Very busy."

"You sound like you're running, Morrison?"

"No, no, sir. Just handing out flyers like candy, sir."

"Really? Do we need to send more down?" his boss said, sounding pleasantly surprised.

"I have someone with questions, sir, may I call you later?" Deek asked, cringing at his own lies.

"Yes, yes, of course. Good work, Morrison, I'm glad you're finally seeing sense and taking the show seriously."

"Thank you, sir, gotta go."

Deek ended the call as he caught up to Nora. She'd stopped to survey the tarmac, and he tried his best to shake off the blatant deception he'd just played on his boss and do the same. Aircraft of varying sizes, shapes and purposes were parked all around the tarmac, but none of them appeared to be in motion. To their left, the rear half of a commercial jet with a Cayman Airways logo on the tail stuck out of a hangar. Farther left was a cluster of charter jets outside the Island Air FBO building.

At first, all Deek could hear was road traffic noise, but then a change in pitch made him search the tarmac once more.

"Hear that?" he asked.

Nora nodded, but neither of them could see the plane whose motor and propeller they could barely hear above the cars.

"There's been nothing this evening," Jeffries said, catching his breath as he hurried up behind them. "Until two minutes ago. But that's Jack Haley taking a tour up, no doubt."

"A tour?" Nora snapped. "Going where?"

Jeffries shrugged his shoulders. "Sunset tour, most likely. He'll fly around the island, watch the sunset from up there, then come back. Sometimes he does a longer tour over to the Sister Islands, ninety miles away. Jack's a good guy. He calls himself GCM Charters & Tours."

Deek and Nora looked at each other. "We need to stop him taking off!" Nora ordered.

"What for?" Jeffries retorted. "Jack's not about to fly his Cessna 172 to Florida in the dark. He'd have to stop twice, or even more if he flew around Cuba."

Nora was already jogging out onto the tarmac to get a better view.

"He could be dropping our guy on one of the smaller islands, or more likely, Daniels will do what he did to the last pilot that flew him," Deek babbled.

"What was that?" Jeffries inquired.

"Killed him and threw him out midair."

"Holy mother of…" Jeffries trailed off as he dialed a number on his phone.

Deek ran to catch up with Nora.

"There!" she growled, pointing to the other side of the apron where a small plane was now taxiing toward the runway.

She looked around for a better form of transport, and seeing nothing, took off at a sprint. Deek gave chase, but the Norwegian's long legs propelled her much faster than his office bound, out-of-shape muscles could match. He also wondered what on earth she planned on doing if she reached the airplane.

Fifty yards away, Deek could see there were two people in the cockpit, and the man sitting right seat was looking their way. It was hard to make out details as the low sun glinted off the plane's windows and both men wore headsets, but Deek knew it had to be Wayne Daniels. And if that Cessna took off, he'd have lost his trail once more.

Up ahead, Nora drew alongside the taxiing plane and kept running until she was slightly ahead. Turning, she slowed and franticly waved her arms.

"No!" Deek yelled, terrified they'd steer the plane and its thrashing propeller straight at the policewoman.

Nora stood her ground and the pilot suddenly stomped on the brakes and brought the Cessna to a halt a few feet from her. She made the cut-throat sign and the motor slowed until it spluttered to a stop, the pilot's door flying open and a man leaping to the tarmac.

"Are you freakin' crazy, lady?" the pilot yelled. "I looked up and there you were right in front of me! I could have killed you."

"Stand clear of the plane," Nora ordered, her eyes locked on the passenger and her hand resting on her Taser.

Jack Haley took a few steps away from his precious plane, looking back and forth between the policewomen and his client. "What the hell's going on?"

Nora ignored Haley and stayed focused on the passenger as Deek arrived heaving and wheezing. He stood well clear and watched as the passenger door opened.

"Come out! Slowly!" Nora commanded, moving closer.

The man extricated himself from the snug airplane and stood on the tarmac with his hands in the air. Deek's first thought was that

Daniels would certainly have a gun, but then he wondered if the man could have hung on to a firearm while escaping the downed plane. He looked more closely at Daniels.

"He looks different," Deek said, glancing over at Nora then back to the man before him.

"What's your name?" Nora asked.

"I'm Trent Mayfield," he replied in an American accent. "You wanna tell me what the hell this all about?"

"*Fy faen*," Nora swore and took the Cayman Islands driver's license the man offered her, verifying his name.

"Where are you going?" she asked.

"I was taking my client up for a sunset tour," Haley said, coming around the nose of the plane.

"Did anyone else approach you today about taking them anywhere?"

"No," Haley replied, shaking his head. "Just this guy's people."

"His people?" Nora questioned.

"Sure. He had someone call and make the booking this afternoon," Haley explained. "Was that your office who called me, Trent?"

His client smiled. "Yeah."

Deek was ready to walk away, but Nora didn't move.

"They call you on your mobile?" she asked, looking at the pilot.

"Yeah," he replied.

"Let me see the number," she ordered and held out her hand.

"Ma'am, clearly you have the wrong people here," Trent said. "How about you let us go so I can get my sunset flight while the sun's still setting?"

"Fly west, it'll still be there," Nora snapped back, and took the pilot's cell phone from him.

Deek stepped over and she showed him the number.

"You live here?" she asked Trent.

"I do," he replied.

"But your office is in Florida?"

"No, but I have friends all over the place."

"Can we go now?" Haley asked impatiently.

She handed the phone and license back. "Sorry," she said, sounding more disappointed than apologetic, which Deek guessed to be the truth. It was how he felt. "I'll let air traffic control know you can go on your tour," Nora added.

They began walking away, then Nora stopped and spun around. "Hey, one more thing," she said and the two men who were about to get back in the plane paused. "How did you pay for this tour, Mr. Mayfield?"

"He paid me in cash. Hundred-dollar bills," Haley answered for him, patting his pocket.

Nora turned to Deek and whispered. "Give me a hundred dollars."

Deek frowned. "Uh... I kinda need the little I have left for a hotel."

"Hey lady, we need to go," Mayfield insisted, but Nora ignored him.

Instead, she growled at Deek. "You can sleep on AJ's sofa. Now give me a hundred dollars."

Deek dug into his pocket and peeled five twenty-dollar bills from his shrinking watch money, handing it to Nora.

"Mr. Haley," she said. "Exchange one of those hundred-dollar bills with me."

The pilot shrugged his shoulders. "Sure. If it means you'll let us be on our way."

He handed Nora a hundred-dollar bill and received the twenties in return.

"Enjoy your flight," Nora said, then turned and walked away with Deek in tow.

"What was that about?" he asked, but she didn't answer as a security vehicle sped toward them. When it stopped, Officer Jeffries and an airport security man in uniform stepped out.

"Wasn't your guy?"

"No," Deek said.

"Control can clear them," Nora added, looking back at the Cessna.

An SUV appeared from behind the buildings, and drove over, joining them on the tarmac. Detective Whittaker got out.

"False alarm?" he asked, and Nora shook her head.

"Maybe not," she replied, and Deek looked at her, puzzled.

"Do you remember that phone number?" she asked Deek.

He shrugged his shoulders. "Yeah. Numbers are kinda my thing."

"I figured that much," she said. "Let's track this number, sir," she explained. "It's a Florida 305 area code. And I suggest we detain the passenger, a Trent Mayfield, when they land."

"He's not Wayne Daniels, Nora," Deek said. "He's similar build and age, but it's not him."

"I know," she told Deek, then turned back to her boss, holding up the money she'd exchanged. "I think you'll find this is one of the hundred-dollar bills which will match the cash paid out from the bank today."

"Damn it," Deek cursed, realizing what she'd concluded. "He was a decoy."

Nora nodded. "I think so, but we won't be able to confirm that until the morning when the bank opens."

"And we get a warrant from a judge," Whittaker pointed out.

"That'll be too late," Deek blurted. "Daniels will have found another way off the island by then."

"Sorry, Deek," Nora said. "But I'm sure he already has."

"Boat?" Whittaker queried.

"Almost certainly," Nora replied.

"To another island," Deek added, feeling desperate once again. "How will we know which one?"

"We won't," Nora replied. "But it doesn't matter."

"Of course it matters," Deek moaned. "I've lost him again."

"No you haven't," Nora contradicted. "You know exactly where he's going."

Deek looked up. "Oh yeah. I guess I do."

The horizon blazed an array of orange and yellow hues as the sun dipped below the ocean off the stern. Between the low drone of the diesel engine, the swaying of the boat, and the beer he was drinking, Angler was beginning to feel exhausted. He'd had an eventful day, even by his standards. He looked at his phone. It was down to one bar of reception. Quickly, he went through the critical protocols of connecting to the blog site via a secure VPN, and typed a message.

"Fair winds and following seas. Back on course tomorrow."

Hitting send on the message, he moved on to a text, updating Grady Foster on his adjusted schedule. Thirty seconds after he hit send, "no service" flashed on the screen. With a smile, Angler took another swig of beer, and tossed the cell phone over the side.

The wheelhouse door slid open behind him and he turned to face the captain.

"You said I was to let you know," the man said in a thick Jamaican accent. "We just past da twelve-mile mark. We in international waters now."

Angler tipped his beer bottle the man's way in thanks, and the captain went back to the helm.

25

On the island of Grand Turk, a young couple watched the sun dip toward the horizon. Two dogs lay in the sand beside them, yards from the gently lapping waves on Pillory Beach.

"Cheers, mate," the petite blonde said, clinking a stubby bottle of Red Stripe against her companion's. "I know you fancy your craft beers and all, but sometimes I hear Jamaica calling."

"Won't hear me complaining," the tall, lanky man replied, extending a long leg and burrowing a bare foot into the sand.

"Ahhhh..." Emily Durand sighed with pleasure after her opening swig. "Hooray beer."

Boone Fischer smiled and reached down to scratch behind the ears of Mama, the senior dog that lay snuggled up against his thigh. Their younger dog, Brixton, jumped up in a flurry of sand and made a mad dash for the surf, pouncing on the foam as the water retreated. Both dogs were rescues, Brixton from Belize, and Mama from here in the Turks and Caicos Islands.

"Gonna miss our little pot brownies," Emily said wistfully.

Boone chuckled. Em had started calling them that just last week. Strays here were called "potcakes." In Belize they were "potlickers." And Brix and Mama were both brown.

"They'll be in good hands. They love our landlady and her pups," Boone assured her. "And we're only gonna be gone for the weekend,"

"Yeah, about that... I still think you should visit your mum in Tennessee, since we'll be in the States anyway."

"We're divemastering in South Caicos on Tuesday," Boone reminded her. "Another time."

"Speaking of mums... since Mama's spayed now, and all puppied out... wonder if we should give her a new name?"

"Got anything in mind?"

"Should be something with a similar sound..." Emily mused, taking a contemplative sip of her beer. "How 'bout—"

Her words were cut off as "Wannabe" by the Spice Girls blared from the phone in her pocket. Boone recognized the familiar ringtone Emily had assigned the caller.

Em clawed the green-cased phone out of her pocket and answered, tapping the speakerphone icon. "'Allo, AJ! How's things in Grand Cayman? You all packed?"

"Thinking about it," AJ responded. "We had a bit of excitement over here, so I'm running behind."

"What sort of excitement?" Boone asked.

"Hi, Boone! Oh, you know... crashing seaplane, international intrigue... I'll fill you in on the drive from Miami to Fort Myers."

"Oh, bugger!" Em cursed. "I forgot to book the hire car!"

"Actually, that's why I called," AJ said. "You don't need to. I'll be flying in with an American federal agent bloke I met. Turns out he's heading to the boat show, and he's got a car in airport parking at Miami."

"Works for me!" Em said. "What kind of agent? FBI? CIA?"

"Umm... no, nothing like that. Hey, you two ready to do some boat shopping?"

"Not entirely," Emily admitted with a sigh.

"Em's still in the grieving stage," Boone said.

"Boone is too!" the blond divemaster protested. "He just hides it, with his strong-'n'-silent-type bollocks."

"We definitely need a new boat," Boone admitted. Bubble Chasers Diving had lost their dive boat recently, and had been subbing with some of the local dive ops on Grand Turk and South Caicos. It was fun working with new people on a variety of boats, but the two divemasters were eager to get back to running their own op.

"You have anything in mind?" AJ asked.

"Well, I want speed," Em declared, "and Boone wants something with a shallow draft."

"Several of the dive ops over here on GT have boats you can bring right up to the beach," Boone explained. "Pretty convenient for resorts without a dedicated dock. East Bay Resort is gonna get some catamaran dive boats from Aventura, and I saw they had a vendor booth at the boat show, so hopefully we can start there. Provided I can keep Emily away from any six-engine Cigarette boats."

"Good luck stopping me!"

AJ laughed. "Back to the planning... assuming our flights aren't delayed, we're landing at about the same time. Share your location with me once you clear customs, and we'll meet up near the exit."

"Good thinking," Boone said. Cell phone use wasn't allowed in US Customs, but once they passed through, they could ping AJ's phone with their own.

"'Course it's good thinking, we Brits are a clever bunch," Emily said, her thick South London accent considerably less posh than AJ's.

"No argument there."

"Well, I should get going," AJ said. "Got to get back to my cottage and make up the sofa bed for Secret Agent Man."

"Ooh! Can't wait to meet 'im!" Emily gushed. "Right-o, see you stateside." She hung up and pocketed her phone.

"Secret agent... American... but not FBI or CIA," Boone mused, then shrugged and raised his beer to his lips. "Well, we'll know soon enough."

Deek leaned to the side while Constable Sommers took the Jeep through yet another roundabout on the Esterly Tibbetts bypass, as the group made their way north from the airport. Nora took the first exit, causing the surprised Deek to bump shoulders with Jazzy as they joined the two-lane West Bay Road, driving parallel to the ocean for a few minutes. Just as the water appeared in clear view on their left, Nora made a left turn then pulled into a small, sloped parking lot next to a colorful little hut.

AJ jumped out. "See you in a mo," she said, walking towards the hut.

Nora backed up, pulled out onto the road, then backtracked the way they'd come.

"You sure AJ won't mind me crashing at her place?" Deek asked, leaning between the front seats.

"Why should she mind?" Nora replied, arriving at a four-way intersection they'd driven through a few minutes earlier. "That's what sofa beds are for."

Turning right at the stop brought them to a low wall facing the ocean. A tight left then took them by a brightly painted food shack named Heritage Kitchen on the inland side with strings of lights decorating its walls and outdoor dining area.

"Best food, ever," Jazzy said, pointing to the little eatery.

Continuing south on the narrow road, the seawall and the faint remnants of sunset gave way to large, waterfront homes, and at the end of the road, Nora parked beside a gate in a wood fence just past an expansive home.

"She'll be right behind us," Nora commented, turning off the Jeep.

Her phone rang and she looked at the caller ID. "It's Whittaker," she said, putting the call on speaker and setting the phone on the dash. "Sir, I have Deek with me."

"Constable… Mr. Morrison… I have something for you."

"The phone or the money?" Nora asked.

"Both. Rasha works fast. The bill is definitely from the withdrawal made at the bank earlier today."

"And the phone?"

"From the number you got from the pilot, we were able to determine its last-known location—thirteen miles east-southeast of East End. But all signal was lost at 7:33 p.m."

"*Faen,*" Nora cursed. "He's on a boat."

"Likely. And outside our territorial waters."

"East-southeast isn't heading for the Sister Islands," Nora commented.

"No, I bet he's going to Jamaica," Deek said. When Nora looked at him, he shrugged. "Maritime Administration analyst, remember? I've got maps of the oceans and sea lanes tattooed on the inside of my brain. Detective, was there any Automatic Identification System signal transmitting in the vicinity of that last ping?"

"Unfortunately, no," Whittaker replied. "But it's not uncommon for boats to turn off their AIS."

Deek was well aware of that fact. While there were a few legitimate reasons for a skipper to switch off their identification transponder, often the reasons were more nefarious: drug and weapons smuggling, illegal fishing, human trafficking—even nation-states might send their oil tankers out "dark" to avoid international sanctions.

"If you are able to pull up additional pings from that phone, you may be able to determine the course and speed," Deek suggested. "And I'd recommend you reach out to the US and Jamaican Coast Guards, to see if they can't line up an intercept. The nearest commercial airport with international flights is Montego Bay... Wayne Daniels may try to fly out from there."

"Given your connections in the Maritime Administration, Mr. Morrison... shouldn't you reach out to the US Coast Guard?"

"Uh... no. You'll have much faster results, I promise you."

"Very well. I'll let you know if we learn anything else. I have Rasha looking into Mr. Daniels's phone to see if we can determine where it was purchased and where and when it was first activated. You are flying out tomorrow, yes?"

"Yeah... with AJ. I'm actually at her place right now."

"Well, have a good evening, and come back and visit another time when you can take the time to relax and enjoy our island, Mr. Morrison."

"I'd like that," Deek replied, but he seriously doubted international travel lay in his unemployed future.

Nora rang off, and looked up at the rearview mirror where a single headlight in the distance made her squint. "She's here."

Nora pocketed the phone and got out with Deek following suit. A deep, throaty rumble approached, and in moments a rider coasted to a stop atop a sleek, expensive-looking motorcycle. A leather riding outfit added some bulk to her otherwise slim figure, but Deek was certain this was AJ—a fact confirmed when she removed her helmet and shook out her purple-streaked blond hair.

"Sorry for the delay! Had to nip down to the shops for a few items for the trip." She guided the motorcycle through the gate. "You two have any luck tracking down that bloke?"

"Some," Nora said, and summed up what they'd learned as AJ wheeled her Ducati next to a small cottage in the grounds of the large house.

"I should get the kid home," Nora said. "Enjoy your trip, AJ. Good luck, Deek."

"Thank you for your help, Constable," Deek responded, as he clawed one of his Maritime Administration cards from the sparse supply in his wallet. "If you find out anything more, don't hesitate to contact me."

"Hope you get the bad guy," Jazzy added as the young constable glanced at the card, then tucked it into a pocket.

"You need better cards." Nora declared, then walked back to the Jeep, letting the gate swing closed behind her and her teenage charge.

AJ was chuckling as she zipped open her riding jacket. "Nora's not exactly a people person. Come on inside, let me see if I can scrounge some clean sheets for you. It's an early flight, and we'll want a proper sleep."

Angler stared up at the stars as he lay on the deck, a few life jackets standing in for a mattress, and his waterproof duffel tucked beneath his head as a makeshift pillow. Below, the engine of the inboards imparted a vibration to the surface of his makeshift bed, the numbing sensation bringing to mind those old vibrating beds in rundown motels—more distracting than relaxing. He needed to get some sleep, but his mind kept chattering at him. Before his brain would allow him to nod off, he needed to think through his timetable and see what could be kept on track, and what might need to be shifted.

Prior to sending his final message to Hildebrand, Angler had texted an associate to request transport out of a small airstrip in Negril, the closest possible option. If his calculations were correct, at their current speed, they'd reach Jamaican waters at about eight in the morning. If he could be in the air before nine, he'd be able to reach Florida in time to slip into his prior plans without too many adjustments. Unfortunately, there had been no confirmation before he'd lost signal and deep-sixed his phone.

As soon as the coast was in sight, he'd insert a fresh SIM card and activate his remaining burner phone. He would check on the status of the requested transport, and if there was no response, he'd have to cajole the fishing boat's captain to take him further up the coast to Montego Bay and try to get a commercial flight out. On the other hand, his transport man was usually solid. Usually. Angler thought back to the previous pilot he'd been forced to eliminate. *Best not to repeat that experience with this one,* he thought. *Three plane crashes in one week would be pushing it.*

26

"Rise and shine!"

Deek blinked, turning over. Reflexively, he reached for his watch on the nightstand; his hand hit air. There was no nightstand along the side of the sofa—his watch was currently marking time in an Islamorada pawn shop. Deek rolled over and spotted his phone on the floor. He reached down to tap it, bringing the lock screen to life.

"Four-thirty? I set my alarm for five... the flight isn't until seven."

"Seven-ten," AJ said, clanking about in the kitchen. "But I need my coffee and I hate rushing. I let you sleep while it brewed, so count yourself lucky."

"Well, thanks for that," Deek said, sitting up and yawning.

"Sofa bed treat you right?"

"Yeah. Comfy. Thanks." He accepted a proffered mug of coffee and took an experimental sip. "Wow. That's good."

"Costa Rican. A guy in the Keys turned me on to it."

"I thought you Brits liked tea."

"It'll do in a pinch, but coffee gets the job done faster. Grab a shower... you're a bit whiffy, if you don't mind me saying. I'll suss out some breakfast. Reg'll be along to pick us up in thirty."

Four and a half hours later, AJ and Deek's Cayman Airways flight descended into Miami International. After disembarking, they passed through immigration and headed down to baggage claim. Deek didn't have any luggage, but AJ had a bag to collect, having brought some of her diving gear, in case she had a chance to do some diving. Her bag in hand, they slow-walked along the line to customs, before finally emerging near the exit to ground transportation.

"No location ping from Emily yet," AJ said as they stepped from the air-conditioning into a warm, humid day. "Probably still in customs, but shouldn't be long. I saw Providenciales on the baggage claim screen, so they're probably right behind us."

Deek fired up his own phone and found a single voicemail from his boss. Taking a deep breath, he played the message. Oddly... there wasn't one. There was a nanosecond of rustling, then the message ended. *Probably was just slow to hang up, when I didn't answer,* he thought.

"So... where did you park? Dolphin or Flamingo?"

"Hmm? Oh, the parking lot. Flamingo, I think." Deek took out his wallet and confirmed the lot, then stared forlornly at his dwindling supply of cash. "Hope I've got enough for the parking," he said.

AJ glanced up from her phone. "Oh, they take credit cards, no worries."

"Umm..."

"There she is!" AJ held up the map on her phone and showed Deek the pulsing dot with the name Emily floating beside it. AJ's phone dinged and an overlay of a text popped up. Deek squinted at it and saw: *AJ!* with an army of additional exclamation points, followed by *Be there in a tick!*

They waited only a minute before AJ laughed and pointed toward a large crowd approaching the exits. "There's Boone. You can always spot his head above everyone else's. Emily, not so much."

Moments later, a piercing squeal split the humid air and a pint-size blonde burst from the pack and made a beeline for AJ, rolling a lime-green suitcase behind her, an enormous pair of pink sunglasses above a button nose and a dazzling grin. Apparently, the suitcase was slowing her down too much and she abandoned it in her headlong charge.

"AJ!" she cried, nearly bowling her friend over with an aggressive hug. "Been a long time, yeah?"

"Too long," AJ agreed, hugging her back. "So good to see you, Emily." She squinted at her. "What happened to your green shades?"

"Oh, yeah... lost my favorite sunnies when we lost the boat. Haven't found the perfect pair, yet."

"Pink suits you, too," AJ said. She looked over the blonde's head—quite easy to do, as she had several inches on her—and called out, "Hi, Boone!"

Boone waved as he paused to retrieve the stranded suitcase, then strolled up to them, dragging all of their luggage. He appeared to have both of their checked bags and a pair of carry-on backpacks, either in his hands or slung over his shoulders.

"Always the pack mule, eh Boone?" AJ said with a laugh.

Boone smiled and shrugged as much as his encumbrance would allow. "Good timing on the flights," he commented. "You been here long?"

"No, just got here. Deek, this is Boone Fischer... and the one stuck to me like a remora is Emily Durand. And Boonemily..." she said, pronouncing the pair as one word, "this is Deek Morrison."

"Deek! That's a cool name," Emily proclaimed. "Is it short for something?"

"Derek. But back in elementary school, a teacher left out the 'R' on her roll call sheet and, well... I've been going by Deek ever since."

"Ace. I love Deek. Deek it is. Maybe Deeky if I'm feelin' cheeky. I go by Em sometimes... if someone's in a hurry, comes in handy."

Deek smiled. Em's thick British accent was quite different than AJ's, and her enthusiasm was infectious. Boone, on the other hand, seemed extremely laid back. The two were an unusual pair, both in energy and appearance. While Emily looked like she was straining to attain five feet in height, Boone was quite a few inches over six feet tall, long arms and legs giving him a lanky appearance—although judging by the musculature under his T-shirt, he certainly wasn't skinny.

"I hear you're giving us a lift to the boat show," Boone prompted, setting Emily's suitcase down beside her and turning it so that the handle was ready for her to grab it. "We certainly appreciate the ride."

"My pleasure," Deek said. "AJ and her friends were very helpful on Grand Cayman, so it's the least I can do. I'm parked over in the Flamingo Lot."

"The national bird of the island of Bonaire," Emily intoned like a professor. "Ooh, what kind of car does a secret agent drive? Will we all fit in an Aston Martin?"

"Pretty sure it's a Hyundai." Deek raised an eyebrow at AJ. "You told them I was a secret agent?"

AJ grinned. "Not exactly, but I may have exaggerated a smidge."

While Deek explained his actual job, the group made their way into the parking lot and piled into the rental car. Nearing the exit, Deek spotted the fees for overnight parking. "Uh... I wonder if I could trouble any of you for a little help with the parking. My credit card has been having issues."

Angler looked out the window as the pilot taxied off the runway at Page Field, a small general aviation airport in Fort Myers. The journey had been an interesting one: after Angler had come ashore in Negril, he had received notice from his contact that a plane wouldn't be available at the nearby aerodrome until 10:00 a.m. At 9:57, a Learjet 36A had arrived.

Fortunately for Angler—and perhaps, too, for the pilot—the man in the cockpit for this flight was a consummate professional. A brief conversation with the Fixed Base Operator in Negril, followed by a quick handoff of an envelope, and they were back in the air in record time. Thanks to the pilot's contacts—and an additional fee, paid by wire—they'd been able to secure a short-notice Cuban Overflight Permit, drastically reducing their flight time. It would have been even faster, but the pilot had opted for a quick stop in Key West to clear customs and immigration, rather than doing so at the Southwest Florida International Airport in Fort Myers; apparently because he "knew a guy" in Key West and "had an arrangement" here at Page.

The pilot brought them to a halt on the west ramp alongside the FBO, and Angler rose from his seat and retrieved his duffel. Unzipping it, he extracted two bundles of cash and held them out when the pilot stepped out of the cockpit.

"That'll cover it," the man said, after taking them and giving one of the bundles a cursory glance.

"You got Wi-Fi on this plane?"

"Of course." The pilot gave Angler the password.

Angler quickly downloaded his preferred VPN app. The burner phone offered some protection, but he liked layers. Once it was installed, he nodded to the pilot. "Appreciate the lift. Much better experience than the last charter. Wouldn't mind using you again sometime, Mister...?"

The pilot smiled. "No names."

Angler chuckled. "Oh, I like you even better. 'Til next time, amigo."

"You need ground transport?" the pilot asked as he engaged the cockpit door and stairs.

"Nah, I got it covered." Angler stepped out into the blistering sun and made his way to the road. Squinting across Fowler Street, his stomach grumbled. Retrieving his phone, he sent a text to Grady Foster. *Pick me up at the Steak 'n Shake by Page Field.*

Ten minutes later, Angler set a take-out bag down in a corner booth. Reaching inside the bag, he extracted the double cheeseburger and set it on the table. It took all of his willpower to keep from tearing into it, but he took out the burner phone and typed in the number of the captain of the *Beeracuda* from memory. He texted: *Ready to go fishing. You at the marina I told you about?*

A moment later, a reply came. *There now.*

I'm still a few hours out. Meet you at Doc's. Have a rum on me.

Angler set the phone down, took the empty take-out bag and stuffed it into the waterproof bag beside him. That done, he proceeded to murder the double cheeseburger.

Rolling along the flat expanses of the Everglades on I-75, Deek cut across Florida, explaining as best he could what he was doing here.

"So... you think this Wayne Daniels guy is Satan?" Emily poked her head between the seats, her raised voice competing with the music playlist she'd insisted on blasting from the rental's speakers.

"Shay-tahn," Deek replied, correcting her pronunciation. And no. I mean... yes. I did think that at first. But now I think this Daniels is an operative, working for Şeytan."

"So... who's Şeytan?" AJ asked.

A powerful billionaire with control over a fleet of oil tankers, Deek thought, but did not say. "Someone who might be untouchable," he said instead. And after he said it, he realized it might well be true. Hildebrand had motive, and had paid the man going by the name of Wayne Daniels, but other than that... what other proof did Deek have?

Boone turned to him from the passenger seat. "And you think they're trying to disrupt these peace talks?" Boone asked. "Possibly with a terrorist attack of some sort?"

"Perhaps. I'm not sure of the exact method that might be used."

"I assume you've called the police, yeah?" Em said. "Or the FBI? Or your bosses at the Maritime whatsa-whosit?"

Deek sighed. "I've tried to convince them, but my boss hasn't been particularly supportive." His phone buzzed from the holder on the dash and he glanced at it. "Oh boy... there he is now." He reached over and switched off the music.

"Right in the middle of Lady Gaga?" Emily protested. "Deek, you philistine."

"My boss thinks I'm working the Maritime Administration booth at the convention," Deek blurted quickly. "Handing out flyers and such."

"Oh, so you need crowd noise!"

"No noise might be better." He sent the call to the car speakers and answered it. "Deek Morrison!" he shouted, doing his best to approximate the sound of someone busy and harried.

"Morrison!" his boss shouted right back, but with an odd cheerfulness in his voice. "How are you? How's the convention? As busy as it was yesterday?"

"Umm... yes sir! Surprising amount of interest."

"Well, good! You there right now? I don't hear much hustle and bustle..."

Deek saw Emily lean forward between the seats and start to open her mouth, but he quickly shook his head at her. "Uh, just getting back sir! Ran out of flyers so had to run across to the printers and make up some more."

Emily gave Deek an enthusiastic thumbs-up and AJ snorted a laugh from the backseat. Deek's phone suddenly chimed as another call came in.

"How are the flyers looking, Morrison?"

"Uh..." Deek was staring at the phone, trying to remember where that area code was from. Keys, he thought.

"Everything all right, Morrison?"

"Yes, sir… a call is coming in. I'll let it go to voicemail."

"No, no! You take that call! Could be important. I'll wait on the line."

"I… well, okay, sir."

Boone, who had been listening quietly, reached over and tapped the incoming call button.

"Deek Morrison."

"Deek, this is Kate."

"Kate, yes, how are you?"

"All's well on my end. You still in Grand Cayman?"

"Just got back."

"I've got something for you. Well, my friend Michelle did the actual getting. The billionaire you were looking at… his super yacht is the *La Fiamma Azzurra*, right? If I didn't mangle the, what is it… Italian?"

"Yes, that's Hildebrand's yacht. And you said it perfectly."

"Michelle tracked down the blueprints for it. The builder had them behind an encryption wall. She thought that was odd, and looked at some of the other yachts under construction; none of the others had that layer of protection."

"That's odd, but not too surprising," Deek said. Billionaires often have a dose of paranoia."

Kate laughed. "Yeah, I was just reading an article on one that built a big bunker for when the poor rise up to go after the rich. Anyway, I thought you might like to take a look. The blueprints are a pretty big file, so I'll send you a download link once I'm stopped. I'm on my way to that boat show you mentioned. You still planning on working a booth?"

"That's the plan. I'm on my way now. Oh! Actually, I have to go… I've got someone on the other line."

"Maybe see you there. Bye for now!"

Deek tapped the call waiting. "Mr. Powell? You there?"

"Yes, Morrison. I'm here. Important call, I take it?"

"Oh, not really. It was… a local I met, with excellent boating skills and knowledge of the waters around the Keys," Deek said quickly, deciding on a little truth, before diving back into the lies. "She expressed some interest in the work that the Maritime Administration does. Might be a prospective hire. Listen, uh… I'm just getting back with the flyers so I probably ought to hustle."

"Wonderful. Wonderful. You can let me know how it all goes, when I see you again. I can't wait to hear about it all, face to face." The call ended.

Deek frowned. Something had sounded "off" to him.

"What's wrong?" Boone asked.

"He was nice."

"So, Deeky," Em began, "if you think there's an attack coming… why are you going to a boat show?"

Deek sighed. "Because I don't want to lose my job. But as I mentioned, I think Hildebrand's super yacht is part of this, and it's supposed to be at the boat show. And while I sit there, handing out flyers, I'll have time to think… see if I can put a few pieces of the puzzle together."

"Hey all, time-sensitive request," AJ announced. "I realize we're in the middle of a swamp-surrounded interstate, but do you think they have rest stops? I could really use the loo."

"I saw a sign for one coming up," Deek said.

Fifteen minutes later, after a brief respite at the Collier County Rest Area, Deek drove onto the entrance ramp to rejoin I-75, but slowed as flashing lights entered his peripheral vision. A police motorcycle drove by, followed by another, followed by a convoy of four black SUVs and a single police motorcycle bringing up the rear.

"Whoa!" Emily announced. "Make way for the fancy folks."

"Diplomatic plates," Deek observed.

"Wonder who it is?" Boone mused.

But Deek thought he knew who they were… and where they were going.

"They are on their way, sir."

"Thank you, Monsieur Roux," Hildebrand said. "Have you liaised with their respective security teams?"

"But of course," his bodyguard replied. "They will arrive at the Edison Ford Marina in Fort Myers in one hour and twenty-two minutes."

Hildebrand stifled a smirk. Barbeau Roux's time in the French Foreign Legion had led to a regimented, precise way of doing things; it was part of the reason he'd hired him. He was surprised the Frenchman hadn't given the ETA down to the second. "Charters ready?"

"They are. Two hand-picked crews, one boat for each delegation, positioned at different piers."

"Good." Hildebrand snorted. He'd placed their boats far apart to cut down on potential scuffles between the two groups. "Of course, one will probably complain about having to walk farther than the other."

The Frenchman frowned. "I hadn't considered that eventuality," he said with some annoyance.

"It's a joke, Barbeau. Just be sure to put the Azeris on the one without the full bar. I'm sure some of them don't strictly adhere to their religion's stipulations, but they'll need to ask for a drink if they want one. Can't risk insulting them. Far too much money riding on this."

Laura cleared her throat. "Sir, with your permission, I'd like to make another pass through the two guest houses."

"Yes, do that."

"I should make another sweep as well," Roux said. "I will accompany you."

"That's not necessary..."

But Roux was already exiting the room. "I need to pick up the multi-frequency finder from my security room," he announced over his shoulder.

Laura watched him go, then turned to Hildebrand. "Well, I'm not waiting. Far too much to do."

Hildebrand nodded as she left. "Indeed. So very much to do."

27

Deek crossed the Cape Coral Bridge and made his way through densely packed little homes to the marina and hotel complex off Glover's Bight where the Great American Boat Show was being held. Upon reaching their destination, Deek was informed that on-site parking was full, and he was forced to backtrack to a privately owned, cash-only lot. There, a florid Florida man perched on a folding lawn chair under an umbrella separated Deek from forty dollars of his remaining money. After Boone had covered his airport parking, he couldn't bring himself to beg again. Before leaving the car, Deek grabbed a backpack containing a much-needed change of clothes and a toiletries bag.

At the convention site, while Boone, Em, and AJ checked into their hotel rooms and stashed their luggage, Deek popped into the hotel lobby bathroom, changed out of his clothing in an empty stall, then brushed his teeth and washed his face. Unfortunately, he hadn't packed a razor or shaving cream. He looked in the mirror, running a hand over his stubble. *Meh. Good enough.*

Returning to the lobby, he waited until the others came down, and then the quartet made their way toward the convention and approached the reservations tables. They didn't get very far, when Emily abruptly shouted, "Blimey! Mermaids!"

Off to the side, near the entrance to the main convention floor, two "mermaids" sat: a brunette with a red shimmering tail, and a blonde with a blue tail. Both women wore half-tees with a dive flag formed from the words "Scuba Radio." They flanked a table covered with swag and "World of Boating" and "Just Plane Radio."

"Sorry, mates... but I have to get some pics with the mermaids. I am powerless to resist! C'mon, AJ! Your dive op is Mermaid Divers, so you don't have a choice either!" Emily grabbed AJ by the hand and tugged her toward the Scuba Radio table. "Boone, you're our cameraman!" she called back over her shoulder. "Get your arse over here."

Boone shook his head with a smile plastered on his face. "She's kinda got a thing about mermaids. You go on ahead. Once she's had enough, we'll get some tickets and head in after you. Where's your booth?"

"Back left corner of the exhibition hall."

"Well, we'll find you." With that, he strolled after Emily and AJ.

Deek approached the entrance, digging into the backpack for his boat show ID lanyard. *Not here? Is it in the car?* Shaking his head, he went to the registration desk and extracted his driver's license and one of his business cards. "Deek Morrison... Maritime Administration, Department of Transportation. My apologies, but I'm afraid I've mislaid my ID."

The woman at the table gave him a quizzical look, then adjusted her glasses and peered at her list. "Maritime Administration. Booth #76?"

"Sounds right."

"Funny, I just made up an ID for a gentleman for that booth."

"What? Who?"

"A Mr. Ansari."

Deek's stomach did a flip. Mo Ansari was a fellow analyst in his office—and a Class A suck-up to the higher-ups. *What on earth...?* "Uh... okay. Well, could I get a replacement?"

"Of course, one moment." The woman was already digging through a box on the floor beside her chair. "Let's see your ID again?" She wrote on a card with a pen and slid it into a plastic cardholder. "Mr. Deek Morrison. Here you go." She handed him a lanyard. "Don't lose it!" she said cheerfully.

Deek took it. "Thank you, ma'am," he said, already jog-walking toward the entrance. He spared a glance at the Scuba Radio table. AJ and Emily were currently posing with the mermaids, and Boone was on one knee, clicking away on a smartphone. Deek directed his attention to the entrance, flashed his badge, then plunged into the convention.

A few actual boats were inside the hall, but many of the vessels on offer were represented by large, high-def photos on posterboard—a number of these were docked in the adjacent marina. Deek rushed past booths for Sea Ray, Grady-White, Valhalla, and Newton, before he paused to get his bearings.

"Would you like a T-shirt?" an attractive presenter asked as he passed a booth for Penn fishing gear.

Deek took the T-shirt without thinking, mumbled a thank you to the young woman, and was twenty steps away when he realized he'd forgotten where he was going. What was the booth number? *Seventy-six, back left corner,* his panicked mind managed to recall.

Now with a destination, Deek allowed himself to scan some of the exhibits as he passed. Many of the items—rigid inflatable boats, remotely operated underwater drones, rebreathers—sent his mind down a rabbit hole of all the possible ways they could be used to attack a ship full of diplomats.

Deek scrambled along an aisle to the far wall and dashed down to the back corner, turned right… and froze.

"Morrison! So glad you could join us!" his boss called out, a radiant smile on his face. There was nothing friendly about that smile.

Grady Foster pulled into the parking lot shared by the Gulf Star Marina and the Fort Myers branch of Doc Ford's Rum Bar & Grille. "I love this place," he said, killing the engine. "If we have time, I wanna get a grouper sandwich!" He started to get out.

Angler stopped him with a hand on his arm. "Wait." With a practiced eye, he scanned the other cars in the parking lot, then expanded his gaze to include the surrounding buildings.

"This is where you told him to wait, right?" Foster asked.

"Yeah."

"Something wrong?"

"That's what I'm trying to determine." Angler was still concerned about that chase in Grand Cayman. It was likely that his spectacular plane crash and a few CCTV cameras here and there might have put them onto him, but what if his communication had been compromised? Satisfied with what he saw, he nodded his head—now topped with a baseball cap for the Tampa Bay Rays—and grabbed the brand-new duffel bag at his feet. The waterproof bag from Grand Cayman lay within, but he'd decided that was a bit too conspicuous to be carrying around. "Okay. Let's go."

"You, uh… you might wanna take care of that." Foster pointed at Angler's face.

Angler twisted the SUV's mirror and looked at the beads of blood on the side of his chin. After the chase in Grand Cayman, he'd wanted to lose the goatee, but a quick field shave in the Steak 'n Shake bathroom hadn't gone off without a hitch. Muttering, he licked a thumb and swiped at the damage, then pressed the heel of his hand against it. "Gimme a sec."

A few minutes later, Angler entered the restaurant. On the outside balcony, he found the skipper of the *Beeracuda* sitting at a table overlooking the marina. The man looked up as they approached. "Who's he?"

"A passenger." Angler shared a glance with Foster, then nodded toward the bar inside. "Grab that fish sandwich you were talking about. I'll come get you later."

Foster shrugged and went inside. Angler sat and set the duffel down beside his chair. The skipper's eyes followed it to the floor.

"Where you at?" Angler asked.

"Right down there, end of the pier." He nodded at the dock that ran parallel to the restaurant's balcony.

Angler spotted the boat. "You have the dinghy I requested?"

"Yep."

"Motor good?"

"Inspected it myself. Oil change, new spark plugs... good to go."

Angler nodded. "We'll be here tomorrow morning at seven."

"Half up front," the man reminded him.

"Up front can mean a lot of things," Angler rumbled. "Could be now... could be tomorrow when we board the boat for our little trip. So I'll give you half of the half now, another quarter tomorrow morning."

The skipper looked like he was going to object, but Angler was already unzipping the bag on the floor.

"You eat lunch here while you waited?"

"Yeah."

"What'd you have?"

"Shrimp tacos."

"That's not enough. Have a burger." Angler dropped the takeout bag from his lunch onto the table.

The man looked at it. "I like burgers."

"'Course you do. You're a red-blooded American." Angler stood up and hefted the duffel. "Next burger, you'll get tomorrow morning. Then a couple more once we reach our final destination. I'm a man of my word."

Mr. Powell continued to smile at Deek. Dressed in a full suit, his boss had a lanyard and badge hanging in front of a red tie.

"Sir..." Deek managed, sparing a glance behind his boss. The booth was immaculate and Mo Ansari was busy hawking flyers and beer koozies to the few passersby who had made it to the back wall of the convention. "I... uh... I can explain."

"Oh, that's not necessary, Morrison... how about I explain *for* you? You lied to me yesterday and said the booth was doing well. Then you flew to the Cayman Islands. And on my end of this little charade, I basked in the warmth of your glowing report about how well things were going for about five minutes, before I realized that was all likely horseshit. Mr. Ansari, how many people have actually signed up for our newsletter?"

Ansari snapped to attention. "Three, sir. Four, if you count the guy who signed up as 'Gene Poole' and gave an email address of youmustbekidding@blowme.com."

Powell's cheek twitched. "And how many brochures have we handed out in the past two hours?"

"Lost track, sir... maybe... ten?"

"You see, Morrison? That's a dishearteningly realistic number for an offshoot of the Transportation Department at a boating show. But yesterday, you told me you were—and I quote—'handing out flyers like candy.' Well, once I fully absorbed the ludicrous nature of that statement, I called down here and asked if someone could deliver a message to Booth #76. I was informed there was nobody to receive my message, as Booth #76 was no more than an unoccupied, plastic fold-out table with a haphazard pile of stickers and pamphlets."

"I was just—"

"At which point I booked two last-minute plane tickets for Ansari and myself to come down here and 'show the flag' for the Maritime Administration, since we'd already spent a considerable amount of department funds to book this slot in the convention!"

"Sir, I was right!" Deek blurted. "Şeytan Taciri's operative received a large amount of cash from a bank in Grand Cayman. I have reason to believe he departed in a boat that had gone dark with its transponder off and—"

"What did I say to you two phone calls ago, Morrison?" Powell bellowed, snuffing out Deek's attempt at explanation.

Mo Ansari gave Deek an innocent, raised-eyebrow look, wondering if Deek did, in fact, remember his boss's words.

"I provided you with a very simple if/then statement, Morrison. *'If* you're not behind the counter of our booth when the boat show opens... *then* you will no longer be employed by the Maritime Administration.' Now... were you behind the counter when it opened yesterday?"

Deek swallowed. "No, sir."

"Then you're fired. Give me your badge."

Deek lifted the boat show lanyard. "This, sir?"

"No, you imbecile! Your Maritime Administration badge!"

"I... I don't have a badge, sir."

"You lost your badge, too?" Powell roared in disbelief.

"No, sir. Analysts don't have them, sir."

"They don't?" He turned to Ansari. "You don't?"

Ansari shook his head.

"I have business cards," Deek said quietly.

"Well... give me those."

Deek handed over the three remaining business cards from his wallet. Powell snatched them from his fingers and squinted at them. "These are terrible." He handed them to Ansari. "Make sure we have better cards."

"I'll get right on it, sir!" the sycophant promised.

Deek was already striding away, face flushed, as his boss shouted after him, "Don't expect a letter of recommendation, either!"

Yamaha, Cummins, Shimano, Abu Garcia... Deek surged past presentation booths for marine engines and fishing gear, his awareness of the world shrinking to a tiny pinhole just ahead of him as he searched for the exit. Suddenly, a face entered his narrow focus. "Hey... Deek... what happened?"

Deek halted, blinking. AJ Bailey stood in front of him.

"Boone spotted you and said something was wrong," she said.

"Has something happened?"

Deek looked around, seeing Boone and Emily behind AJ, looking on with concern. "I... uh... I've been fired."

"Oh, shite, I'm sorry mate!" Emily declared, moving to his side and placing a hand on his arm.

"To be honest, I'm surprised he didn't can me a couple of days ago," Deek said, with a sad half-smile on his face.

Emily hugged him from the side while AJ placed a hand on his shoulder. Boone abruptly leaned down and spoke.

"Let me get this straight... you just got fired, because you were supposed to be standing behind a booth handing out brochures and stickers?" he said, a note of disdain in his voice.

"Boone, lighten up, the bloke's just—"

"But meanwhile, you've got a possible terrorist in your sights, with at least some idea of motive," Boone interrupted, "and if you'd been here picking your nose behind a wobbly table, you wouldn't know half of what you know, right?"

Deek nodded. "Yes, that's about right."

"Well, now you've got nothing holding you back."

"I also have no official governmental abilities to help me with my investigation."

"Were they all that helpful before? From what you told us in the car ride, it didn't sound like you were getting much support from your department. Except for... who was it that helped you with tracking that plane? The one you followed to Grand Cayman?"

"Oh, that was my buddy, Pete. But he's not with the Maritime Administration."

"So, that's something you two now have in common," Boone said matter-of-factly.

"Boone!" Emily punched him in the arm.

"No, he's right..." Deek said, frowning.

"Unlike your boss, Pete actually helped you," Boone pointed out. "And he's got some useful skills, right?"

"Yes. He's a fellow boat spotter, but he's got an additional interest in tracking executive jets and private planes. Has a lot of next-level software."

"Perfect," Boone said. "That guy you were chasing? His trail ended on a boat with no transponder, right?"

"Oh! And you think he was heading for Jamaica, yeah?" Emily added. "Probably fly back here from there; so maybe some planes for your mate to track. That's a good next step, innit?"

"Yes… good. I can tell him what to look for, and he can sort through them quickly."

"Right!" AJ added, piling on. "And Roy—Detective Whittaker—likely has some more data by now, so maybe you can determine course and speed. Figure out when they'd have reached the Jamaican coast."

"And maybe the phone came back online at that point," Deek mused. His firing was by no means forgotten, but at least it now had some company in his head. "AJ, can you contact the detective for me? See if there's anything more?"

"Sure thing."

"I'll reach out to Pete; ask him to compile all outbound traffic from Jamaica to South Florida from dawn until now. And there's Kate—that Keys divemaster who called on the drive from Miami? She has quite a few resources at her disposal, too. In fact, I should connect her app-designing friend with Pete. And maybe I can track down Sam Waters. She's the deputy who jumped on the seaplane while it was taking off."

"Brilliant! See, you've got a whole crew, already!" Em pointed down the aisle of exhibits. "And while you wait to hear back from them, why don't you help us look at boats, yeah? I've been salivating at several prospects."

28

Sam Waters continued her patrol around the approaches to the boat show, paying particular attention to the choke point between Glover's Bight and Shell Point. After the incident with the seaplane, Sam's higher-ups had decided to beef up security on the approaches to the boat show. Here, the Caloosahatchee River dipped down from Fort Myers, passing Cape Coral on its way toward San Carlos Bay and Sanibel Island. Aside from pleasure boaters and fisherman, there hadn't been too much traffic—the waters here were relatively shallow, and larger boats were rare.

She was just about to call Dusty and see about a lunch and bathroom break, when a small motor yacht came into view from the direction of Fort Myers. What caught her eye was a tri-color flag flying from a staff aft of the bridge: it looked like a Colombian flag, though the yellow band was more of an orange. As the boat passed, she noted the American flag at the stern. It was unusual to see a foreign flag on a pleasure craft of modest size; Sam estimated the boat's length at no more than fifty feet or so. Sam noted the name on the hull: *Smooth Move*, home port of Fort Myers.

As the *Smooth Move* passed by, Sam spotted another motor yacht of similar size passing Shell Point, and again, this boat was flying a foreign flag, one that Sam didn't recognize. Also tricolor, this one had blue, red, and green bands, and in the center... what was it? She squinted behind her polarized sunglasses. *A star and crescent.* Dropping to idle, Sam took out her smartphone and googled "flag with blue red green and crescent." Google informed her it belonged to Azerbaijan.

"I wonder..." Sam made an assumption that the orange-tinted yellow on the previous flag was indeed orange, and looked up flags with red, blue, and orange. "Curiouser and curiouser," she mumbled, when the result was Armenia. These must be the delegations that Deek had told her about.

Sam scanned the waters near the boat show one last time, before grinning and throttling up, temporarily abandoning her post. She fell into line behind the two boats as they headed into shallower waters to the west.

They passed by Sanibel Island to the south, and Sam hoped the captains knew what they were doing. Last year, Hurricane Ian had roared into the coast, altering many of the channels local boaters had known like the backs of their hands. Sam herself had nearly gone aground on two occasions, in spots that once had several feet of depth.

It wasn't long before the barrier island of Captiva came into view, and the boats turned north. As they neared Baskin Island, they slowed.

"Well, that's interesting," Sam said aloud. She watched the boats as they motored slowly toward the piers alongside the houses on Baskin Island that Hildebrand was staying at. Sam debated following, but figured she better get back to her duties. On the return trip, her phone rang. She half expected it to be Dusty, wondering where the hell she was, but instead she saw the name Jo Jo Tanner on her screen.

"Jo Jo. What's up?"

"Sam," the voice crooned. "Huge yacht just passed by Baskin on the Gulf side. This thing is sexier than Gina Lollobrigida. Where you at, darlin'?"

"Halfway back to Cape Coral. The yacht... can you make out the name?"

"Something Italian. Too far off to make out, now."

"*La Fiamma Azzurra*?"

"That was it. Hot damn, Sam... when a British babe speaks Italian, that's almost too sexy for my old heart."

"*Grazie*," Sam said with a laugh, thinking something similar about the former rock star's velvety voice. "Which way was it headed?"

"North."

"Weird. That yacht was supposed to be the highlight of the boat show," Sam mused.

"The one in Cape Coral?" Jo Jo said with disbelief. "Good luck getting it safely in and out of there. My guess is, it's headed for Boca Grande Pass. Deep enough water to anchor just inside."

"What the hell do you mean, you aren't at the boat show?" Hildebrand shouted into his phone. "Where on earth are you going?"

"I'm sorry, Mr. Hildebrand," the yacht's captain said. "But the water is too shallow in Glover's Bight. And the channels between Sanibel and the boat show are right on the limit of *La Fiamma's* draft in the best of conditions, and after Hurricane Ian, there are still some hazards in the water. The harbor pilot strongly recommended against it."

"You should have told me!"

"Your assistant, Ms. Smythe, signed off on the change of plans, sir."

"What? She's the one who suggested the boat show in the first place!"

"I wouldn't know about that, sir. She sent the pilot out to the ship as we neared Sanibel."

"Laura!"

When there was no reply, Hildebrand stepped out on the balcony and looked toward the two buildings the delegates were housed in. He spotted Laura below, striding purposefully away from a group of security men and aides working for the delegates. She saw him on the balcony and raised a cautionary finger, then waggled it toward the entryway of his home.

Hildebrand raised the phone to his ear as he went back inside. "I have to go. Where are you planning on anchoring tonight?"

"Inside the bay near the Boca Grande Pass," the captain replied.

"Very well. I'll speak to you later." Hildebrand hung up and descended the stairs to the foyer where Laura was waiting for him.

"We have a bit of a problem."

"Yes, I just spoke to the captain."

"What? Oh, that. No, this is something else. The Azeri delegation is complaining that their accommodations are inferior to the Armenians'. I'd like to shift them to Enoch's house to the south."

Hildebrand frowned. "But it's exactly the same."

"Yes, but I took the lead aide aside and told him it was the cleanest of the three, and had the best water pressure."

"Is that true?"

"No idea. But what really sold it was pointing out that the balcony up top would give them the best view for qibla."

"I'm not familiar with that term."

"It's the direction to the sacred shrine in Mecca. For daily prayers."

"Ah... very good. Have you checked with Enoch?"

"Yes, sir. It took some persuasion, but eventually he was amenable. So, with your permission... I'll have the staff prepare it."

"Yes, go ahead." When Laura turned to go, Hildebrand stopped her. "Wait. What's going on with *La Fiamma Azzurra*?"

"Yes, I'm sorry about that. Amendments had to be made. I was unaware of the changes to the depth around the boat show due to the recent hurricane."

"That's not like you," Hildebrand observed. "Using the boat

show as a cover for the negotiations aboard the yacht was *your* idea."

"I apologize. I'm afraid I had too many balls in the air. But the harbor pilot I found suggested an alternative plan. In fact, he's suggested an excellent spot to anchor for the negotiations, off the Gasparilla Island Lighthouse."

Hildebrand sighed. "Fine."

"Tomorrow morning, the captain will bring her back out to the Gulf and position her near Captiva Pass," Laura continued. "The security teams will then go over and sweep the boat. Once they are satisfied, we can send the delegations over."

"Does Monsieur Roux know all this?"

"Not yet. I haven't seen him in several hours."

"Did you call him?" When Laura shook her head, Hildebrand frowned. "Why on earth not?"

Laura shrugged. "I don't particularly like him."

Hildebrand laughed. "Well, that's an honest answer. Roux is an acquired taste—a bit like a stinky French cheese. Never mind, I'll fill him in on the changes."

After she left, Hildebrand sent a text: *Change of plans.*

On the outskirts of town, Angler and Foster removed the last of the bags from the storage locker and placed them in the back of the SUV. Angler's phone buzzed and he pulled off one of his gloves with his teeth and retrieved the phone to check the text that had just come in. A second message came up as he was reading the first and he scanned the details of the newcomer.

"We on?" Foster asked, when Angler returned his phone to his pocket.

"We are. A few changes, though."

"No plan ever survives contact with the enemy," Foster intoned.

Angler snorted. "I've lost track of how many adjustments we've had to make. This one's no different. In fact... looks like an improvement."

Foster rolled the self-storage unit's door closed. He took the lock in a gloved hand and snapped it into place. "We just gonna leave it empty? Do we gotta cancel the lease?"

"It'll cancel when the prepaid debit card we booked it with runs out. C'mon, let's get on the road."

While Foster navigated back toward Fort Myers, Angler looked at the GPS coordinates he'd just been provided. The original location for his op had been north-northeast of Sanibel, but now the anchoring had changed. The new location was nearly twenty miles to the northwest, just offshore from Gasparilla Island. "Better."

"What's that?" Foster asked.

"Where we're going tomorrow. Better location. Less boat traffic, fewer people. I wasn't thrilled with our proximity to Sanibel and Fort Myers Beach. And the visibility will be a hell of a lot better for us than in the bay." He looked over at Foster. "How long since you last dived?"

"Been a year or two, but hey, it's like falling off a bicycle."

Angler continued to look at his phone, running through some contingencies. Finally, he nodded and looked at the road ahead. "Okay. It's on."

"There's Aventura!" Emily announced. The group angled toward a corner booth with beautiful posters displaying an array of catamaran boats. Deek trailed behind, looking at his messages. An email had just come in from Kate down in Shark Key. There was a transfer link tied to a sizeable PDF; he tapped on it and watched the glacial pace of the download.

"Check it out," Boone said, pointing at one of the photo-posters. "They make a sargassum harvester. The Aventura Clean Cat."

"Ace!" Emily turned to AJ. "In South Caicos, we met a woman from the States who had designed one."

Boone approached one of the men at the booth and began asking questions.

"I better get in on this, Aidge," Emily said, inventing a new nickname for AJ on the spot. "Otherwise, Boone will pick something without enough pep!"

AJ laughed and looked around at Deek, who was engrossed in something on his phone. She peeked at the screen. "A watched pot never downloads."

"Hmm? Oh. Yes. These are the blueprints for Hildebrand's super yacht that Kate's friend managed to locate. Or… steal, probably." His phone dinged in his hand and he glanced at the pop-up. "Actually… she's here!"

"Who? Kate?"

"Yes! I forgot, she said she might come and check out the boat show."

"Tell her to come and see the Aventuras," AJ suggested.

Ten minutes later, Kate arrived, dressed in cargo shorts and a black tank top, with a frayed plaid flannel her only nod to the season. Deek made the introductions, and Emily instantly treated Kate like a bosom buddy.

"Shame you aren't British, though," she mused. "We'd've had a trifecta. Although, with a name like Kingsbury, I think we can let you into the club as an honorary member."

"Do I have to drink tea?"

"Oh, God no. AJ and I are java junkies."

"Deek, did you get the blueprints?"

"Should have them by now." He looked at his phone. "Yes, download complete."

"Something very interesting in there," Kate said. "After the overall plans in the beginning of the PDF, the diagrams are stacked by floor. Scroll down to the bilge."

"Okay…" Deek did so, then frowned. It looked like there was a hatch in the bottom of the hull, amidships. "What on earth is that?"

"Back up one level to the first deck above the bilge."

"Looks like a… what do you call that? They had something like that in the movie, *The Abyss*."

"It's a moon pool. They have them on some marine research vessels and drilling platforms. Provides divers with easy access."

"Maybe they have an expedition submarine or something," AJ suggested, as the others gathered around to look at the screen.

"Too small for that," Boone said. "And not much of a wet room. Almost looks like it opens into a storage area."

"And look, it's right next to the galley and the pantry. That's weird, innit?"

Kate brought the blueprints up on her phone, so they wouldn't have to crowd around a single screen. After the group examined the super yacht in more detail, the rep from Aventura came over.

"Sorry to interrupt, but I just completed the background check for you and your dive company, Mr. Fischer and Ms. Durand. I'm sorry to hear about the loss of your boat, but am glad you came to us. Were you interested in test driving one of the multi-hull dive boats tomorrow?"

"Yes! Do you have an Arawak here?"

"Of course. Excellent choice. Top speed of twenty-four knots, excellent fuel economy, and with only two and a half feet of draft, she can do beach pickups."

"Great. We'd love to take her out in the Gulf and do a dive from it. We'll pay you for your time."

"Well, I won't be driving, you can arrange a payment with the captain, Ernesto."

"Ladies and gentlemen, may I have your attention," please, the convention sound system announced. "We are sorry to report that *La Fiamma Azzurra*, the featured super yacht of the Great American Boat Show will not be displayed, due to a change in her itinerary. However, there will be plenty of other vessels to enjoy. We apologize for the inconvenience and thank you for your time."

Everyone looked at Deek, who was staring into the middle distance, thinking hard. He fumbled with his phone and opened his boat tracking app. Hildebrand's super yacht was bookmarked and he pulled it up.

"Where is it?" Kate asked.

"Just inside the bay, below Boca Grande. Not far from Baskin Island, where Mr. Hildebrand is staying." He looked up. "Do you mind if I come on the test drive tomorrow? Turns out my schedule is quite clear."

"Sure thing!" Emily said. "Do you dive?"

"No, but I'd like to be aboard. But speaking of diving..." He held up the map on the tracker app and pointed to the area around Boca Grande. "Could you maybe ask if there are any dive sites near here?"

29

The sky on the bayside was glowing with the imminent sunrise, when Hildebrand joined Laura at the docks where the tenders from the yacht would soon arrive. Hildebrand was wearing one of his power suits and Laura had on a light blue pantsuit.

She gave Hildebrand a nod. "The Azeris have finished their dawn prayer and both security teams should be here shortly. The captain of the yacht just launched the tenders."

"Yes, yes... good." Hildebrand seemed distracted, glancing at his phone.

"Everything all right, sir?"

"Just some... business." He pocketed the phone. "I'm not used to being kept waiting when I text someone."

"Would you like me to...?"

"No. Personal matter. So! Are we ready for the big day?"

"I believe so," Laura said. "Ah, here they come."

The security teams for the two delegations approached, the Azeris on one side and the Armenians on the other. Monsieur Roux walked between the two groups, ensuring everyone behaved themselves. Both teams consisted of three men: two aides/bodyguards and one ambassador.

"Welcome!" Hildebrand said. "The captain of *La Fiamma Azzurra* is offshore and her tenders should be coming through Captiva Pass shortly."

One of the Azeri security men spoke. "Whichever tender comes first, we will take that one. The Armenians had the first boat coming here. We will go first now."

A burly Armenian bodyguard started to argue. The Armenian ambassador, a somber man with a heavy five o'clock shadow, placed a hand on his argumentative aide's shoulder and shook his head. He spoke in accented English. "This is fine. It is fair. But we search the yacht at the same time."

"Yes, that is the plan," Hildebrand said. "The security sweep will be conducted simultaneously. Monsieur Roux will accompany you and ensure everything is done properly." Both ambassadors nodded.

The argumentative Armenian acquiesced, then looked over at one of the Azeris who appeared to be the oldest of the three. He caught the Armenian's eye and gave a single nod.

"See?" Hildebrand said, beaming. "Common ground already!"

"Permission to come aboard?" Angler asked. The captain of the *Beeracuda* looked up.

"Depends. You got a burger for me?"

"Cooked to order, medium rare," Angler said. "But I'm fresh out of to-go bags, so let's do that song-and-dance out of range of marina security cameras, what do you say?"

The skipper laughed. "Works for me. Come aboard."

Angler stepped across and turned back to Foster, who started handing four gear bags across.

"Hey dude, welcome aboard," a youthful voice said. "Where do you want these?"

Angler turned his head to see a young man who would probably be categorized as a "surfer dude" reaching down to grab one of the gear bags.

"Don't touch that!" Angler roared, channeling his drill sergeant from basic training.

The kid jerked his hand back, like he'd touched a hot stove. "Whoa, chill dude, chill..."

"Who the hell are you?"

"Justin, man."

"He's my first mate for your little excursion," the skipper said, intervening physically between the two. "He's a good waterman, and he doesn't ask questions."

Angler gave Justin a hard look, then swung that gaze onto the captain. "You're vouching for him, then?"

"Yes. I need him for the crossing to... well, to your 'southerly destination.' That still part of the plan?"

"It is. After we get back from the dive."

"And if you want to operate the dinghy away from the *Beeracuda* while you two do whatever it is you're going to do, then you need one of us in each boat. No way in hell I'm leaving the *Beeracuda* unattended."

"We'll be handling the dinghy on our own," Angler said. "If you need him for the crossing... fine. But collect his phone."

The captain nodded. "Fair enough."

"Foster... run back to the SUV and get the rebreathers."

"What is this?" the beefy Armenian asked.

"It is called a 'dumbwaiter,' I believe," Roux replied. "It's a small elevator that brings up food and drink from the galley."

An Azeri bodyguard frowned at the curved door on the wall opposite one end of the conference table. "Why is it stupid?"

Roux looked at the man like he'd lost his mind, before realizing the double meaning of the word. "Oh... no... it is the English word 'dumb' that means unable to speak. A waiter that brings you food or drink but doesn't talk."

He muttered to himself in Azeri and the Frenchman instinctively knew the man was complaining about the complexities of English.

The other members of the security team were busily scanning for listening devices and cameras. This dining room would be the site of the actual negotiations, and was receiving a thorough examination.

The big Armenian punched a button on the side of the dumbwaiter and the doors slid open, revealing two cling-wrapped plates of grapes, cheeses, olives, and bread. "The word galley. Is kitchen?" the security man asked, frowning at the spread.

"Yes. On a boat, a kitchen is called a galley. And a bathroom is called a head."

Overhearing this, the Azeri bodyguard rolled his eyes and muttered anew.

"You can't blame all the English for that," Roux said with a chuckle, "just the sailors. And if you think English words are a mess, you should see all the nautical terms."

"I want to see this… galley," the Armenian said.

"You shall examine every deck, if you wish," Roux said. "I thought we should start here, in the conference room, since this is where the delegations will carry out the negotiations." Roux leaned forward and pressed the button beside the dumbwaiter, sealing the door. "Let us continue to the bridge, then I will take you to the lower decks."

Aboard the bridge, Roux introduced the men to the captain. Both teams asked the man a number of questions, until Roux checked his watch and cleared his throat. "Each delegation may assign one security member to the bridge, if you wish."

The burly Armenian held up a hand. "What about the jamming you promised. No information of these negotiations may leak to the outside world."

Roux nodded. "You will be pleased to know Mr. Hildebrand has outfitted this vessel with the latest in electronic jamming equipment. Once active, no cell phone or radio will function within five kilometers. Additionally, drones will lose their signal if they approach."

Both teams seemed pleased and Roux gestured toward the exit. "We're running behind. Let's proceed to the other decks."

Twenty minutes later, the sweep reached the bottom level. Roux took them through the galley, letting the teams check the kitchen, freezer, and pantry.

"Why is this door locked?" an Azeri asked, pulling on the handle of a hatch beside the galley.

"The room beyond is not yet complete, and there are hazards. Mr. Hildebrand ordered that it be sealed off. No one aboard has access."

"What is there?"

"At the moment, nothing. Now, if everyone is satisfied, we should return to the shore and pick up your diplomats for the negotiations. Mr. Hildebrand has a precise timetable in mind."

In the hotel lobby, Deek was nose down in his phone. A text from Nora had come in, confirming the money the tour guide had been given had indeed come from the funds that had been withdrawn in Grand Cayman. Furthermore, the phone number that belonged to a "Wayne Daniels" that had gone dead off the coast had not been active since. Neither of these data points were anything Deek hadn't expected.

On the other hand, his own research had borne fruit late last night. With his buddy Pete's help, they'd been able to examine flights coming out of the airports in western Jamaica yesterday morning, and there had been several commercial flights from Montego Bay... but Deek was now certain "Mr. Daniels" had not flown out of there. An unscheduled flight had landed in a small aerodrome in Negril, a coastal town that was much closer to Grand

Cayman. The plane—a LearJet 36A—had landed at 9:57 a.m. and taken off again fifteen minutes later.

Then things got interesting. The plane flew across Cuba, which wasn't something you could typically do on short notice. Then, it landed in Key West. At this point, Deek had felt a tinge of disappointment, until Pete pointed out that it had taken off twenty minutes later and flown to Fort Myers, but instead of landing at the main airport just out of town, it landed at Page Field, a general aviation airfield closer to the river.

"If this is your guy, why go to Key West first?" Pete had asked.

"He wanted to clear customs somewhere else," Deek had replied. He'd asked Pete to see if that particular plane had done any other unscheduled trips in the last six months, and if there were any ties to Hildebrand or any of his companies. Then, he'd allowed himself to nod off in a plush chair in the lobby. A man from the front desk night shift came over to check on him, and Deek had explained that "marital troubles" had led him to seek solace in the lobby.

Now, after a fitful sleep and another lobby restroom sponge bath, he felt quasi-human again, as he sipped burnt hotel-urn coffee and looked at the blueprints for the super yacht. His attention was drawn to the superstructure, which had an unusually large number of antennae, above and beyond what he'd seen on most pleasure craft.

He was debating a coffee refill from the hotel's complimentary breakfast nook, when he raised his head and found Kate and AJ looking down at him.

"Oh… hi. I mean… good morning."

"You okay, Deek?" Kate asked.

"Yeah, no offense, mate," AJ added, "but you look like shite."

"Uh… problem with my room. Long story. Is it time to go?"

"No, we're not due at the dock until 9:00 a.m.," AJ said. "You've still got an hour, but…" She grinned and looked at Kate.

"Hold out your hand," she said. When Deek did so, she dropped two pills in his hand.

"What are these?"

"Motion sickness pills. They take about an hour to take effect. You may be in a profession involving boats, but I have a vivid memory of the shade of green your face was, the last time we were on a boat together."

Deek's face turned a shade of red and he gave a rueful chuckle. "The irony isn't lost on me. But it looks like I might be looking for a new line of work, anyway." He looked at the pills. "One or both?"

"Two may make you drowsy, so maybe start with one."

"Thanks." He used the remainder of his cold coffee to take one of the pills.

Kate pointed at Deek's chest. "You fish?"

"Hmm?" Deek looked down and realized he was wearing the Penn fishing gear T-shirt the booth presenter had given him yesterday. "Oh, this… no. Someone gave it to me at the boat show. I'm running short of clean clothes."

"We're going for breakfast at the restaurant by the water," AJ said. Boone and Emily are already there, and Em said we'd better hurry or Boone'll clean 'em out."

Deek stuffed his laptop into the backpack. "Lead the way."

"Good morning!" an older man in an Aventura polo shirt called out from the dock. "I am Ernesto, your captain for today." He spoke with an accent of some sort, likely Dominican. Deek had looked them up last night, and had learned the company was founded by a French naval architect, and were based in the Dominican Republic. A young man was with Ernesto, wearing a logo shirt as well.

"Beautiful boat!" Kate declared, as they came alongside the catamaran.

"Thank you! I agree. The Arawak is my personal favorite. Fast… large, but not too large… and can handle very shallow water. I see you have your gear. How many of you will be diving?"

"Three," Boone said. "Deek and I will stay up top and check out the boat, but these three ladies will be doing the diving."

"*Bueno.* And I understand all of you are divemasters or dive instructors, yes?"

"We are indeed," Emily said. "And we signed that waiver thingy, so you're covered."

Ernesto laughed. "Very good. Since you are all skilled, may I ask that you assist with the running of the boat? Young Carlos here, is needed on another charter."

"Fine by us," Boone said. "We're hoping to do most of the skippering anyway. Test drive and all."

"Yes, of course. And I understand you have requested to go out in the Gulf to test the top speed, and then dive up near Boca Grande?"

"Well… that's assuming there are any dive sites up there," Kate said. "This area isn't exactly a hotbed of scuba diving."

"Actually, there is a relatively new wreck dive up there!" Ernesto declared. "I asked around, and learned that a small pleasure craft sunk during Hurricane Ian. They added a dive mooring to the spot only last month. I have the coordinates."

"Then let's get this show on the road," Boone announced, stepping across to the Arawak and turning back to help bring aboard everyone's gear.

"You see that buoy there?" the captain of the *Beeracuda* asked. "That's the new wreck dive they just added."

"What's the depth?" Angler asked.

The captain glanced at his gauges. "Just over thirty." He turned and called out, "Justin! Hook the mooring line."

"Belay that!" Angler barked.

"Be-what?" Justin asked, boat hook in hand.

"We're not diving now and we're not doing it from this boat. That's what the dinghy's for." Angler looked toward the distant shore. The houses along the beach were just visible. "I want you to take us further into the Gulf, eight miles from this spot."

The captain raised an eyebrow, then shrugged. "It's your charter."

Angler went aft and Foster rose from a bench. "I hear you right? Eight miles?"

"I want this boat to be completely out of view from any vessels close to shore. Given the height of the yacht's superstructure, they'll be able to detect it, but it'll just look like a fisherman." Angler checked his watch. "We'll bring the dinghy back and tie up to the mooring. I want to be in the water by 10:45."

30

Sam brought her boat closer to Baskin Island and slowed to an idle. Retrieving her binoculars, she trained them on the shore. The docks beside the cluster of homes were crowded, with the two motor yachts she'd trailed yesterday tied up on either side of one pier, and Hildebrand's own motor yacht, the *Aeolus*, snugged up against another one further to the south. There was quite a bit of activity on shore at the moment.

She had talked Dusty into scrounging up a replacement to play harbor patrol near the boat show; this seemed like where she needed to be this morning. Sam glassed the group near the northernmost dock. Two expensive-looking, open-topped limousine tenders were tied up there, no doubt from *La Fiamma Azzurra*.

Two separate groups of men boarded each tender. On the shore, two men and a woman remained. Sam recognized one as the billionaire Harold Hildebrand, and the woman was Laura, whom Sam had met a few days ago. The other man was unfamiliar, but from his military bearing and alert posture, she imagined he was a bodyguard of some kind.

Hildebrand and the other man then split off from Laura and boarded one tender, while Laura went aboard the other. In moments, crew members cast off, and both tenders motored toward Captiva Pass to the north. Sam set down the binoculars and throttled up, keeping a respectable distance.

"Welcome aboard *La Fiamma Azzurra*, gentlemen," Hildebrand said with a beaming smile. "Monsieur Roux, would you take our guests up to the conference room?"

"But of course." The bodyguard gestured toward a set of stairs at the far end of the tender bay. "This way, if you please."

The trip from the bay had been uneventful, and the limousine tenders were currently tied up at the extendable swim platform. While the ambassadors followed Roux, Hildebrand gestured for Laura to come join him.

"Is everything aboard ready?" he asked.

"Yes, sir. Do you wish to go over the materials for the negotiations?"

"No need," Hildebrand said, tapping his temple. "It's all up here." He laughed. "I was about to say I wrote most of it, but I didn't... *you* did, actually. And a very fine job you did, too. You absorbed the intricacies of the Azeri-Armenian conflict and the specifications of the pipeline project in record time."

"I've always been a quick study, sir."

"Still, I'm grateful. When your predecessor passed away so suddenly, I confess I was ready to delay this entire venture! Meeting with you that very day was a godsend. And your skill with languages, that was an added bonus!"

Laura blushed. "Thank you, sir." She looked toward the stairs that led to the upper decks. "Are we going up?"

Hildebrand looked at his watch. "No... not yet."

A crewman came over. "Shall I bring the tenders aboard, sir?"

"That won't be necessary," Hildebrand replied. "Leave them as they are."

"Woooo!" Emily cried as she skippered the Arawak across the shallow waters of the Gulf. "Good to be behind the wheel again! How's your tummy doin', Deeky?"

"I don't want to jinx it, but… so far, so good."

The boat sped along the coast of Sanibel before turning north along the barrier islands. Deek looked toward shore as they passed Baskin Island, scanning for any activity in the nearest channel.

"Em, if you're diving, better get below and gear up," Boone suggested. "Ernesto, okay if I take the wheel?'

"Of course! That is the point of a test drive, after all."

While Boone piloted and Kate, AJ, and Emily geared up below, Deek examined the GPS on the console. "Ernesto, this waypoint is the location of that wreck dive?"

"Yes. We should be there very shortly. Boca Grande is just to the northeast."

Deek took out his phone and tapped on his boat tracker, but the app seemed to be having trouble connecting. *Strange, we're not that far offshore. Should be plenty of signal.*

A moment later, Ernesto gasped. "*¡Caramba!* Look at the size of her!"

Deek looked up from his phone and spied the super yacht up ahead, anchored in the Gulf.

"That is the yacht that was supposed to be at the boat show, I believe," Ernesto said.

"*La Fiamma Azzurra*," Deek breathed. He pocketed his phone. No need for the tracker, now. There she was, plain as day.

Emily came up the ladder, outfitted in a three-mil wetsuit with lime-green sleeves and side-stripes. "Cor blimey, she's stonkin' huge, yeah?"

"She looks like she's at anchor," Deek said, squinting in the sun. He had no idea what had happened to his sunglasses.

Emily took off her huge, pink shades and handed them to him. "Here, mate. I won't need these shortly."

Deek put the enormous sunglasses on, and Emily stifled a snicker.

"Suits you," she assured him.

"Are they anchored at the dive site?" Boone asked.

"No, the buoy is right up ahead. The yacht is probably a half kilometer away. But there's another boat already on the mooring."

"Oh, bollocks," Em muttered.

"It's all right, we can keep station," Ernesto said. "I'd prefer that to waiting for them to come up."

As they approached, they could see it was a small dinghy, empty of occupants.

"They might just be spearfishing," Boone suggested. "We can always hook on later, if they come up while you're down."

"Right-o! Time to get wet!" Emily descended to join the others.

In short order, Emily, AJ, and Kate were suited up and Boone surrendered the wheel to Ernesto and went below to assist the divers. Deek came down to watch. All three women were highly experienced divers, so the assistance was more of a courtesy than a necessity. The divers dropped in and gathered near the dinghy, ducking their heads, searching.

"I can see the wreck," AJ called back to the boat. "No divers, no bubbles in sight."

"Well, keep an eye out," Boone cautioned. "If they are spearfishing, they might attract a shark or two."

"Hope so!" Kate called. "I love sharks!"

Emily laughed. "Well, we'll steer them your way. Okay, let's blow some bubbles!"

The three descended.

Skimming over the sand, Angler gripped his outstretched left arm with his right, the compass on that wrist positioned below his eyes. In moments, the massive hull of the super yacht came into view, casting a shadow on the bottom. Angler glanced over at Foster. The younger man clearly remembered his diving skills and was easily keeping up. He flashed an "OK" sign at Angler, indicating he'd seen their target.

Approaching along the bottom, Angler spared a glance up at the looming hull of the vessel. Normally, an underwater assault such as this would be done at night, but in this case the meeting was set to begin at noon, and they only had this window between the security sweeps and the beginning of the conference. Each diver wore a LAR V Draeger rebreather, which eliminated the telltale stream of bubbles that a standard scuba unit would emit. In addition, each had a drybag strapped to their chest. Both men had some personal gear, and Foster's bag contained their payload while Angler's had all of the remaining money from Grand Cayman. He had decided that leaving it aboard was an unnecessary risk. While he was sure the captain of the *Beeracuda* was well aware that motoring away with the cash while Angler was diving would be signing his own death warrant, he'd rather avoid the hassle of having to track the guy down and kill him.

Reaching the underside of the yacht, Angler spotted the moon pool hatch and swam up to it. He detached a fob that was clipped to his vest and held it over a plate by the edge of the hatch. There was an audible clunk, and the hatch slid open sideways. Angler held up a hand to Foster. *Wait.*

Ascending into the pool, Angler lifted his mask from the water. The room was pitch black. Retrieving a headlamp, he strapped it over the balaclava diving hood and switched it on. The room was twenty-by-twenty, with several unfinished walls and surfaces. A variety of construction materials lay in corners. Angler ducked back under and signaled Foster to join him.

He hauled himself up onto the edge of the moon pool and removed the rebreather system and drybag, then turned to assist Foster.

"Whew! That was a workout!" the man said, when he had removed his gear. He stripped off his mask and started to take off his hood, but Angler stopped him.

"No. Leave that on. There might be some kitchen staff in the galley. We shouldn't encounter any, but just in case. Harder to ID us, if we're spotted."

"And if we *are* spotted?" Foster asked, unzipping his drybag and extracting a pistol with an attached suppressor.

"We do this right, none of the wage-earners get hurt," Angler said. "And I'd prefer to keep it that way. You use that only if we encounter security."

"Roger."

Angler examined the fore and aft walls. "Engine room is back that way, and the galley, pantry, and freezer are all on this side. And if my 'benefactor' was telling me the truth, there should be a ventilation panel behind this empty shelving unit. Gimme a hand."

Foster assisted, and the two men shifted the metal shelving aside, revealing a large vent at deck level. He twisted the metal catches on the corners and removed the grate.

Foster leaned over and looked through. "Not exactly an HVAC vent, is it?"

"Window dressing," Angler said, then got on his hands and knees and crawled through. "Hand me the bag," he said, once he was inside the shaft.

Foster pushed his drybag into the opening and followed it. The two men found themselves in an alcove of a large pantry.

"Sweet! Barbecue potato chips!" Foster exclaimed, grabbing a snack-sized bag.

Angler shushed him, then removed several large containers of cooking oil from a shelf. "Here we go."

"That the backdoor access to the elevator thingie?" Foster asked, indicating a small panel behind the shelving unit. He quietly tore open the chips and shoved a handful in his mouth, crunching loudly. When Angler gave him a look, he said, "C'mon, that was a long, hard swim. I need the carbs." He grabbed another packet of chips and shoved it into his bag. "And one for the road."

Angler sighed and turned his attention to the panel. There was a small control unit to the side with a green button, a red button, a button with the image of a padlock on it, and up and down arrows. He punched the green button and the panel opened, revealing an empty shaft, illuminated by cracks on the far wall. *Probably the main access to the galley on the other side,* he thought. He checked his watch, then punched the "down" button. "Give me the device."

Foster opened his bag and extracted the curved metal box. Angler took it and waited. After a moment, the dumbwaiter arrived from above with a cling-wrapped tray of appetizers. Angler smushed the device into the tray of olives and cheeses and stepped back. He pressed the red button and the panel slid closed, obscuring the device's embossed warning: FRONT TOWARD ENEMY.

Angler punched the lock button and it lit up orange. "Done. Go." He dropped to his knees and scrabbled back to the room with the moon pool, the crunch of potato chips following behind. Three minutes later, the two men were geared up and back in the water.

Emily, Kate, and AJ had given the wreck a thorough examination. Having gone down during Hurricane Ian, the pleasure craft was still in good shape, with many of its fittings in place, although saltwater corrosion had begun its dirty work in some spots. The name on the hull was still visible, and seemed appropriate for the unfortunate vessel: *Ship Happens.*

The boat had settled upright and marine life had found this new artificial reef and made themselves at home: squirrel fish were tucked into various places and a school of glassy sweepers were hiding out in the V-berth. The antennae of several lobsters waved from an opening under the hull at the sandy bottom.

The trio of divers were currently in the sand, examining a pair of tiny pipefish in a bed of seagrass, when Em spotted movement on the far side of the wreck. Visibility in the Gulf varied greatly depending on the tides, and she guessed there was about fifty feet of viz at the moment. She ascended from the sand and gave a quick flutter kick toward the submerged boat.

As she rose above the deck of the wreck she spotted two divers in wetsuits on their way to the mooring line, swimming fast. Both wore full hoods and had bags strapped to their chests, but what stood out the most was the lack of bubbles. In lieu of a tank of air or Nitrox, the two men had boxy contraptions on their backs.

Not your run of the mill recreational divers, Emily thought, *and they're in a hurry.* She turned around to find Kate and AJ looking up at her. She fired off a rapid series of hand signals: she pointed at herself, then pointed two fingers at her eyes, raised the other hand and held up two fingers, then flattened both palms and paddled her hands like fins. *I... see... two... divers.* As AJ and Kate finned toward her, Em pulled out the little slate she kept in a pocket of her BCD. Using the attached pencil, she scrawled a single word and turned the slate to face them. *Rebreathers.*

Kate looked at the slate, then took the pencil and wrote *Yacht?* Then she pointed off to the northwest.

AJ nodded, then jerked her thumb up, suggesting they ascend. Kate and Em flashed "OK" signs and all three kicked hard for the dive boat.

"Woo!" Foster whooped as he broke the surface and started to shrug out of his gear.

"Pipe down," Angler hissed, pushing his Draeger into the dinghy. "Sound travels far across open water."

Foster rolled over the side and into the boat, then helped Angler join him.

Angler pulled off his mask and hood, but froze as he heard the sound of an idling motor.

"We've got company," Foster said.

Angler looked up and spotted the catamaran a hundred yards away. There were several men aboard, dressed in casual tropical clothing. One man, wearing overly large pink sunglasses, looked right at him. A tall man at the wheel said something to his companion.

"Oh, shit."

"What?" Foster asked, releasing the mooring.

"I know that guy. In fact, I think I know the tall guy next to him, too… from a few years ago." Angler settled in by the motor. "Stay frosty, but keep it chill. We're just two divers, done for the day. I'll head for shore, then change course once we're out of sight."

Angler throttled up to cruising speed, trying his best to look casual.

"That's him!" Deek said. "He's shaved his goatee, but I'm sure it's him."

"This is gonna sound weird, but he looked familiar to me, too." Boone slipped a hand into a pocket of his cargo shorts and grabbing a compact set of birding binoculars, he trained them on the dinghy.

"You carry binoculars?"

"When I had my own boat, they were always by the wheel. Been carrying them ever since… whoa, hang on. I know that guy."

"Which one?" Deek asked. He didn't recognize the younger man who was with Daniels.

"The older one who looks like he could snap you in half without breaking a sweat. He's a mercenary."

"How on earth do you know that?"

"That's a whole 'nother story for some other time," Boone said, his binos still trained on the boat as it sped away. "Ernesto, can you radio the Coast Guard?"

"I'm already trying, but there's something wrong with the radio. It's static." A moment later, he added, "And there is no signal on my phone!"

"Those aerials on the bridge of the yacht!" Deek blurted. "They must be some form of jammer. We've got to get after them!"

"No can do," Boone said. "We've got divers in the water, and besides… there isn't a doubt in my mind that they're armed. And we aren't."

Beside the mooring buoy, bubbles appeared, and AJ, Kate, and Emily broke the surface. Ernesto pulsed the engine and coasted toward them.

"Boone," Emily cried out, "did you see the two guys get in the dinghy?"

"We did. Grade A certified bad guys, we think. You three okay?"

"Yeah, but… Boone, they had on rebreathers… and I'm pretty sure they came from the direction of the yacht."

"The hatch!" Deek shouted. "The… Kate, what did you call it?"

"A moon pool. Yeah, they could've gotten on the yacht, dropped something off…"

"Like a bomb," Deek said.

"Radio them!" AJ shouted. "Warn them!"

"No can do, Deek thinks that yacht is throwing off some kind of electronic jamming."

"Well, then we'll have to do this the old-fashioned way," AJ said, swimming for the Arawak. "Drive up and yell at them! C'mon, let's get aboard."

31

Bobbing in the Gulf just north of the super yacht in her Lee County Sheriff launch, Sam examined it with her binoculars. She could see a man with an assault rifle on a catwalk alongside the bridge. *And if there's one on this side, there's likely one on the other,* she thought. She had watched the two groups of men exit the tenders and board the ship, along with Laura, Hildebrand, and the bodyguard. This must be the meeting that Deek was concerned about. If there was indeed a terrorist, were they already aboard?

Both limousine tenders lay moored at the aft platform. Sam was debating approaching the vessel and demanding a "routine inspection" when a small boat appeared from behind the yacht, dashing for the shore. *La Fiamma Azzurra* was so massive, it had obscured that boat, and she guessed it was about a quarter mile south of the yacht. It looked to be a small dinghy, and looking through her binos she could just make out two men. She immediately throttled up and moved to intercept, but once she'd cleared the obstruction of the yacht she saw a second boat; a catamaran of some kind. Since the dinghy was moving at a good clip, she might not be able to catch it anyway, so she turned her attention to the catamaran.

Moments later, she came alongside it and found three women and three men aboard. And one of the men...

"Sam?"

"Deek? What are you doing here? And what on earth are you wearing?"

"What? Oh, these." Deek stowed the pink sunglasses on the neck of his T-shirt. "Sam, thank God you're here! Two divers just came from that yacht. The ship has a moon-pool hatch on the underside, amidships. We think they may have left some sort of bomb."

"Bugger! I'll call it in!"

"You can try, but..."

"What's up with the radio? All static."

"Jamming from the yacht. We were just on our way to warn them."

"I'd advise against that. You were right about the Armenia and Azerbaijan meeting, and they've got a lot of security. Some blokes with some big guns are aboard."

"Blimey, are you English, too?" Emily called out, then sobered. "Sorry, not the time for bonding banter. What do you suggest we do?"

"I'll warn them. You can follow, but keep a respectable distance."

Boone turned to Ernesto. "I realize this isn't what you signed up for..."

"I was in the Dominican Navy for six years," the man said, steel in his eyes. "If we can save lives, we should do so."

"We'll keep well clear, all the same," Boone said.

"Look, I realize this is a little crazy," Kate ventured, "but maybe we should stay geared up. If they won't let Sam approach, we could go to that underwater hatch ourselves."

"I'm game if you are," AJ said to Emily.

Kate held up a hand. "Umm... just so I'm clear here... there may be a bomb aboard?"

Deek went to look at his watch, only to find a band of pale skin. "Dammit. What time is it?"

Emily lifted her wrist and looked at her dive computer. "Quarter to twelve."

"I bet they start the negotiations at noon. If there *is* a bomb, and I'm right about the timing... whatever happens will probably happen when all the delegates are in the same room."

As Sam turned her boat to the north and throttled up, Boone followed.

"Right-o, so we've got a few minutes before kablooey," Em said. "Wonderful."

"We'll begin the negotiations shortly," Laura announced. "If all of you will take your seats around the table. Ambassadors here, on either side of the head of the table. Mr. Hildebrand will sit here between you, and act as a referee."

"Where is he?" an Azeri bodyguard asked.

"He will be here shortly, I assure you. Last minute business. He insisted you begin without him."

"Is there any food?" the Azeri inquired.

The burly Armenian security man pressed a button on the side of the dumbwaiter; it elicited a stubborn buzz and remained closed.

"A fresh plate is likely being prepared this very moment," Laura said. "Now, if you would please take your seats and look at the research materials we've provided you, I will go fetch Mr. Hildebrand."

Laura exited the conference room; the door clicked behind her. Roux was waiting down the hall. "We're leaving now."

Laura followed the Frenchman to the aft recreational platform and boarded the tender, where Hildebrand sat at the wheel. "I hope you know what you're what you're doing," she said.

Sam reached the yacht just as a tender pulled away and headed for shore. *Was that Hildebrand?* Now alongside the massive vessel, she placed her engine in neutral, retrieved a bullhorn, and was about to shout a warning when a powerful jet of water smashed into her with the force of a cannonball, bowling her over the side and into the drink.

"They've got one of those anti-piracy water jets!" Deek shouted. "Merchant ships use them off Somalia. They hit hard, she might be stunned!"

Boone increased speed, angling toward the empty sheriff's boat. "Em, if you gals want to make for that hatch, I'll freedive after you, once I've picked up Sam."

"Right-o! In we go!"

Kate went in first, followed by AJ and Emily. Boone came alongside Sam's boat, but a burst of automatic weapons fire echoed across the water and a slicing pain seared across his shoulder. He jerked the wheel hard to starboard and angled away, pushing the throttle to the stops to put some distance between them and the shooter.

"Ernesto... take the wheel," Boone grunted, stepping aside.

"I see Sam!" Deek yelled. "She's waving an 'OK' sign and jerking her thumb down."

"She's telling us she's fine, and she's going to descend... probably freedive for the hatch," Boone snarled through gritted teeth, clamping a hand over his bleeding shoulder. "But I think they're on their own, for now."

Deek pulled off the swag T-shirt from the boat show, wadded it up, and gave it to Boone.

"Thanks," the young man said, pressing it to the wound. He

winced, but then his face changed and he looked past Deek. "That tender that left the yacht… it's just sitting there."

Deek turned his head and spotted the tender several hundred yards away, between the super yacht and the shore. He turned back to ask Boone for his binoculars and found them already being offered up. Deek took them and looked at the boat. Hildebrand was aboard, along with a woman and a man with a military bearing he'd never seen before.

"What on earth is he doing?" Deek asked aloud.

Emily dove for the bottom, following Kate and AJ. In moments they were under the yacht. Kate made a beeline for a square of shimmering water inside an open hatchway. Emily started to follow, but spied AJ off to the side, grabbing at something trapped on a lifting strake on the underside of the hull. It looked like a packet of crisps. *Good ol' AJ, environmentally conscious even in the face of mayhem.* Emily watched Kate's fins disappear up the hatch, and she followed.

Breaching the surface, Em encountered a darkened room, the only light coming from the water below. She hauled herself up with a splash, the sound muted and echoey in the dark space. "Kate?" she whispered, digging in her BCD vest for the small light she always carried for looking into cracks and crannies for various marine beasties. Her fingers had just found it when a voice came from above.

"Here," Kate said, flicking her dive light on.

AJ popped up and looked around.

"Welcome to the party, Aidge," Emily whispered, turning her own light on.

"Why are we whispering?" AJ asked as she pulled herself up into the room.

"The ambience demands it," Em replied, removing her gear and fins. "What did you snag down there that was so important?"

AJ triggered her light and shined it on the plastic bag. "Barbecue crisps. But what caught my eye, was… they're unopened."

"That's weird, innit?" Em offered, then shrugged. "Some clumsy snacker probably dropped 'em."

"We better get a move on," Kate urged, shining her light around. There was an obvious hatch leading out of the room and she reached for it.

"Hang on a tick," Em said, pointing her beam at a shelving unit that was pulled away from the wall. A substantial amount of water lay on the floor behind it, and at the base of the wall, a grate lay on the ground.

"A vent cover's been pulled off!" AJ exclaimed.

A splash came from the moon pool and Emily aimed her light that way, "About time Boo… you're not Boone."

Sam pulled herself up. "Boone had to take the boat away from the yacht when the crew fired shots."

"Is he all right?" Emily blurted.

"I think so, but I was still disorientated from being knocked ass over teakettle. I only heard the shots and saw them veer away." She saw where Kate and AJ were looking. "What've you got?"

"A vent that doesn't look like much of a vent," Kate said. "With a lot of puddled water in front of it. And in it," she added, looking inside. "There's a room beyond. I'm going in."

Kate crawled into the passage which was only about four feet long. The others followed, and soon the group was in a darkened pantry.

Emily stood up and something crackled under her foot. She reached down and chuckled when her fingers found another packet of barbecue crisps. "Here you go, AJ… something for your collection."

"This one's empty," AJ remarked.

"A lot more water over here, in front of this set of shelves," Kate said, shining her light on the floor. "And a bunch of jugs of cooking oil lying around."

"Shine your torch on this empty shelf, would you?" Sam requested. "I see a little orange light back there."

Kate did so, and the others clustered around. "Looks like a little hatch of some kind. Some controls on the side there."

Sam reached through and pressed the illuminated button with a lock icon on it. It clicked and the orange light extinguished. "Okay..." She looked at the other buttons. "Green means go, I guess." She pressed the green button and the panel slid open.

"Holy—!" Moving as one, all four women threw themselves to either side when the contents were revealed: a plate of appetizers with a curved, metal box on top, its surface embossed with an all-caps warning.

"Front toward enemy!" Em gasped. "We're on the killy end, yeah? I don't know what you call that, but I've seen it in movies."

"It's a claymore mine," Sam said, recovering somewhat from the shock.

"Oh my God," Kate said softly. "The blueprints. I don't remember this being in the pantry, but I took a good look at the main dining room up top. It had a huge table in the plans, and at one end there was a box in the wall marked 'dumbwaiter.' This has up and down buttons. And if I were going to hold a conference on board..."

"What time is it?" Sam asked quickly.

AJ held up her wrist and looked at her dive computer. "Two minutes to noon!" she hissed.

Sam shined her light around the corner. "Looks like there's a timer on the back of it." She looked at the rest of the large pantry. Someone give me their light." She grabbed AJ's. "Everybody, get out of this alcove and go to the far corner!"

"Why did you leave the talks?" Laura asked. "And what are we waiting for, exactly?"

The limousine tender bobbed in the waves, a hundred yards

from *La Fiamma Azzurra*. Hildebrand looked up from his watch and smiled. "As you both know, I've quietly tripled the size of my oil and gas shipping fleet over the last few years. A pipeline agreement between Armenia and Azerbaijan would not be good for my bottom line, to say the least, but since most of my shipping is under different holding companies, the negotiators don't know that. As to why I'm not there, I don't want to be associated with what is about to happen. I have an operative who will by now have passed a weapon to one of the delegates… *after* the thorough security sweep. The meeting should begin at noon, but several minutes into the remarks, that delegate will pick a fight with the other side; an altercation that will lead to sudden violence. He will shoot one of the opposing negotiators."

"How do you know this?" Roux asked.

"Because I've paid him handsomely; the more violent he is, the more he'll be paid. And it helps that his wife is in dire need of expensive medical treatment." Hildebrand again checked his watch.

"I suppose that's *one* way of sabotaging the talks," Laura said, turning to look back at *La Fiamma Azzurra*.

Sam put the dive light in her mouth while AJ, Em, and Kate dashed around the corner to find cover. Wasting no time, Sam reached in, grasped the edges of the claymore, and gently lifted it from the grapes, olives, and cheeses. She spared one moment to examine the timer at the back, but instantly decided on a surer course of action. *These men are pros, and it might be booby-trapped,* she thought, as she scrambled through the vent, into the adjacent room. Throwing herself to the floor, she leaned over the open hatch, pointed the business-end of the claymore downward, and released it into the water, hoping it didn't roll "bad side up."

Sam knew this was an anti-personnel mine, so the front end should be packed with sharp bits of metal for a fragmentation explosion, and therefore should be heavier, keeping the lethal end pointed down. In theory. Rolling away, she prayed that her theory was correct.

Once Sam had vanished through the vent, Emily bolted toward the wall beside it, ready to assist the sheriff's deputy if something went horribly wrong. She heard a hum behind her and flashed her light back over her shoulder just in time to watch the dumbwaiter suddenly rise, vanishing from sight.

"He said to begin without him," one of the Azeri delegates said.

The Armenian across from him nudged the folder on the table in front of him. "Has everyone read over the materials? If so, I say we—"

He was interrupted by a hum and a click. Beyond the head of the table, the dumbwaiter slid open, revealing a smushed plate of olives and cheese.

"Should we eat first?" the Azeri asked.

Hildebrand frowned at Laura, who was looking back at the yacht. "What do you mean, that's *one* way of sabotaging the talks?"

She had no time to answer, as there came a sudden, muted BOOM. A spout of water shot up from the side of the yacht and several seconds later, the limousine rocked like they'd passed over a wake.

Hildebrand stared at the ship. "What on earth was that?"

"The yacht is under attack!" Roux cried. "We should head for shore and call for help! Out of the range of the jammers!"

"An explosion!" Ernesto cried.

"Underwater," Deek said, pointing.

Boone stood up from the bench, still clamping Deek's T-shirt to his shoulder. "We need to get alongside! They could be hurt!"

Deek spotted movement on the far side of the yacht. "Hildebrand's tender is heading for shore!" He laid a hand on Boone's arm. "You two, go render aid… if the yacht security men let you. But take me to Sam's boat! I'll go after Hildebrand… but more importantly, I'll get out of the range of the yacht's jamming, and call for help."

Ernesto nodded and aimed the catamaran toward Sam's vessel. "It's a good plan."

"You know how to drive a boat?" Boone asked.

"I've been along for the ride all week… I think I've picked up a thing or two."

"The radio… call for help on—"

"Sixteen. I may be a desk jockey, but I know the basics. And my cell will probably start working again at the same time."

Ernesto brought the cat alongside the smaller vessel—a rigid inflatable center console—and Deek stepped across gingerly. He looked at the controls and surprised himself by getting the boat moving with minimal trial and error. Pushing the throttle forward, he looped around the super yacht and headed toward Boca Grande, his eyes searching for the limo tender. Grabbing the mic, he pressed the call button and started speaking, repeating over and over, "Mayday, mayday, mayday… this is the… actually, I have no idea what this boat's name is… can any law enforcement or emergency services hear me? Mayday, mayday, mayday."

32

"Are you all right?" Kate asked Sam. The explosion had been muted, but they had all felt it shake the hull.

"Banged my shin on some piping trying to get some distance from the hole, but otherwise I'm hunky dory."

"I hate to mention it," AJ began, "but… we don't know if that was the only bomb."

"True," Sam said. "We have to get them to shut down the jammers, call for help, and be prepared to evacuate the ship. We need to get to the bridge. Without getting shot."

"Kitchen staff!" Emily blurted. "They're probably right on the other side of this room and the pantry. "They'll know the quickest way."

"And they're probably wondering what the explosion was," Kate offered. "Let's inform them."

In moments, the quartet had found a reasonably level-headed crewman who understood their explanation, and was guiding them through the crew passages toward the bridge. When they came to a passage to an outer deck, Emily stopped.

"You three go on," she said. "I'm gonna get outside and see if I can spot Boone."

Alongside the yacht, Ernesto and Boone braced themselves for gunfire, but the security men weren't in sight. Reaching the spot where they'd seen the eruption of water, Boone tossed the bloody shirt aside, took a lungful of air, and dived in. The shallows were shrouded in sand and silt kicked up from the explosion, limiting visibility. After a thorough search, he returned to the surface.

"I don't see them!" he shouted. "I think they must've gotten aboard."

"They did!" a familiar voice rang out.

Boone looked up to find Emily above, leaning over a railing. "Em! Thank God!"

Emily's smile slipped a notch. "You're bleeding!"

"It's just a graze."

"Well, get your arse out of the water before your 'graze' attracts a bull shark, yeah? Hey, where's Deek?"

Deek looked down at the console, trying to determine what the noise was. He spotted a phone in a holder, the screen lit up with the name "Dusty." *Sam's detective friend!* He tapped the accept button. "Dusty! This is Deek Morrison!"

"Deek? The maritime guy? Where's Sam?"

"On Hildebrand's super yacht. I think."

"What do you mean 'you think?' Why do you have her phone? I've been calling for the past hour, it keeps going to voicemail."

"I'm on her boat and the phone was aboard. Listen, there's no time. We need Coast Guard and police units out to the super yacht, *La Fiamma Azzurra*. And I might need some police assistance myself. I'm chasing Hildebrand."

"What the hell are you talking about?"

"There's been an explosion. A bomb. I think Hildebrand is responsible."

"For bombing his own yacht? Wait, never mind… where's the yacht. Where are you?"

It's offshore from Boca Grande, directly across from… I see a lighthouse."

"White? Metal supports on the sides?"

"Yes."

"That's Gasparilla Island Lighthouse. And you're there?"

"No, I'm southeast of there. I think Hildebrand is heading for Baskin Island."

"Okay. I'll call the cavalry. I'll divert one unit to Baskin. Don't do anything stupid!"

As Dusty ended the call the boat's marine radio squawked. "Unidentified vessel, this is the United States Coast Guard, what is the nature of your emergency?"

Deek quickly repeated what he'd told Dusty as his boat continued to gain on Hildebrand's tender.

Laura's thoughts whirled, as she replayed the explosion, the eruption of water at the side. The explosion had likely occurred under the water, *not* aboard the ship.

"There is someone following us," Roux said, looking astern.

Laura followed the Frenchman's gaze and spotted the boat. What's more, she recognized it; the oncoming boat belonged to that sheriff's deputy who had been to Hildebrand's house on Baskin Island. *How on earth did she…?* Laura thought quickly, her eyes flicking to Roux's shoulder holster, revealed when the whipping wind fluttered his jacket.

"Damn… there's a police boat coming out of Captiva Pass!" Hildebrand cursed, turning the wheel to starboard. "I'll make for Redfish on the south side." He increased speed, the roar of the engine filling the air.

Laura looked at the distant boat, a light flashing atop the cockpit. She glanced back at the pursuing boat. *They're both much faster than we are.* Another moment's thought, then she made her decision and sat down. Sliding open a compartment beside one of the seats, she removed the false bottom and retrieved the contents, keeping her hand at her side on the padded bench.

"Monsieur Roux, I don't believe our pursuer is friendly," Laura said loudly enough for only Roux to hear over the engine. "If your weapon's safety is on, I suggest you remedy that. And crouch down... you're too exposed!"

The Frenchman looked back at her, noting the fearful look on her face. He nodded and extracted his handgun. Crouching, he turned his head toward the boat behind them and thumbed the safety off.

Laura raised a Walther PPS compact pistol in a freshly gloved hand and popped off two rapid rounds into the side of Roux's head. He stiffened and collapsed to the deck just as Laura threw herself down beside his falling body. His weapon bounced off a table post and Laura pinned it, dragged it to herself. She tossed her own weapon toward the wheel, took Roux's gun, then sat up and lifted it in a two-handed shooter's grip. By now, Hildebrand had turned at the sound of the shots.

"Laura! What—?"

Laura Smythe shot her boss twice in the chest.

Deek was gaining on the tender when it abruptly turned to the south, and the man and woman in the passenger compartment ducked down. *Damn, they've seen me*, he thought, but then spotted the flashing light of the police boat coming out of the pass on the north side of Baskin. He was about to try and reach them on the radio when two loud pops echoed across the water, followed by two more. Looking back at the tender, he now saw that no one was at the wheel.

What the hell? Deek was already at top speed, so all he could do was continue his pursuit as the unmanned boat continued plowing through the waves. The police boat to the north turned south and joined the chase. Deek was fifty yards behind the tender, when the woman rose from the deck and staggered to the wheel. Deek watched as she tentatively held her hands over the controls, then grabbed the wheel and throttled down. In moments, the boat slewed back toward the Gulf and coasted to a stop.

The woman turned to face Deek, tears streaming down her cheeks. Blood seeped from a wound on her forehead. "Don't shoot!" she cried, raising her hands.

As the police boat came alongside, the woman cried out, "My name is Laura Smythe. I'm an assistant to Mr. Hildebrand. I... I'm not sure what happened, but he... his bodyguard..." She trailed off, swayed, and abruptly collapsed to the deck.

Thirty minutes later, Deek stood near a marina on Pine Island, near the Lee County Sheriff's Gulf District Office. He recognized a nearby pier as the location where the small fishing boat had mysteriously caught fire several days ago. Perhaps that had been no coincidence, that the fire had occurred so close to the police marine unit's station, which was situated nearby.

Deek waved as the catamaran dive boat approached with Emily at the wheel. In moments they were tied up and the occupants began stepping across.

"Where's your shirt, Deek?" AJ asked.

"I donated it to Boone's shoulder wound," he replied. "Boone, you all right?"

Boone was shirtless as well, and indicated the large adhesive bandage atop his shoulder. "I'm okay. You?"

"Exhausted."

"I bet!" Emily sympathized. "We're right knackered, too. Got the yacht crew to listen to us and shut down their jammy thingie, and the Coast Guard showed up."

Sam, AJ, Em, and Kate recounted their ordeal aboard the yacht.

"So you were right about terrorism," Kate said at the end. "That man you've been chasing... he and another diver set the bomb, right?"

"Yeah," Deek said, then turned to Sam. "It looked like they were headed for shore... you should—"

"Already had Dusty put out a BOLO on them," Sam assured him.

"But... was it Hildebrand that hired them, you think?" Kate asked.

"Not sure. It might have been his bodyguard. The surviving witness, Laura Smythe? She was Hildebrand's executive assistant. She said the bodyguard was ex-French foreign legion, so he probably had a lot of overseas contacts."

"And they killed each other?" AJ asked. "Hildebrand and the bodyguard?"

Deek nodded. "That's what Ms. Smythe said."

"I met her on Baskin Island," Sam said. "She had been tied up by an intruder, remember?"

"Right. Pretty sure it was the same man who set the bomb."

"As I recall," Sam said, frowning, "when we found her and freed her... she wasn't exactly a blubbering mess, was she?"

"No..." Deek said, recalling. "She was pretty calm and collected."

"Not... crying and fainting or anything."

"No."

"Where is she right now?" Sam asked.

"Ambulance left with her about fifteen minutes ago," Deek answered. "She had a nasty cut on her forehead, and the EMTs thought she might have a severe concussion. Kept passing out while the police were questioning her."

"What exactly did she say happened?"

"She said Hildebrand had a pistol stored near the captain's chair. He turned on the bodyguard but the man must've seen it coming. They shot each other. She thinks it was a double-cross, but she wasn't sure who did the double-crossing."

Sam frowned. "You see it happen?"

"No. I was looking toward an approaching police boat when it happened." He thought for a moment. "Laura and Roux were ducked down right before I turned away," he mused.

"Where were Hildebrand and Roux shot?" Sam asked.

Deek shuddered. "It was messy. Hildebrand was shot in the chest. Roux…" He stiffened. "I think he was shot in the *side* of the head, now that I think of it."

Sam clawed out her phone and made a call. "Dusty! It's Sam… I'm fine, no time for that! The ambulance that just left here with the witness, can you find out what hospital it's going to?"

Her eyes went wide as she listened. "Call me the moment you hear anything!" She hung up. "Deek… the ambulance was found just off the road. Both EMTs were unconscious, and the witness is gone."

"Laura Smythe" thanked the Uber driver, tipping him generously. His account registered a five-star rating from the beautiful woman. "Thank you, Miss Wilson!"

"Don't mention it," she replied, a Southern twang in her voice. "You earned every penny."

"And I'm sorry about your head," he said, nodding toward the small adhesive bandage on her upper forehead.

"Why, thank you!" she said with a brilliant smile on her face beneath a pair of dark sunglasses. She laughed. "I swear, I've got to be more careful around low branches. Drive safe now, y'hear?"

Laura turned away from the car and the smile vanished. Walking with purpose, she entered long-term parking for the airport, sliding on a fresh pair of gloves as she reached a white SUV, rented with a pre-paid debit card—the same card that "Miss Wilson" used for her Uber app. She unlocked the vehicle with a key fob and got into the front seat.

Turning on her phone, she opened a home screen folder with

several innocuous icons in it. Tapping one, she triggered an app that wiped all data, factory-reset the operating system, and then bricked the phone. With practiced ease, she popped the SIM card out and pocketed it. She opened the glove compartment and dropped the phone inside, then retrieved a purse and a blond wig from within. Sliding the wig over her black bob, she winced as she pressed against the cut on her forehead.

Deliberately smashing her head against the metal support aboard the tender had been a spur-of-the-moment decision, but had paid dividends in minimizing the questioning by authorities. Laura arranged the bangs to cover the small bandage and gave herself a quick check in the SUV mirror. Satisfied, she took a new phone from the purse and brought it online. She swiftly brought up available flights and purchased a seat on one that was leaving in less than two hours. Laura placed the phone back inside the purse beside a wallet and passport.

Exiting the front seat, she got into the back and retrieved a carry-on suitcase and unzipped it. Looking around and determining no one was nearby, she changed out of her pantsuit into a simple sundress, then gave the suit a quick fold and stuffed it into the carry-on. She took a moment to close her eyes and let out a long, slow breath. Not everything had gone to plan, but enough of the train had stayed on the tracks. The closest she'd likely come to having everything unravel had been when Angler had unexpectedly showed up at one of the houses, with that sheriff's department deputy and the government pencil-pusher right on his heels. Tying herself up had been a spur of the moment decision—if everything had gone south then-and-there, playing the victim card would have been her best bet.

Exiting with the bag, she locked up the rental and shoved the gloves into an outer pocket of the carry-on. The nitrile gloves she'd worn when shooting Roux and Hildebrand had been disposed of in the Gulf as the tender raced along, long before the police boat arrived, floating away on the tides—if ever discovered, they would likely be far, far away from the incident. She walked briskly to the airport shuttle, and luck was with her; one pulled up just as she reached the shuttle stop.

As the shuttle moved through the parking lot, Laura opened another innocuous-looking app on her new phone. This one showed a series of bank transfers. She smiled when she came to the latest batch, which had been scheduled to trigger at noon. Hildebrand had been entirely too careless with his banking information, and it had been a simple matter to insert some of her own software into his systems. More challenging had been her intervention into his plans to sabotage the negotiations. A sneer came to her lips. *A single scuffle… one man shot? Half measures.*

She had intercepted Hildebrand's and Angler's messages and played the middleman, allowing some messages through while altering others, steering the mercenary toward her much more ambitious goal. A minor shooting from a zealot? She didn't want a little hiccup in the pipeline deal… she wanted outright war between Armenia and Azerbaijan, scuttling any chance of an agreement ever occurring.

If the device had gone off as planned, the entire conference room would have been shredded by high-velocity shards of metal propelled by a block of C-4. A series of false communications would appear in several of the delegates' email and social media accounts, and both sides would suspect the other of committing the heinous act. And further "proof"—much more extensive and detailed—would be discovered in the coming days, revealing the mastermind of the entire plot to have been Hildebrand himself, with damning communications and payments coming directly from Hildebrand's shipping and energy companies. The payment routed to Angler in the Cayman Islands alone would be sufficient to send investigators digging into his accounts. And with the man himself now dead, there was no one to refute the evidence.

But something had gone wrong with the device. Perhaps Angler was dead, blown to bits in the shallows beneath the yacht. But just in case… Laura cancelled a pending transfer of funds and deleted the recipient from the system. After all, she didn't pay for failure.

On the other hand, plenty of funds would soon be making their way into her own unmarked accounts all over the globe. Hildebrand had invested a lot of money in his shipping company in anticipation of his own plans coming to fruition, but with his terroristic scheme soon-to-be revealed, the highly-valued stock of Hildebrand Energy and Hildebrand Shipping would tank. Which would be enormously profitable to anyone who had shorted those stocks. Which, of course, she had… to the tune of nearly a half billion dollars. And she'd have plenty of money to buy up bargain-basement stock for the Georgia pipeline, the only viable alternative left standing.

Inside the airport, she approached the departures counter for the flight she'd selected. By some miracle, there were two agents open, a man and a woman. She chose the man and flashed him her pearly whites. "Good afternoon," she said in a thick Scandinavian accent. She held out her passport which listed her has Astrid Svensson, then showed the agent the reservation on her phone.

"Good afternoon, miss!" the man said, checking her out. "Where are we flying today?"

"New York. Then Stockholm," she said. *Then on to Istanbul.*

Zehra "Şeytan" Taciri took her boarding pass and strolled away from the counter.

33

Varadero, Cuba

Reclining in a beach chair under a thatched cabana, the man known as Angler took a sip from the perspiring can of Cristal and looked out at the ocean. A fishing boat floated in the waves, and he watched it for a time. The Florida Keys lay a hundred miles beyond; doubtless the *Beeracuda* would have returned to its homeport by now. The captain had earned his pay, waiting for Angler to reach him even as police and Coast Guard radio traffic had begun to swarm the airwaves. Angler had taken the dinghy straight in toward shore until out of sight of the yacht, before hooking out to sea and circling around to rendezvous with the *Beeracuda* in the Gulf. The crossing to Cuba had been surprisingly uneventful, after the events of the last week. That odd young man, Justin, had turned out to be an able seaman, and Angler had tipped him an extra three hundred dollars when they dropped their passengers off near Havana.

Angler briefly wondered what Grady Foster was up to. Having paid the man with funds from the Cayman Islands withdrawal,

Angler had given the man the slip in downtown Havana. Foster didn't have the kind of discretion to lie low, and now that the job was complete, there was nothing to do but take the final payment, and get out of this line of work. Seek a new life.

Angler picked up his latest burner phone and glanced at the time: 9:59 a.m. He watched the time flip to ten, then triggered the VPN and tapped the banking app. Angler stared at the balance in the account. Zero.

He took a breath. Perhaps the transfer would take a while. Maybe the 10:00 a.m. time he'd been told was the transfer time on Hildebrand's end. And it probably wouldn't be a direct payment; too easy to trace. Who knew how many detours the money would take?

Angler drained the Cristal and signaled a waitress for another, then settled in to wait. An hour later, the balance still read zero. He drained his second beer and thought a moment. He and Foster had maintained radio silence and destroyed their previous phones during the voyage. A feeling of dread washed over him as he opened the browser on his phone and brought up the news.

There, at the top of the feed was the headline: *Billionaire Harold Hildebrand shot dead by bodyguard.*

The old merc sighed and dropped his phone into the sand beside his lounger. Apparently, fate wasn't ready to let him move on with his life just yet. Crushing the beer can, he caught the waitress's eye and signaled for another. It was a beautiful day at the beach. Might as well enjoy it.

Islamorada, Florida

Deek Morrison parked his rental car and exited the air-conditioned interior into the Florida sun. He had just left the parking lot when his phone rang. It was his boss. Well... his former boss. He answered it. "Deek Morrison."

"Morrison, this is Powell. Listen... some information has come to light, and apparently... well... apparently, I owe you an apology."

Deek didn't answer, just walked to the sidewalk and strolled toward his destination.

"Morrison? You there?"

"Yes, sir, I'm here."

"Well... as I was saying... I owe you an apology. Apparently, you were right about the whole terrorism thing. And... well, I'd like to offer you your old job back."

"Thank you, sir. But that's not necessary."

"No, no, I insist! We need men like you."

Deek laughed.

"What's so funny?"

"Well, sir... that's exactly what the man from Homeland Security said."

"I don't understand."

"It seems my research and diligence in regard to this plot reached someone at the DHS. Apparently, my skills would compliment a number of their divisions. So, as I said... your offer to hire me back? It's not necessary. I'm interviewing with them tomorrow."

"Morrison—"

Deek hung up and entered the pawn shop. When the man from Homeland Security had asked him to travel to their offices for the interview, Deek had admitted that he really didn't have any funds on hand to make the journey on short notice. When he explained why he had no funds, the Department had provided him with a generous travel stipend. Generous enough that he'd have sufficient money to get to DHS HQ and still have enough left over for something else he needed to do.

Deek went straight to the glass cases with the watches. The

pawn shop owner came over and Deek pointed at the Omega Seamaster Professional he'd pawned several days ago.

"That one."

"You sure? It's pretty beat up."

Deek smiled. "We've been through a lot."

Discover more books in the genre, and sign up for our newsletter with new releases and great deals at
www.TropicalAuthors.com

ABOUT THE AUTHOR

Author of the Miami Jones Private Investigator Mystery series and the Baskin Island Mysteries

A.J. Stewart is the *USA Today* bestselling author of the Miami Jones private investigator series and the Baskin Island mysteries featuring Sam Waters.

He has lived and worked in Australia, Japan, the UK, Norway, and South Africa, as well as San Francisco, Connecticut, and of course Florida. He currently resides in Los Angeles with his two favorite people, his wife and son.

AJ is working on a screenplay he never plans to produce, but it gives him something to talk about at parties in LA.

For more information and a free ebook visit AJStewart.com

ABOUT THE AUTHOR

Author of the Shark Key Adventures series

Chris(tine) Niles has been telling stories since she was a lying kid. Now she's figuring out how to make a career of it. Because she likes to eat, she tried for about fifteen minutes to write romance. But her characters kept killing each other, so she switched to thrillers.

Her heart is buried deep in the hammock north of Sugarloaf Key, and you can only find it from a kayak. Despite that, her body lives in northeastern Indiana with her husband, two adult daughters, and a hungry four-legged sack of fur named Franklin.

For more information, newsletter, and a free ebook visit
ChrisNilesBooks.com

ABOUT THE AUTHOR

Author of the AJ Bailey Adventure series and Nora Sommer
Caribbean Suspense series

A *USA Today* Bestselling author, Nicholas Harvey's life has been anything but ordinary. Race car driver, adventurer, divemaster, and since 2020, a full-time novelist. Raised in England, Nick has dual US and British citizenship and now lives wherever he and his amazing wife, Cheryl, park their motorhome, or an aeroplane takes them. Warm oceans and tall mountains are their favourite places.

For more information and a free ebook visit HarveyBooks.com

ABOUT THE AUTHOR

Author of the The Deep Series

Born in East Tennessee, Nick Sullivan has spent most of his adult life as an actor in New York City, working in theater, television, film, and audiobooks. After recording hundreds of books over the last couple of decades, he decided to write some of his own. An avid scuba diver for many years, his travels to numerous Caribbean islands have inspired The Deep Series.

For more information visit NickSullivan.net

Made in the USA
Las Vegas, NV
21 October 2023